Praise for the novels of
MaryJanice Davidson

"A hilarious romp full of goofy twists and turns, grea
for fans of humorous vampire romance." —

"Delightful, wicked fun!" —Christine Fe
    #1 *New York Times* bestselling author of *Water l*

"Move over, Buffy. Betsy's in town and she rocks!
don't care what mood you are in; if you open this l
you are practically guaranteed to laugh . . . top-notch humor
and a fascinating perspective of the vampire world."
    —ParaNormalRomance.org

"One of the funniest, most satisfying series to come along
lately. If you're [a fan] of Sookie Stackhouse and Anita
Blake, don't miss Betsy Taylor. She rocks."
    —*The Best Reviews*

"*Undead and Unwed* is an irreverently hilarious, superbly
entertaining novel of love, lust, and designer shoes. Betsy
Taylor is an unrepentant fiend—about shoes. She is shallow,
vain, and immensely entertaining. Her journey from life to
death, or the undead, is so amusing I found myself laughing
out loud while reading. Between her human friends, vampire
allies, and her undead enemies, her first week as the newly
undead is never boring . . . a reading experience that will
leave you laughing and 'dying' for more from the talented
pen of MaryJanice Davidson." —*Romance Reviews Today*

"A hilarious book." —ParaNormalRomance.org

wonderfully witty."
    —Catherine Spangler,
    author of *Touched by Light*

Anthologies

Cravings
(with Laurell K. Hamilton, Rebecca York, Eileen Wilks)

Bite
(with Laurell K. Hamilton, Charlaine Harris, Angela Knight, Vickie Taylor)

Kick Ass
(with Maggie Shayne, Angela Knight, Jacey Ford)

Men at Work
(with Janelle Denison, Nina Bangs)

Dead and Loving It

Surf's Up
(with Janelle Denison, Nina Bangs)

Mysteria
(with P. C. Cast, Gena Showalter, Susan Grant)

Over the Moon
(with Angela Knight, Virginia Kantra, Sunny)

Demon's Delight
(with Emma Holly, Vickie Taylor, Catherine Spangler)

Dead Over Heels

Mysteria Lane
(with P. C. Cast, Gena Showalter, Susan Grant)

Rise of the Poison Moon

A JENNIFER SCALES NOVEL

*MaryJanice Davidson
and
Anthony Alongi*

ACE BOOKS, NEW YORK

THE BERKLEY PUBLISHING GROUP
Published by the Penguin Group
Penguin Group (USA) Inc.
375 Hudson Street, New York, New York 10014, USA
Penguin Group (Canada), 90 Eglinton Avenue East, Suite 700, Toronto, Ontario M4P 2Y3, Canada
(a division of Pearson Penguin Canada Inc.)
Penguin Books Ltd., 80 Strand, London WC2R 0RL, England
Penguin Group Ireland, 25 St. Stephen's Green, Dublin 2, Ireland (a division of Penguin Books Ltd.)
Penguin Group (Australia), 250 Camberwell Road, Camberwell, Victoria 3124, Australia
(a division of Pearson Australia Group Pty. Ltd.)
Penguin Books India Pvt. Ltd., 11 Community Centre, Panchsheel Park, New Delhi—110 017, India
Penguin Group (NZ), 67 Apollo Drive, Rosedale, North Shore 0632, New Zealand
(a division of Pearson New Zealand Ltd.)
Penguin Books (South Africa) (Pty.) Ltd., 24 Sturdee Avenue, Rosebank, Johannesburg 2196,
South Africa

Penguin Books Ltd., Registered Offices: 80 Strand, London WC2R 0RL, England

RISE OF THE POISON MOON

An Ace Book / published by arrangement with the authors

PRINTING HISTORY
Ace mass-market edition / August 2010

ISBN: 978-0-441-01904-5

ACE
Ace Books are published by The Berkley Publishing Group,
a division of Penguin Group (USA) Inc.,
375 Hudson Street, New York, New York 10014.
ACE and the "A" design are trademarks of Penguin Group (USA) Inc.

PRINTED IN THE UNITED STATES OF AMERICA

10 9 8 7 6 5 4 3 2 1

*For Christina, who has not had a book
from us all to herself in fifteen years.
How did THAT happen?
Huh. Sorry, kid. Here you go. Love you.*

In taking revenge, a man is but even with his enemy; but in passing it over, he is superior.

—SIR FRANCIS BACON

PROLOGUE
The Elder's Diary

August 5, 8 P.M.

No. I'm not doing this.

August 6, 8 P.M.

Seriously. Not gonna.

August 7, 8 P.M.

Mom, Dad: you can shove this blank book and a pen in my face every evening for the next fifty years, and I'll never write more than twenty words. Okay, thirty.

Also, we're out of milk. Also also, I hate how powdered milk tastes. I know we've got to make sacrifices. But I dislike milk in powder form. Just sayin'.

August 8, 8:30 P.M.

Phlllbt.

August 9, 1 P.M.

Honey—this isn't entirely about you. As your father has told you, it's important to tell your story. People are counting on you. Not just now, but in the future. They need to see what you've seen, learn the lessons you've learned. It may not seem fair, but you owe them that.

August 9, 8 P.M.

MOM!!! YOU READ MY DIARY! AND YOU'RE WRITING IN IT! WHAT KIND OF MOTHER DOES THAT?!? DO YOU EVEN UNDERSTAND HOW COMPLETELY TWISTED THAT IS, OR ARE YOU TOO BUSY BEING A PSYCHO TO GET IT?

August 10, noon

Hey, ace. Don't be mad at your mother. She knows this is important to me—to all of us, really—and she volunteered to sneak a peek at what you've done so far. Can't say either of us are totally impressed; but we're still hoping *you'll come around. You know, almost better than any of us, how deep the abyss is that we're all staring down. (This isn't <u>Seventeen</u> magazine, ace, and your privacy isn't more important than our survival.) I don't believe this town can last through another winter. What may be left of us is on these pages. So what say you crank it up a notch and write a note or two for posterity?*

August 10, 12:30 P.M.

Ugh, I knew I should have moved this thing to another hiding place after Mom invaded my privacy. ('Scuze me, the privacy that isn't as important as our survival, vomit vomit vomit.) No point now—both parental slugs have left their eternal slime in this journal, and now there's nothing to be done.

I'd burn this thing tonight if I didn't think we'd need to save every bit of paper to make it through another winter.

August 11, noon

Jennifer, I guess you're going to be totally annoyed that I'm writing in here; but your parents begged me so I'm writing this while Gautierre and I came to visit you today. You just stepped out of your room to take a pee break. Did you know you take forever? (How long can it take, Jenn? I mean, geez.) Gautierre thought it was weird, but I said it was a girl thing, so he dropped the whole thing. They have a point. Your folks, I mean. You gotta do this. Gautierre agrees. Okay, you flushed so I gotta go; good-bye!

August 11, 12:03 P.M.

Having thrown Susan, the artist formerly known as my best friend, and her boyfriend out of my room for conspiracy to commit phenomenal embarrassment, I would like to state for the record that I, the Ancient Furnace, do NOT pee or flush. I am more powerful than that. I can simply will my urine away.

Away, urine! See? (I'm no longer pretending this is any sort of a private document.)

Okay, everyone, I'll make you a deal. If you can all go twenty-four hours without molesting my journal, I will start serious entries tomorrow. Deal?

August 12, 12:04 P.M.

All right. Thanks, everyone, for refraining from sharing further tales of my bathroom habits. Guess I should keep my end of the deal.

My name is Jennifer Caroline Scales. I live in a town called Winoka with three major problems.

First, those of us who turn into dragons don't call it Winoka. We call it Pinegrove, because that was the name it had before a woman named Glorianna Seabright led an army of beaststalkers here, wiped out the inhabitants, and renamed it. That was about forty years ago.

Second, last November Mayor Seabright died, and on that night a barrier rose that blocks off this town from everything else around it. It's enormous and translucent and blue and round, like my ass when I'm in dragon form.

The only thing that makes it through is weather—snow, rain, sun, wind, okay you probably know what weather is! For a while, electricity made it through fine, too—but then a bad January storm knocked out more of the grid than we could repair with what we had. The town began rationing fuel. Since then, it's gotten harder.

Third, everyone outside this barrier appears content to wait for us to die. More on that tomorrow.

CHAPTER 1
Andi

Winoka—or Pinegrove, as Andeana Corona Marsabio knew some called it—sat in a river valley. The Mississippi cut a wide boundary to the north and east, and the only crossing for miles was Winoka Bridge. Its aging gray steel arch connected the eastern higher ground to the western lowlands, where the town's city hall and oldest neighborhoods lay.

"It's beautiful," she murmured as she took it all in from her perch atop the riverside cliffs. The shimmering blue dome that covered it all only made it look more magical. There had been nothing like this in the dark places where Andi had once lived. Here, she found beauty. Here, she found light.

Here, she found Skip Wilson.

"It'll look even better after they're all dead," she heard him say.

She turned to where he was sitting, a few feet behind her and to the left. The rising sun made her squint. She wondered if he placed himself like that on purpose. He was drawing now, letting a sketch pencil fly across a large pad. Maybe he was drawing her. Sometimes he liked to do that, when he wasn't drawing creatures.

"They don't need to die," she reminded him.

"I disagree." The pencil didn't stop.

Is this turning me on? she wondered. *Or scaring me? Or boring? Boring would be bad.* Her arms crossed, and she massaged the insides of her forearms with her thumbs. "They have as much right as you and me to live."

"I disagree."

"It's inhumane."

"I dis—"

"Yeah, well, you disagreeing doesn't mean piss to me." Andi turned back to the trapped city. (Asked and answered: this was *not* turning her on.) Rainbows bled through the eastern half of the dome; a wisp of mist from a recent shower had slipped through the barrier that let almost nothing else through. "I should let them out."

Finally, she heard the *skritch-skritch-skritch* of his pencil pause. "We've gone over this. We don't know enough about the sorcery to bring it down even if we wanted to. Which we don't."

She liked him, yes indeed, but he could be somewhat— what was the phrase? *High-handed. Yes.* Certainly he seemed to have no trouble speaking to her . . . not to mention *for* her. "It doesn't seem difficult. Why not try?"

"Wrong question. Why try at all?"

"High-handed," she muttered.

He didn't notice . . . or didn't care. "We can pass through that barrier. You did twice on the night it went up, didn't you?"

She swallowed. "That's a cheap—"

"Once to leap in and kill your mother, the rotten mayor of that stinking town, and once to make your getaway."

She couldn't believe—she couldn't *believe* he was using her shame and fear to make his point. "I was under the influence of my father's sorcery! I had no choice!"

"Hey, I'm not complaining." Skip smiled and seemed puzzled by her outburst. "Mayor Seabright was a murderous bitch. If your dad were still alive, I'd shake his hand."

"If my father were still alive, he'd have killed you by now."

He chuckled. "Yeah, from what I've heard of him, he was a real piece of work. Who calls themselves The Crown, anyway? Sounds like he might have had some fantasies about sixteenth-century Portugal."

It was a remark designed to piss her off, and they both knew it. Her tan features crinkled, and her blood roiled. "He wasn't European."

"No, that was your mother's side, wasn't it? The beast-stalker side." He snapped his fingers, as if remembering for the first time. "Your father's side was from south of here. Not Texas-south. *Way* south. *Rain forest*–south."

She uncrossed her arms, grabbed two fistfuls of grass, and held on.

"I don't remember much about all those countries down there. My mother and I visited a few years ago, but I was really young. Mostly, I recall lots of vines, strange animals, and simple people who smelled bad."

This is sick, she told herself as she tore herself from the ground and launched herself at him. *He's sick. I'm sick.*

By the time she reached him, he had flung the pencil and pad away and was ready to catch her. They rolled over a few times, her fists pummeling away at him. She started with two, but soon she was pretty sure she had sprouted more. He didn't even try to stop the blows—he didn't have enough arms to do so. She supposed he could turn into something with eight legs, but that wasn't the point.

He laughed at her, an unkind sound meant to provoke more violence. He got it.

A few minutes later, they were sitting across from each other, sullenly examining their wounds. Andi was reasonably certain (more so than usual, even) that this was not in any way a healthy relationship. It was even more aggravating because she wasn't quite sure who needed fixing. Him? Her? Both?

She thought of Jennifer Scales yet again . . . that girl had beat on Skip once or twice herself, hadn't she? What did that say about her—or him?

Probably me, she thought glumly. *I'm the sick one.*

"So," Skip began. He paused, spat a tooth, then tried again. "Ready to kiss and make up?"

"Shut up." She sighed.

"We could just kiss."

"Skip."

"Because I'm ready to let bygones be bygones." He patted his mouth with his sleeve. "Also, I would like very much to stop bleeding from the mouth."

She grinned; she couldn't help it.

"You want—"

Something whizzed past her face like a giant mosquito and slammed into his left foot. As Skip screamed, she recognized the feathered markings immediately. So did he.

"Eddie, you shit! Come out and fight like—"

"Sit still," she ordered, seizing his ankle and trying to keep him from running after the archer. "I'll fix it."

"I don't want you to fix it—I want his eyes out of his skull!"

Aw, she thought, hiding how much this amused her. *That's so romantic.*

Skip jerked his foot away and snapped his fingers. Out of the grass popped twenty beetle-sized shapes, each thinner than paper and waving dozens of antennae.

"Find him! I want to know where's he's hiding!"

"Skip, they never—look, hold your foot still, and I can— you have to get this arrow out." *I had to say that aloud,* Andi thought. *I actually had to tell him that out loud. Because he's way more concerned with getting even than alleviating his own pain. Also,* she realized glumly as she watched the band of two-dimensional insectoids leap through the high prairie like dolphins, *he has made yet more creatures bristling with phallic doodads.*

So, she considered, rubbing her bloody palms on her thighs, *megacool? Or megacrazy?*

"Fuck the arrow," Skip snarled, which was about what Andi expected. "Eddie's getting ready to fire again while you're dicking around with my foot!"

"'Dicking'? I'm trying to help you. And Eddie Blacktooth has never fired more than a single shot, which, if you'd put your angst into park, you'd remember."

"Yeah, he's never *hit* with a shot before, either. Dammit, leave it alone."

Why am I bothering? "I can help."

"Right after Eddie's dead."

"Skip, he's got a head start the length of two football fields. Your little bug patrol isn't going to catch him. If you give me five minutes, I can pull the arrow, staunch the wound, and—"

"I'll get it out myself." In an instant, Skip had morphed into a massive fisher spider. His bloodied boot morphed into a slim tarsus at the end of a long, spindly leg with beige and gray bands. The arrow lost its purchase and slipped free. Skip hissed through his mandibles.

I'm not scared, not exactly, she thought, eyeing the frightening new shape. *And I'm not turned on. Not exactly.*

"You going to try and run after him now?" She already knew the answer.

"I guess you're right—I'll never catch up. Coward knows how to run."

"Funny who's calling whom a coward."

The giant arachnid spun and faced her. "What's *that* supposed to mean?"

"He's a beaststalker, Skip. Maybe you're familiar with the term? Killing ugly things your size is what he's trained to do."

Skip made a sound. A snort. Or a sneer. A sigh, maybe? Hard to read his expression in that shape. "As if that wimp could do any such thing."

"Yeah, you keep telling me he's a wimp, that you kicked his ass last year in a parking garage, blah blah blah. I never met that Eddie Blacktooth, Skip—but I've met *this* one. Do you have any idea how hard it is to put an arrow so close to us, every time, from two hundred yards or more? You're lucky he hasn't decided to split your heart open. Maybe there's a little wind each time, or maybe he's toying with you. Either way, I get why you wouldn't get any closer to him than you have to."

"He's the one who'd better keep his distance."

"Hmm. Well." She coughed. "He *is* the one with the compound bow."

He began kicking up tufts of grass and hollering through his mandibles at an enemy he could not catch, and Andi could only squint at the far tree line. She was pretty sure Eddie was gone, but with the shot taken downwind and so far away, who could be sure?

And how, she wondered, *do I feel about that, exactly? Do I wish he were still taking shots? Do I wish he'd stop toying with Skip?*

She looked down at the arrow. It was good that Skip

could take care of that by himself. Andi's healing would have required sorcery, and sorceries cost the caster—usually in years of life. The man who had cast the dome over Winoka, Edmund Slider, had slipped into death after exerting too much power.

If this was to be only the first of many times Skip would be injured, Andi would have to give up some years.

Her years. Time she would never, ever get back.

For Skip.

Maybe Eddie knows that, she told herself. *Maybe he'll try to whittle us to death—Skip with arrows, and me with my own sorcery. It'd be like him. It'd be . . . polite.*

She still could not bring herself to hate the boy. Or his girlfriend, Jennifer Scales.

Skip shifted back into the form of an angry, brown-haired boy with a limp. "This whole thing is going to crap."

"What is?"

"This!" Skip flung his arms wide, emphasizing his disgust with (a) the dome, (b) the universe, (c) the weather, (d) the beaststalkers, and/or (e) her. "This . . . whole . . . thing! Edmund Slider did an amazing sorcery, this supercool *event*, he *made* it *happen*, and for what? Huh? Andi?"

"I'm sitting forty inches away, I can hear you perfectly," she snapped. "And I know. I know! Edmund made this noble sacrifice, killed himself, for peace."

"Yeah, he—um, no."

"What?"

"No, Andi. He sacrificed himself to help us all—to destroy the town!"

"I don't think 'help' means what you think it means."

"Geez, did you have a brain tumor for breakfast?"

"Not that I know of."

"Why do you trap something under glass? To *help* it?"

"Um, I don't . . ."

"No. You trap it under glass to suffocate it. To watch it die slowly. To show it what it gets when it screws with you."

She tried not to let her skin crawl away. "So great. The town's dying slowly. They've lost power, and there's no way they have the fuel and food to get through a second winter. So what's your problem?"

Skip actually spun around in a small circle, looking not unlike a Hopi Indian about to embark on a snake dance. "It's taking too long!"

"Taking too long?" She knew she sounded like an idiot parrot. Trouble was, this time she honestly had no idea what his malfunction was.

"At some point," Skip frothed, "you want to lift the glass and crush what you've trapped."

"Charming. So how do you plan to lift the bowl?"

"You and I don't have to. We're not going to go in. We're going to ship in the crushing."

The thin beetles he had sent after Eddie returned and crawled up his leg and body, to settle and chirp on his shoulder. Andi had rarely seen anything so gorgeous and repellent at the same time.

She motioned to them. "Looks like they didn't find Eddie after all."

"Screw Eddie. We'll make more and destroy Winoka."

"Destroy what with who now?"

"Destroy Winoka. With these creatures. It's perfect, Andi! It's so *us*. We've worked together to make them. I create them, you bring them into the world."

She snorted. "You mean, you draw them, and I sing to make them all poofy and three-dimensional . . ."

"Don't mock what we do. We're gods, Andi."

She blinked and said nothing.

"Right!" he added, as if she'd agreed, or required more

information. "We're gods, and we can make an army. An entire army programmed to do whatever we want. They'll spy for us, fight for us, die for us."

"Like Hannah Montana fans."

He frowned.

"What?" she asked. "I've been in this world long enough to learn about Hannah Montana."

"We'll program these armies to make an impact."

"What kind of impact?"

"Take things out. City hall, school, people—"

"People?" *It's got to be a joke. Or perhaps testosterone poisoning. Maybe when the entire world is a sizzling cinder in space, he'll be content.*

"Yeah! Kill enough of them, and they'll start fighting each other."

"They're already fighting."

"Not much. Not anymore."

This much was true, Andi had to concede. Best they could tell, an uneasy cease-fire had formed. Dragons and those town residents who could stand them—led by Dr. Elizabeth Georges-Scales—clustered near the hospital, while those most hostile to the newcomers kept close to city hall. A good deal of the town didn't care who was what or where, as long as everyone left them alone.

But not everyone did. And now, Skip wanted to add to their troubles.

"Edmund wouldn't have wanted them to die," came a third voice from behind.

They turned and saw Tavia Saltin, Skip's aunt. Andi self-consciously smoothed out the front of her jeans and tried to unmess her hair.

Skip got to his feet. "Aunt Tavia, listen. Mr. Slider put that barrier up for a reason. He's given us an opportunity! We should take it."

Tavia was a frail, middle-aged woman with wisps of dark hair and broad teeth that flashed easily, but she was not smiling now. "His last act was an effort to buy you time, so that you could come to your full powers. Out of respect for his wishes and what I believe your own father would want for you, I've let you set your pace. I've gone along with living out of abandoned houses and restaurants on the edge of town, so you could indulge your visions in peace and quiet. But these fantasies of yours are getting riskier. We have been scraping out an existence on the edge of a dying town for over a year, and all you have done is sketch creatures in the sand, play with your girlfriend . . . and now, this daydream about burying a town that would die on its own if you walked away and left it alone. Focus on improving yourself, Skip, not on tearing down others."

"Aunt—"

"Don't interrupt me. I'm losing patience. Our kind is on the verge of extinction, and it's time you paid attention. I've suggested before that we bring in my remaining brothers and sisters, so you can learn from—"

"I'm not interested in any more relatives!" Skip's tone was so vehement, Andi scrambled away from him. "No more Saltins, no more Wilsons! If they're not ditching me, they're slapping me around or getting themselves killed! You're all useless—I'm not looking for any more like you. You want to find your pathetic siblings, go right ahead. Andi and I will stay here and get this done ourselves."

Andi stared at Tavia as Tavia stared at Skip. She wasn't sure what she wanted the older woman to do. Leave them alone? Take Andi with her? Help them kill Winoka?

After a few moments, it was too late to ask. Tavia turned without another word and left.

CHAPTER 2
Susan

"Welcome to another edition of *Under Big Blue*, with Susan Elmsmith. I'm Susan Elmsmith. It's Day 300, and we're—well, we're still under the dome. We're broadcasting from the parking lot of Winoka Hospital, a beacon of hope for this troubled town. The, er, hospital, not the parking lot.

"This is the place where the wounded come for healing and comfort, where medical professionals work tirelessly to keep the spark of life . . . um, sparking . . . and where Death fears to tread!"

"Good heavens, Susan—"

"We have a special guest today, to celebrate our three hundredth day of survival. Dr. Elizabeth Georges-Scales, M.D., leader of the town—"

"Susan." The emerald-eyed, blonde woman seemed embarrassed. "I'm not the leader of the town. I'm the head of surgery for this hospital."

"If you say so. Your job has become more difficult this past year, hasn't it?"

"It has. While the violence of last winter and spring has died down, we are running out of medical supplies . . . and everything else."

"Can't we reuse some things?"

"Replenishment is possible in some cases—we began recycling certain resources and growing some simple medicinal herbs once it became clear the dome would be with us for a while.

"And we are figuring out ways to keep our building's generators going with biomass—wood, animal carcasses, that sort of thing. However, most of modern medicine is too sophisticated—pharmaceuticals, plastics, and so on. Our second winter is coming. The only thing that penetrates this dome is weather. We need the outside world to be thinking about this problem and helping us forge a solution."

"And how do we know they aren't already working hard on this problem, Dr. Georges-Scales?"

"Because we have received virtually no transmissions from the outside world. In fact, from what we can see ourselves through the few media outlets who carry excerpts of your reports, there is no evidence anyone is paying attention to our town at all."

"Could you elaborate on that, Dr. Georges-Scales?"

"No one—not media, not university research, not private industry, not law enforcement, not military—has responded to our repeated requests for assistance. At all. People need to understand that there are real people in here, hurt and dying."

"Why don't they respond, Dr. Georges-Scales?"

"Your guess is as good as mine. Perhaps some are frightened by what this town holds. Perhaps they want us to go away. This town is not a danger to anyone. The only danger here is that people will suffer needlessly. Please, if you are listening to Susan's transmission: reach out to us. You will be saving lives. We would be so grateful. Thank you."

"You've done your own share of lifesaving, haven't you, Dr. Georges-Scales?"

"Oh." Susan held her breath and tilted her brunette locks as she watched the doctor pause at this deviation from their agreed-upon script. "Well. Yes, we have saved some lives here. The staff at Winoka Hospital is highly trained and professional. I am honored to work with them."

"And you lead them, against all odds."

"That's a dramatic overstatement, Susan."

"So it contains a kernel of truth, then, Dr. Georges-Scales? Sources credit you with keeping this town together in a crisis. They point out your trademark focus and discipline. They talk of your accomplishments: you were a favorite disciple of the late Mayor Seabright, you finished med school one year early, you sing beautifully in the shower when you think no one's listening—"

"My husband put you up to this, didn't he?"

"I can't comment on that, ma'am," she said primly. "But sources also say you fell in love with a dashing young man who should have been your enemy. The danger thrilled you, and hurling caution to the winds, you embraced it with a surprising vigor and passion."

"I'm going to hurt him. Jonathan, if you're watching this transmission . . . shame on you. You should be taking Susan's broadcasts more seriously."

"Argh. Pause it, Gautierre." Susan made a cutting motion, and her tall, black-braided boyfriend lowered the camera. "C'mon, Dr. S. I'm trying to spice it up."

"With mixed metaphors focused on my personal life?"

"Folks outside the dome need to see a little hope in here. You give people hope, and even people in this town want to know more about you. I figure maybe part of the reason we're not hearing anything is because all we have to share is depressing . . . or boring."

"You're worried that we're boring them."

Susan swallowed and managed a smile. "Not that boring is bad, mind you! Except it is, in journalism."

"You'd prefer a return to the daily killings, from a few months ago."

"Geez, Dr. Georges-Scales, no! I'm not talking about being exciting that way. I was thinking of something more fun. For example"—she motioned to Gautierre, who faithfully raised the camera again—"some of our listeners may want to learn: what is it like to love a dragon?"

"Come again?"

"Loving a dragon. What is that like?"

Elizabeth stared at Susan, then the camera, then the boy holding the camera. "I . . . I don't suppose it's any different from loving anyone else. I've only had one love in my life, and that's Jonathan Scales. He's a wonderful man. I wouldn't trade my life with him for anything."

"That's sweet. But our viewers' concerns may be . . . more specific. More practical."

The older woman shifted. "Such as?"

"What's the experience like?

"The experience."

"Yeah. The act."

The doctor's face paled. "Susan. I'm not talking about this on the Internet."

"Don't think of it as the Internet. Think of it as posterity.

You've experienced something no other woman has, yet—a physical expression of passion with a man who could literally tear you apart. Surely, you have some tidbits you could share, some advice—"

"Susan . . . okay, first of all, I could just as easily tear *him* apart. And I might, if he put you up to this. Second, if you and Gautierre have questions for me, I am happy to answer them . . . *in private*."

"Arrrgh! Gautierre, cut! We'll have to edit that out, too."

"Susan, maybe Dr. Georges-Scales is right . . ."

Susan didn't blame her boyfriend for siding with the older woman. Even though he was a lovely boy who was utterly devoted to his perky and clever girlfriend, Dr. Elizabeth Georges-Scales could intimidate the heat away from a fire. Susan bit her lip and nodded as Elizabeth walked to Gautierre, seized the camera from him, handed it to Susan, and said, "This interview is over."

"Yes, ma'am."

"You should edit quickly and transmit."

"Yes, ma'am."

"Electricity is at a premium, Susan. I support your use of hospital computers and power outlets because you are doing important work and because you're usually good at it. But you need to stay focused on the crisis at hand."

"Yes, ma'am."

"Lives depend on you, as much as they depend on me and my colleagues."

"Yes, ma'am."

Elizabeth sighed as she walked away. "Oh—and, Susan."

"Yes, ma'am?"

"The 'experience,' as you call it, is absolutely outstanding. But it has nothing to do with what the man can do under a crescent moon. It has everything to do with his love for you, his depth of commitment, and his . . . willingness to learn."

Susan grinned. "Yes, ma'am."

"One more thing. As far as Jennifer knows, you and I never had this conversation."

"Yes, ma'am!"

CHAPTER 3
Jennifer

Jennifer Scales caught her mother as she was coming in from the hospital parking lot. Beyond her, Susan and Gautierre were smiling and fiddling with their electronic equipment.

"How'd the interview go?"

To Jennifer's surprise, Elizabeth turned bright red. "It went well. What do you need?"

"What do you mean, what do I need? Watch shift. I'm headed up to the roof."

"Ah. So where's Catherine?"

"I think she's already up there. She volunteered for last shift, too."

"She's been pulling an awful lot of shifts."

"You're complaining? She's a quick study with that rifle."

"I'm noting that as recently as two months ago, she was in daily rehab learning to walk again."

"Yes, well, she's fine now. You cleared her yourself."

Elizabeth nodded. Catherine Brandfire, granddaughter of the late Winona Brandfire, had spent much of the last year in a hospital bed recovering from a vicious wound to her spinal cord. The cut had meant to hobble her out-of-dragon form and cripple her limbs, but Jennifer's powers as the Ancient Furnace and Elizabeth's skill as a surgeon had restored Catherine's ability to walk and shift.

"I still wouldn't suggest she try flying soon."

"You and me both. She's a trampler. She always sucked at that. Can't even whomp worth a damn."

"Sniper duty sounds about right, then."

"Um, Dr. Georges?"

"Georges-Scales," Elizabeth said automatically, looking over her daughter's shoulder. Jennifer felt a surge of irritation—not at being interrupted, nor at the incomplete use of her mother's name, but at the fact that the doctor never seemed to catch five minutes around here. Everybody looked for her.

Everybody found her.

"Right. Um. Hi, Jennifer."

Jennifer nodded tersely at Anna-Lisa, formerly an administrative assistant in the administration wing, now a war scout. Anna-Lisa and her team of determined medical secretaries explored the town for medical supplies of any kind. It had become difficult work once the pharmacies were empty, because recognizing the most useful supplies required both basic medical knowledge (to avoid duplicative effort) and excellent reflexes (to avoid attacks from enemies).

Anna-Lisa turned to Elizabeth. "Dr. Georges-Scales?

Um, we were thinking? That maybe we would try the homeopathic remedy store? In the strip mall by the cinema?"

Jennifer loathed it when women said things as questions? Because it was so annoying? Not to mention wishy-washy? She had never heard a man talk like that.

She had mentioned it to her mother once, who had pointed out that Anna-Lisa was busting her ass with limited military medic training. If she talked like this? It wasn't worth quibbling about.

Still, it was as irritating as a centipede navigating a groin rash?

"That sounds fine, Anna-Lisa. I doubt you'll find much real medicine, but bring the homeopathics back. They may have a useful placebo effect in some situations."

The petite brunette, who apparently grew new freckles across her nose and cheeks by the day, nodded.

"Okay, so, we'll do that? But the reason I came out?"

"Someone needs me back inside."

"Yeah. They do. And Dr. Paige thinks Mrs. Gremmel's foot is going to have to come off."

Elizabeth nodded grimly. Jennifer knew that expression. She also knew Mrs. Gremmel's case—a nice sixty-eight-year-old woman who had suffered exactly zero attacks from any dragon, spider, beaststalker, or rogue raccoon in town. She was simply diabetic, with poor circulation. She'd received the town's last known dose of insulin back in July. She now sported a gangrenous foot, and Dr. Georges-Scales had limited options. A few antibiotics. No propofol. No halothane. No nitrous oxide. No thiopental. Very little ketamine. Even fewer fentanyl. Maybe a little bit of etomidate.

Soon, Jennifer figured, they would all be reduced to hitting patients over the head.

Hey. Then I can be a surgeon, like Mom!

She had banished the inappropriate thought and was about to suggest to Anna-Lisa that she bludgeon Mrs. Gremmel so her own mother could get more than a minute's rest herself, when she heard the air horn and cry outside.

"DRAGON! DRAGON! DRAGON!"

A rifle fired once, then again a few seconds later. Then there was a commotion on the roof—one thump as something landed, then another, then another, and another . . .

Catherine! Jennifer was out the door and sprouting wings before the last of the dragons had landed on the roof. The watch-and-sniper's structure built alongside a roof exit door was crude but sturdy: a ten-foot-high cylinder of balanced bricks and stones transported from ruined houses around town, dotted with plenty of sniper holes and covered with asbestos-lined sheet metal.

Except now, one of the walls had been torn down, and seven dragons were sticking their snouts into the opening and wrestling with the occupants. Flames sprouted from their mouths, ammunition exploded in a fierce staccato, and a man inside screamed.

The dragons were pulling someone else out with their jaws. It was Catherine—who thankfully had shifted into dragon form—but her fireproof scales would not prevent these monsters from tearing her apart.

In a blink, Jennifer was among them, smashing one dragon with her bulk, whipping another's snout with her tail, and clawing at a third with an extended wing. The other four immediately dropped Catherine and backed up to assess the new threat. The largest was immediately recognizable—a middle-aged dasher, at seven feet no longer than the juveniles who surrounded her, but remarkable because her tail ended in two swollen stumps instead of the lethal spiked fork most dashers used.

"Ember Longtail!"

The raiding party's leader straightened up, near-black scales glistening in the sun. The mere sight of Jennifer infuriated her. The peach markings on the undersides of her wings expanded and contracted violently, and a blast of fire came out.

"What is the point of *that*?" Jennifer asked, eyes closed and her head turned slightly. The flames felt ticklish and warm on her skin.

Ember answered with a charge, which caught the younger dragons by surprise and sent them in a somersault—half electric blue scales, half dark spines. Jennifer felt her adversary's teeth dig into her neck, and she cursed herself for her carelessness as blood spilled over her throat.

She didn't dare shift back into human form—it was far more fragile than this one. The only recourse she had was to bite back, and so she did. Ember's left wing was available, albeit not very tasty.

The dasher grunted in pain, but her jaws remained fixed. Jennifer blinked, wondering why she was losing peripheral vision, then realized it was because her jugular was pouring her lifeblood into open air.

Get her off, get her OFF. Her triple-forked tail swung around and smacked Ember on the back of her spiny head. Nothing. She tried again, harder. Sparks bounced off the other's skull. Still, nothing.

Desperately wishing for a way to melt out of this death grip, she tried plunging a tail tip into Ember's eye socket. A near miss—they were both still moving, and Jennifer's aim was worsening as she lost more vision. She began to feel dizzy. Off in the distance, Catherine bravely fended off the others. Gautierre, thankfully not far away when the attack started, was next to her.

I hope that means Susan is inside and safe.

Now there were new voices—had more allies come out the exit door and worked their way through the rubble?

The answer came in the form of a brilliant shock wave, which took both Ember and Jennifer by surprise. The former unclenched her jaw with an exclamation of pain at the sudden flow of sound and light, and Jennifer squeezed her eyes and ears shut while shifting back into human form.

She wasn't sure if it was the blood loss, or the beast-stalker's shout that had overwhelmed her dragon senses, or both. She blacked out.

CHAPTER 4
Jennifer

Jennifer woke up in a hospital bed with bandages wrapped around her throat. Catherine, Susan, and Gautierre surrounded her in sea-green-cushioned visitor chairs.

Her thoughts went immediately to the dragons' fire, the explosions, and the scream. "Who died?"

"Mark," Catherine answered. Her dark-skinned face was covered in dried tears. "I tried to cover him after they punched through the shelter wall, but they kept pulling me off. There were seven of them, Jennifer! I couldn't fight them all."

Gautierre put a comforting arm around her.

"Anyone else?"

"No." But Jennifer could hear it in Gautierre's tone: Mark was enough. He was one of their sharpest eyes, and a brilliant lab tech to boot. It had been the eager, just-out-

of-college Mark who had hit upon a critical countermea-
sure to enemy creepers in camouflage: converting digital
infrared thermal-imaging machines that the hospital used
for diagnostics, to portable equipment for recon sweeps.
Dragons showed up beautifully on infrared. Because of
Mark, Ember had no creepers left in her gang. His was a
powerful loss.

"We get any of them?"

"Jack," he replied.

"Jack?"

"You know—Jack-o'-Lantern? The orange trampler,
roly-poly fellow, blasted the front lobby doors last spring?
He managed to keep his feet after your mother's shout, and
he tried to take her down."

"Oh." Jennifer's heart fell—not for the trampler, who
deserved to die for daring to attack her mother. But Dr.
Elizabeth Georges-Scales had not killed a dragon since she
was forced into a rite of passage on her fifteenth birthday.
Jennifer knew the woman would be wracked with guilt, no
matter how justified she was.

"It wasn't your mother," Susan interjected, reading Jennifer's thoughts. "Gautierre defended your mom. He was
fantastic. Heroic. His tail moved so fast and cut the ass-
hole's throat right before he crashed into your mom." The
girl turned to the boy. "I'm so proud of you."

"Please, Susan. I didn't want to kill him. But something
inside me . . ." Gautierre was a mix of embarrassed and
horrified. Plainly, he was still coming to terms with the kill.
Before today, he was one of the dwindling number of innocents among them. Now he, like the rest of them, knew
what it felt like to take a life. Jennifer felt bad for him, and
grateful.

"Thanks."

"The urge is so hard to control," he continued. He

wasn't talking to any of them. "In that shape. Hearing Mark scream, watching that trampler go after Dr. Georges-Scales . . . I don't feel like I'm defending a single person. I feel like I'm defending family. My own. I—geez! Every attack feels so *personal*." Jennifer could feel herself nodding with him. "There's no room for thinking. Just acting."

Susan rubbed his arm. "It saved Jenn's mom. Maybe yours, too."

"How did Ember get away?"

"Your mother's shout hurt most of them," Catherine explained, "but based on Jack's autopsy, we think they purposely plugged their ears with tree sap. Only the light would have affected them, so they could scramble. If Jack had been smarter, he'd have escaped, too—but he couldn't resist the idea of taking out the great Dr. Georges-Scales."

"Sap in their ears." Jennifer lay back in bed. "That's why they were so bold. They've never landed on the rooftop before. Never risked groups of more than three. Now they'll try again."

"Maybe not. They must be down to—what, now? Twelve? And Jack was one of their most experienced. Everyone else in Ember's gang is a juvenile, some young dumb-ass who came along for the destruction when Winona led the Blaze here. The older dragons still alive under this dome are either allies or loners in the woods by now."

"You are suggesting that attrition can win this conflict." Elizabeth stood in the doorway now, hands on hips; the gaunt form of Jonathan Scales loomed behind her. Jennifer saw relief and irritation in her mother's tired expression; worry and pride in her father's. As wretched as things were beneath the dome, Jennifer never forgot how lucky she was: *her* family, at least, was together under Big Blue.

Gautierre stretched out his hands and stared at his fingertips; Jennifer thought of Lady Macbeth in a ninth-grade

English class an eternity ago, with the Midwestern twist her teach spun on it. *Out out, ya dang spot! Geez, now, out!*

"I don't want to see anyone else die, Dr. Georges-Scales." He sighed. "And it doesn't make up for Mark. But I'm still glad there are fewer of them. They can't keep this up for much longer. Wherever their hideout is, winter's going to be awful for them."

"It's going to be awful for all of us. You are a brave soul, Gautierre Longtail. And I'm grateful you had my back up there on the roof."

"Me, too," Jonathan Scales said quietly, his long, pale fingers grasping his wife's shoulder.

"But dragons are notoriously bad planners, and you are no exception."

"Feted and slammed," Catherine teased, and got the ghost of a grin as a reward.

"Your theory of attrition only works with two assumptions: first, that the unfriendly beaststalkers in this town do not decide to resume hostilities, with us or anyone else. Second, that we can get out of this dome someday soon. Knowing what I do about this dome and Hank Blacktooth, neither assumption seems realistic."

"Oh, *that* weiner," Susan muttered darkly.

"You think Hank Blacktooth will attack again? He hasn't since spring."

"He hasn't attacked *us* since spring. If Ember's on the move again, he and his so-called police force will be looking for her or someone else to kill. If killing doesn't work, then he'll be looking for someone to blame, which will get his people fired up, and they'll go looking to kill. Us, Ember, innocent people—it really won't matter. We're all starting to look the same to each other." She didn't say it out loud, and didn't have to: they were all thinking the same thing.

We look like prey.

"All the more reason for Ember and her gang to die now," Jennifer snapped. "We've got to patrol more aggressively. Try the sewer system. Ember stank like no one's business. Way worse than usual." *Blurgh.*

"Try not to talk, ace," her father advised. "You'll undo all your mother's hard work."

Elizabeth seemed less nurturing. "Aggressive patrols, Jennifer? Would that be anything like Hank's aggressive patrols from the spring? Or the ones Glorianna used to send to other towns, at their 'request'?"

"You know it's nothing like that, Mom." She widened her eyes at her father, a full-blooded dragon in his prime, hoping he would back her up. "Just because it's an idea someone else had, and used against us, doesn't make it a bad one, you know?"

"I know no such thing."

"Again, ace: no talking. And your mother's right."

Dammit! He's sucking up to her. He's clearly a traitor. Or a seriously whipped husband.

"Dragons ambush, beaststalkers patrol, somewhere out there a few arachnids are doubtless laying traps," her mother continued in the cool, informative tone she used to teach med students how to pull an infected appendix. "It's all perfectly well-intentioned, you see—they're fighting back, or exacting a justifiable price, or ridding the world of an imminent threat, or bringing an unreasonable group into line, or making more room for whatever master race is the flavor of the day. Meanwhile, we celebrate the fact that the older ones are dying, and all that's left to fight each other is children . . ."

Jennifer couldn't help it; she rolled her eyes, knowing her mother hated it, but completely unable to resist the reflex. Besides, her mom had it wrong. "Not what I'm saying, and c'mon, you know that . . ."

"Still using your voice against medical advice," Jonathan reminded her.

"Fine," Elizabeth snapped, ignoring her husband's gesture to end the conversation. "Whatever *you're* saying, *I'm* saying that it's children fighting children. I'm sick of it. Let's not worry about more patrols, people. Let's focus on our mission: healing, protecting, living in peace." Elizabeth stripped off her surgical gloves and stuffed them into the red biohazard box by the door. These weren't for waste removal: a former cafeteria worker or janitor would come by every evening, collect the boxes, carefully sterilize the contents, and return them for reuse. "I'm glad you're okay, honey. Feel better soon."

She brushed past her husband and out of sight.

CHAPTER 5
Jennifer

Later that night, Jennifer felt well enough to morph into dragon shape, which made her feel immediately better. She could feel the tissues around her jugular regenerate, and she decided she was well enough to get up and walk.

Of course, she knew her mother would not agree. Fortunately, Jennifer was nearly as good at camouflage as her father.

Dressed in jaunty, rippling tones of pea green paint and white linoleum (*why, I look like a spring day in the countryside! Ha!*), she made her way calmly down the hall. Her recovery room was within the wing most staff here used as makeshift residences. There was no need to be overly precise with the colors or noise. Most lights were off, and all medical staff would be elsewhere in the hospital, busy tending to far worse cases than Jennifer. The nearest nurses' station, like so many throughout the building, was empty. Down the hall another thirty yards, two seated nurse's aides faced each other, reading and chatting. Jennifer knew they had sharp eyes—but it had been weeks since the late Mark's infrared technology had helped snuff out the last enemy creeper. Camouflage, they were not looking for.

The exit door to the stairwell was more than ten yards from them, and they did not notice it open enough to let a stubborn patient slip through.

This stairwell opened up onto the roof, not far from the stairwell and fortification they used for spotting Ember's gang. Jennifer was relieved to see the rain, which, combined with the twilit gloom, would make her escape virtually impossible to detect. Whoever was standing guard in the rebuilt fortification would be looking up, not over.

She spent some time breathing in the fresh air and looking over the parking lot. The wide swath of concrete lined in yellow was broken only by an occasional grass-lined curb and splintered tree . . . and a volleyball net. Last spring, a few EMTs had stuck the net up to establish some small measure of normalcy. A small league had formed, which had lasted two months before a brutal attack by creepers in Ember's gang convinced them that "normal" and dead was not as good as stressed and alive.

Even with that specific threat gone, no one felt much like playing volleyball. Even several rains later, there were still deep bloodstains and scorch marks on the asphalt.

"Knock it off," she heard.

Flinching at her father's voice, she thought she was busted until she heard her mother's response.

"I'll do no such thing. You need something."

"Save your drugs for someone with an actual medical condition."

They were inside the fortification, Jennifer realized. It was their watch.

"Fine, I'll hold on to the meds. How about a shot to the snout instead?"

He snorted without much humor. "Go ahead and try. I can handle whatever you dish out."

"Such bravery! I'm all atwitter. Seriously, Jonathan. You should take something to keep you awake. Caffeine, if nothing else."

"Coffee? Are you serious?"

"Yes, coffee."

"I don't drink coffee."

"Tea, then."

"Coffee, tea. What's with the fucking breakfast drinks?"

"Jonathan, I don't have a lot of pharmaceuticals to offer. We need you sharp, now more than ever."

He sighed. "You don't *need* me at all."

The doctor's voice remained patient. "What's *that* supposed to mean?"

"It means, I don't see the point. Gautierre was right. Attrition will take care of Ember. She's not the problem. The problem is, we're not getting out of this dome, not without a breakthrough. And Liz—I ain't the breakthrough."

Elizabeth actually chuckled. "Is this what all the irritability is about? You're not feeling useful enough? Jonathan, you're being foolish. You and I are part of a team. We need everyone—"

"Don't give me that team-spirit-crap pep talk. I'm your husband, not some janitor you promoted to medicine scout."

"Great. So as my husband, you should already know that *I* need you. Jennifer needs you. There are others, of course. But you could start there. You two are the irreplaceable ones. The others, as fond as I am of them . . . they're teammates. That's all."

"You're kidding. You haven't needed me for years. And this past year, you've become a leader of this town with no assistance from me whatsoever—you're a surgeon, people need a hospital, they trust you because Glory raised you, and they hate Hank in any event. No one looks at you, and says, 'Eh, I'll follow her because of that Jonathan chap.'"

"Jonathan, this is beyond silly—"

"No, it's not. Nowadays, I'm way more of a hindrance than a help—your beaststalker allies don't trust me, and the dragons still with us are following Jennifer because of who *she* is. Heck, there are one or two elders out there in those woods who'd be a heck of a lot friendlier if I weren't around."

"They're fools. Jennifer is who she is because she's your daughter!"

"*Your* daughter."

"Okay . . . *our* daughter. What's the difference?"

"You've met my other daughter, remember?"

Jennifer let out a low hiss. Evangelina Scales, Jonathan's daughter by his first wife Dianna, was a murderous psychopath (was there any other kind?) with powerful and dark gifts. They had all barely survived her in a fight to the death.

Then, for extra fun, Dianna Wilson (aka Mrs. Scales the First) had managed to manipulate the universe so she could reunite with Evangelina and disappear with her daughter into no-one-knew-what dimension.

"You *must* feel brave, to bring that subject up."

"I'm only pointing out, Jennifer is the way she is because of *you*. Not me."

"Now you're being ridiculous. If you're going to act like

this, go off shift and send someone else up. Someone un-mired in self-pity."

"See, like I said: you'd be fine without me."

"Ugh. Never mind: I'll go downstairs. I'll send someone else up. Someone I dislike intensely enough to inflict you upon."

"Have them bring a cup of coffee, that'll solve every-thing!" he called after her, as the stairwell door inside the fortification slammed shut.

Some things, Jennifer mused as she slinked back to her own roof door and down the stairs, *don't change, no matter what.* She couldn't help smiling at the thought.

CHAPTER 6
Susan

"Welcome to another edition of *Under Big Blue*, with Susan Elmsmith. I'm Susan Elmsmith. It's Day 301, and we're broadcasting from the mayor's office in Winoka City Hall, which is currently occupied by today's *Under Big Blue* guest, Mr. Hank Blacktooth—"

"*Mayor* Hank Blacktooth."

"Mr. Blacktooth, as you know, yesterday rogue dragons attacked Winoka Hospital. Two died as a result of that conflict, and the famous and beloved Jennifer Scales almost died as well. You claim a leadership role in town—"

"Again, I'm the mayor."

"What are you doing to resolve the crisis?"

"Susan, we're working as quickly as we can to eliminate the threat to this town's innocent residents—people like yourself whose families came here for protection. We take our responsibility seriously, and I can guarantee you that by the end of the upcoming winter, Winoka will be dragon-free."

"Dragon-free?" Susan looked nervously at the camera, balanced on a tripod between two of Winoka's peace officers.

Hank leaned forward and repeated quietly and calmly, "Dragon-free."

Unsure of how much this man knew about her personal relationships, Susan returned her focus to the questions she had prepared. "What is the status of your peacemaking efforts—"

"Spare me your mouthpiece questions."

"Um, okay."

"I know the chief of surgery at Winoka Hospital has written most of them for you. I did not agree to have you here so I could waste time answering them. I agreed so I could broadcast a statement, using your web log as a vehicle."

"My web log?"

"Yes. Inexplicably, it gets regular coverage."

"Thanks."

"Gallingly, it is the only dependable way to get my message to the outside world."

"Okay, well. Thanks again. Prob'ly."

"Here's how this will work. I will momentarily give a statement. My assistants here will then take temporary possession of your camera and edit our session using city-hall equipment. They will post the result to your web log, using log-in information you will give them. They will then erase all source information from your camera and return it to you. You will then go back to your friends at the hospital and pretend however much you like to be in charge of your destinies."

Once upon a time, Susan would have found this vastly

intimidating. All right, she still did. But still: she was a journalist. "And I'll give you my log-in information because . . . ?"

One of the peace officers drew his sword. Hank motioned him to lower it.

"Susan. This doesn't have to be confrontational."

"Just surreal and creepy."

"I know your father—he serves in the National Guard, right? Commands a cavalry battalion. He's a good man. He moved here to protect you."

"My mother actually was the one who moved us."

"But he agreed. Surely, he wants what is best for you. He wants you to be safe. And now, by accident of fate, here you are in this dome. He is outside, if I've heard correctly?"

Another threat? Susan nodded. "He was on shift when it happened."

"I'm sure he's worried about you."

"You're not as subtle as you think you are, Mr. Blacktooth. If your goons are going to hurt me, have them get started. I'm not giving you shit."

Hank sighed. "May I please record the statement, and *then* you can decide how intransigent you'd like to be?"

Susan shrugged.

He turned to the still-running camera and tried to smile. "Good evening. I am Mayor Hank Blacktooth. I've asked Susan Elmsmith, a local reporter for this town, to come to city hall and transmit this statement in her web log, and she's graciously agreed to do so. I have two announcements.

"First, in two days this town will have a noon rally on the Mississippi bridge, where our valiant Mayor Glorianna Seabright died over three hundred days ago. Our activities should be visible from beyond the dome, including by press helicopter. I encourage everyone to attend.

"Second, as some of you know, I have a son named

Edward. When the dome appeared, he was trapped on the other side. It has been some time since I have heard from him, and like any father . . . I am worried for him. Here is a recent photo of him." He held up a school photo of Eddie. "If anyone has news of my boy, I'd appreciate hearing it. Susan regularly posts contact points for the city—it's been a long time since anyone used them. We'd love to hear from you.

"I know this crisis has the town, and the outside world, worried. Please know that we are doing all we can to keep the good people of Winoka safe. Thank you all for your prayers and thoughts. Take care."

Once done, he looked at the camera for an edit-ready three or four seconds and then turned to Susan. "Well?"

Susan pursed her lips. She thought of Eddie, alone in the forests surrounding the town. "Edit the statement. Put it on my equipment. I'll go back to the hospital, log in myself, and broadcast it." Pause. "So, what's going to happen at the rally?"

An infuriating smirk was the only response.

CHAPTER 7
Susan

"You *what*?"

Susan attempted nonchalance as she uploaded the edited blog entry. "Your hearing's fine, and you're only standing three feet away, so I know you caught that. Dr. Georges-Scales suggested it, and I've wanted to do this interview for a while, so I said yes."

"He could have killed you!"

"Only with his breath. I guess there are no Tic Tacs here under Big Blue anymore."

"Sooo-zen!"

"Don't yowl; it's not at all sexy. Besides, he wasn't going to kill me. He needed me." She was trying to sound impatient at Gautierre's overprotectiveness, but it was hard. She adored him beyond all reason. She adored his soft cobalt and lavender scales in dragon form, she adored his triple-braided hair in human form, she adored the piercing golden eyes he had in both. She had no idea if first love was this intense, or trapped-in-a-dome love, or he-saved-my-life love. Or a weird-yet-cool combo.

Because she did love him, she was trapped beneath a dome, and he had saved her life. He had walked through fire for her. Literally! It was all she could do to keep from darting across the room and falling on his face and kissing said face for several hours.

Instead, she finished filing the report and squinted outside. "It actually looks decent out there. We should go for a picnic."

"A picnic? Susan, Ember's gang attacked yesterday. You're not going outside. You're not going anywhere!"

"Thanks, Fred Flintstone." It became slightly easier to be irritated now. "I don't recall asking your opinion."

"You want to die? Is that it?"

Hmm. Lots o' drama, even for teens in love trapped beneath a dome. "Gautierre, I'm a reporter. You get why I'm doing this, right? To . . . what's the word? Oh. Right. Report. To tell the truth. I want the whole world to know what we're going through. I do *not* want the world to Area 51 us."

"Area 51 is a verb?"

"Winter's coming," she continued, not cracking a grin. "People will starve. To *death*, okay?"

He straightened his back, which gained him two inches. He tossed his braid gently; a moon elm leaf was woven into the strands. It was the weredragon equivalent of wolfsbane . . . as long as he was in physical contact with it, Gautierre had control over when and where he became a dragon. Without it, he would be tied to the crescent moon. "I love what you're doing."

"No, you don't."

"Okay, I don't. I know it's important. I hate that you risk yourself almost every day."

"Risk? Jennifer's taking risks. Her mom is taking risks, and her dad. The goddamned medical secretaries are taking risks, okay? Me? I'm babbling into a camera and making out with my boyfriend."

"You're not doing either of those right now," he pointed out with a smile.

"Keep it up," she muttered, "and see how much and how often and how long I don't do either of those. Or one of those." *Wait. What? Oh, hell.* He knew what she meant.

She took a steadying breath. *Keep cool. Start over.* "Getting back to it, it does look pretty nice. Want to take a walk?"

"No."

"What, no?"

"Forget it, Susan. It's too dangerous."

"For me, you mean."

Gautierre snorted. "No, for your pet geese."

"I don't own a single—"

"Look, keeping you from getting roasted or skewered is turning into a full-time job. Not that I mind," he added hastily upon seeing her scowl, "but let's not go looking for trouble, okay?"

She slapped her hands onto her hips so hard she almost knocked herself over. "Wait a minute, hose bag! You're not really pulling that chauvinistic garbage on me, are you? What century are you living in? Cute little Susan has to be protected by her boyfriend? Because you can stuff those misconceptions right down your gullet!"

"Susan, pardon the obvious, but *I'm a dragon*!"

"You are not!" She looked again at the leaf. "Well. Not all the time."

"Yes, Susan, even when I'm walking around on two

legs, I'm a weredragon, I was born one and will die one
and will always be one, forever and ever, amen. I fly and
breathe fire and eat sheep."

"Charming."

"You, on the other hand, have only one protection: you're
gorgeous. You don't have scales or a nose horn or wings or
enhanced strength or enhanced speed. It's not chauvinism;
it's reality. You can't protect yourself the way I can. And
you not facing up to that? Pretending it's fine for you to hop
out the door whenever you want, you are woman, hear you
roar? It's not feminism. It's idiocy."

Susan's eyes widened, and she could actually feel her
eyeballs bulge inside her skull. She was so upset her brain
was going into put-down overload. Where to start? With
the idiocy thing? With the pseudofeminist analysis? Hear
her roar? Had he really *said* that?

"You—you—I—arrggle—mmph—"

"Hmmm." Gautierre put his hands out, as if to catch her.
"Are you having an aneurysm? You look really weird."

"—gnnh—mmeh?"

"Here, siddown." He steered her to a wheelchair and
plopped her into it. "Look, I hate the thought of you getting hurt, okay? I'd rather stay under a roof with you and
never fly again if it meant you'd come out of all this okay.
You expose yourself enough by going outside and doing all
those reports."

"Did you just say I expose myself?"

He sighed. "Grow up."

"I love that you look out for me," she began and, when
he looked pleased, added, "in your own horrible, smother-
ing way. But there are plenty of other 'normies' in town
who are risking their safety to go out. Even if I didn't have
to do my reports—"

"You *don't* have to do your reports."

"—I wouldn't spend the day cowering in this hospital, peeking outside, and wishing I could see the sky."

"On that one"—Gautierre sighed—"I think we can both agree. But I think your real reason is, you love seeing yourself on CNN."

"Oh, well." She shrugged modestly. If he only knew, the poor sucker. Loved seeing herself? She loved chocolate. She loved oatmeal. She loved the way towels smelled when they dried on a clothesline.

She *lived* to see herself on CNN. She would wither and die if she had to go back to her old life. The supporting role. The plucky best friend.

No thanks. Tried that the first fifteen years.

"Besides, I'm bigger and stronger than you, and I vote we stay inside for a couple of more hours at least." He ducked, and her hair clip—which she'd yanked out of her ponytail and hurled at him—sailed over his head. "So if we can't go outside, let's put our heads together and see what can we—oooommmpph!"

She had successfully landed on his lips. Touchdown! "The crowd goes wild," she said, smirking.

"Argh, my back," he groaned.

"At least it wasn't a knee in your balls." With that tender thought, she snuggled into his chest.

Dome? What dome?

CHAPTER 8
Andi

They were watching the town under Edmund Slider's dome, the two of them, again. They hadn't talked much in the last couple of days, since Skip had argued with Tavia. Tavia herself had disappeared—presumably to summon her "pathetic siblings," as Skip had called them.

Andi watched Skip carefully out of the corner of her eye. He kept his gaze locked on the bridge.

"What do you think will happen at the rally?" she asked.

"I don't care," he lied.

"Why not go back to the restaurant, then?" The Cliffside Restaurant had been their primary home since last autumn—as a business it was abandoned earlier than the residences nearby, it had a generator that operated easily once grid repair crews stopped coming anywhere near the dome, it had everything from food to television, and only required small modifications to allow for comfortable sleeping quarters.

"Maybe I will." They both knew he wouldn't.

"Hank Blacktooth looked pretty gaunt in that video. Food must be pretty scarce." She thought about what it would be like, to have to ration food and go a little more hungry every single day.

"Susan looks fat enough."

"You're a jerk."

He shrugged. "I didn't mean it as an insult. We're good enough friends, she and I."

"Yeah, I'll bet she's a huge fan."

"She let me feel her up in the back of a Ford Mustang, once."

Andi rolled her eyes. Was this supposed to make her jealous? Having been raised in a void for most of her formative years by the reclusive Dianna Wilson, she really didn't know for sure. She didn't *feel* jealous. Mostly, she felt pity for Susan Elmsmith, who probably let Skip touch her for the same reason Andi did: low self-esteem.

"They're starting," she noticed with no small amount of relief.

Outside Winoka City Hall, a crowd was forming. Some of the participants were coming out of the charming three-story domed brick building. More came out of the police station, which was directly across the street. They all wore white and black dress robes over their clothes, and a few of them sported ceremonial helms that reflected the morning sun.

Then they saw a figure that made them both stand up straight.

"What the *fuck*," he said.

"Oh, no," she whispered. "I didn't think she would."

He turned sharply. "You didn't think she would *what*?"

She motioned uselessly at the scene by city hall. "She said to summon her siblings, she needed to go back to your house and gather a few things. Her sorcery isn't horribly powerful—you know that—and she needed little trinkets from each of them, to make it all work. I offered to help her, so she wouldn't have to return, but she insisted, so—"

"So you let her go into the town?"

"She's an adult! Cripes, Skip, it's her house, she's been living there, she knew the risks . . ." The words felt empty, and she crumbled into silence.

"We've got to go down there."

She did not bother to protest. She simply followed.

As they stepped onto the highway and turned toward the bridge, she saw that nearly three hundred people had gathered on the bridge. Someone had set up a makeshift gallows out of scaffolding and industrial supplies. Four people were standing on it: Hank Blacktooth, two helmeted guards . . . and Tavia Saltin.

The woman's hands were cuffed behind her back and a rag tied tightly over her eyes. Another rag was stuffed in her mouth, and she had bruises and welts all over her face.

Hank, standing in front of her, saw them right away. He pointed and said something, and the crowd on the bridge turned and cheered.

"Skip." Andi pulled back on his shoulder before the boy could run ahead. "They want you in there more than anything. Don't give them what they want."

They came closer, still more than a hundred yards from the edge of the barrier, which split the bridge in two. They could make out weapons on the mob around the gallows—handguns in holsters, swords in sheaths, even a chain saw tossed casually over someone's shoulder.

"They're going to let her go," he muttered so that only she could hear. "They're going to let her go."

She didn't dare answer. She brushed violet strands of hair off her face and thought about the sorcery her father had used to have her execute Glorianna Seabright.

It had been a powerful feeling, tapping into the beast-stalker within. Her father had known that, and what had compelled her to kill had been less a matter of possession than encouraging something that was already there.

Beaststalkers, Andi now knew more than she ever wanted to, lived to kill. The blood in their bones ran warmer when they spilled others' blood, broke others' bones. Knowing that feeling firsthand made Andi absolutely certain of one thing: Tavia Saltin was about to die.

"They come!" Hank Blacktooth called out through a bullhorn. "The mighty spider-folk! Chief of Police, let's give them a formal welcome and salute!"

About two dozen of the crowd, dressed in dark blue uniforms and well-shined black shoes that peeked out from under their robes, stepped forward.

A small redheaded woman with an athletic body and soft eyes pulled out a Kel-Tec P-32 from her shoulder holster. She raised it, and the other police officers—for Andi could now see that they were indeed so—pulled out their own sidearms and pointed them west, away from the gently glowing barrier.

"Prepare yourselves, or prepare your souls!" she cried out in a tinny voice, and two dozen firearms, mostly Beretta and Desert Eagle pistols, went off. The rest of the crowd hooted, and several more unseen guns fired.

The closer they got, the more detail Andi could see: the modern body armor under some of the robes, the Ford pickup truck behind the scaffolding which was lined with modified vehicular armor, the M3 carbines with infrared scopes, the small blades that everyone carried as a second-ary weapon—from hand axes to kitchen knives. The police chief herself sported a catlin, a long, slender, double-bladed knife used for amputations before oscillating saws came into vogue.

She couldn't help it: she admired the knife, and wondered where she could get one herself.

Peering beyond the crowd to city hall, Andi was fairly certain she spotted two shapes patrolling in the tower window. *Snipers,* she guessed. *In case everything else isn't enough.*

It made some sense to be this well armed, of course. They had advertised the event, and dragons were out and about. Even the most powerful dragon would be lucky to get within spitting range without encountering lethal force.

Thinking of powerful dragons made her think of Jennifer Scales. She glanced down the river, up into the beams of the bridge's arch, anywhere she thought the girl might be. Would she be afraid of all of this, too?

Well—she's not here, is she? Question answered.

Skip stopped inches short of the barrier, and Andi tried to hold his hand. He shook it off.

Hank motioned to someone in the crowd with a video camera, then brought up the bullhorn again. "Ladies and gentlemen—and honored guests!—we are here today to celebrate the spirit of this amazing American community. Here in Winoka, we have what I like to call 'town spirit.' Y'all know what town spirit is?"

The hoots and hollers suggested that yes, in fact they did know exactly what it was, but Hank continued anyway.

"Town spirit is about pride in where you live. It's about loving and looking out for your neighbor. It's what keeps us up, when others try to bring us down. Which brings us to today's guests.

"Tavia Saltin," he continued, as his other hand brought up a thick manila folder. "You are a resident of this town—or at least, you pretend to be one as you walk among us. In fact, you are not at all what you seem. According to the town files—files carefully created and maintained by the late, great Glorianna Seabright herself"—he added with a flourish, earning a new round of applause—"you are in fact a monster. Specifically, the eight-legged sort, unnaturally large, unnaturally poisonous, unnaturally vicious.

"While we would normally wait a few days for the waning crescent to present our case, in this case there is no need. Our evidence is legion: your disappearance from public during past crescent-moon phases; your associations with known arachnids like Edmund Slider and Otto Saltin, both implicated in the arachnid plot to destroy this universe and replace it with one overrun with monstrous things; and most recently, your attempt to use your own sorcery within city limits, not more than forty-eight hours ago."

Tavia, who had been working her lower jaw this entire time, finally managed to spit out the rag that had been stuffed there. "The attempt was successful, and my brothers and sisters are on their way. You will have them to answer to if you don't release me at once!"

With a vicious swing, the bullhorn smashed into her thin lips. "Silence her!" Hank snapped (unnecessarily, Andi thought) at the guards, before the bullhorn came back up. Then the Master of Ceremonies was back again, smiling and playing the crowd. "You say your brothers and sisters are coming—perhaps they are already here, watching from the woods? Perhaps they are plotting to save you?"

Tavia, bleeding from her mouth, did not answer.

"Or perhaps all the help we will see for you today stands before us. Here on the bridge we see Francis Wilson, a blood relation of yours, also documented by Glorianna Seabright as an enemy of the town.

"Next to him, his whore, also known as Andeana, also known as the notorious assassin who killed our dear Glory."

Whore? Andi thought, puzzled. *That's a bit—*

"She proved that your kind can slip in and out of this barrier. She proved that you have power over it—power, we can only presume, that includes knowledge of how to end it."

He jumped down from the scaffolding and pushed past the police officers. He was almost touching the barrier now, and his glaring brown eyes tried to burn a hole through.

"Tell me," he continued through the bullhorn. "Would you like to demonstrate that power now, to save one of your own? Would you dare show the secrets of your sorcery, in front of our eyes, so that we may judge how powerful you truly are?"

When they didn't answer, he smiled grimly and extended the hand that held the bullhorn. It plunged into the barrier before Skip's face, and then doubled back above Hank's own arm, pointed at the crowd now. To someone unfamiliar with how the dome worked, it would almost appear as if Skip himself was holding the bullhorn.

"Come on," Hank encouraged them quietly with a wink. "Speak up. Share the secret of this barrier, and we will honor your aunt with a quick death. We can be merciful, even toward our enemies."

"Can you?" Skip didn't sound worried, or upset, or anxious. Merely curious. For some reason, that made Andi more nervous than anything else that had happened in the last ten minutes.

"Skip!" Tavia called out from the gallows, before a guard punched her in the stomach. The older woman doubled over, retching—as was the guard's intention and besides that, as had been Hank's intention.

Andi didn't dare touch Skip. She was certain he was going to go through, and was trying to decide how she would react when he did—defend him to the death, or retreat into the safety of the woods—when Skip actually laughed. *Laughed.*

"Go ahead and kill her, Blacktooth. She doesn't mean shit to me."

Hank frowned and withdrew the bullhorn. "I doubt that. She raised you."

"My *mother* raised me, you strutting, bullying dumbass. I've known my aunt for all of a year. She's a clueless, whining, overbearing loser who needs to wax. A lot. Torture her, kill her, snap her bra strap, see if I care. I have better things to do."

Skip turned and walked away. Andi shuffled back, unsure once again of what to do.

"Jannsen!"

One of the two guards pulled out a bastard sword, held it high behind Tavia with the point straight down, and shoved it down her spine before withdrawing quickly.

The woman collapsed, screaming. Andi grabbed Skip, who had already turned at the sound.

Hank never took his eyes off them. "Again, Jannsen!"

The sword came down a second time, this time corkscrewing through the nerve bundles it had already violated. The sound of metal scraping bone made Andi gasp.

"Again!"

Again the blade came down, and Tavia fell forward. The second guard grabbed her by the shoulders and dragged her back to her knees, so the hobbling could continue.

The sword continued to rape her spine, eliciting a shriek with each plunge. Maybe there were still nerves tough enough to survive the first few thrusts; maybe Jannsen was finding new angles; maybe she was simply still screaming from the first stroke.

Andi began to sob, but Skip stood like a statue. He and Hank stared at each other through the barrier with no facial movement, no signal that anything around them affected them at all.

Skip was not upset about his aunt, and Hank was not enjoying the reaction he was getting from Andi. Not at all.

Finally, the bullhorn came back up. "The rally is over, folks. Let's put her back in her cell. Once the crescent moon is up, she'll start feeling it again. That's when we'll start pulling those pretty feet and hands off."

CHAPTER 9
Jennifer

Jennifer Scales, born of two bloodlines—dragon and beaststalker—flicked back to her human shape while banking in to land on the hospital parking lot. She dropped the fifteen or so feet, caught the impact by flexing her knees, then walked through the front door, acknowledging the armed sentries flanking the west entrance.

It was a measure of how much had changed in the last year that she had flown in as a dragon, switched to human in midair, dropped to the pavement with her swords carefully strapped, and no one blinked. Heck, the only ones who even noticed were the sentries.

Both thirteen-year-olds were nodding back, Jim Tenny cradling a Hechler & Koch S—uh—an S-something-or-other . . . Jennifer had never known much about guns.

Her mother was expert with any bladed weapon, and her father—well. 'Nuff said.

His twin, Jana, was holding the stock of her .12-gauge in one hand, the shotgun barrel resting on her left shoulder. They looked weirdly alike, which was unsettling as they were fraternal, not identical, twins. In fact, except for the length of their hair, they really were identical. They even bore identical, slight smiles.

Susan's right. The Boy Scouts/Sniper Team are creepy. Especially when they drag their sisters into it.

"Have you seen my dad?"

In times of crisis, she knew her mother drew inward, while her father extended outward. Together, they were a formidable team. But what she needed now was the one who would talk with her and help her process what she had seen less than twenty minutes ago.

Jim and Jana shrugged, so Jennifer went inside.

The next person she ran across was Anna-Lisa, looking harassed as usual, barely flicking a glance her way as she walked by on the way to the supply room, talking to herself. "Oh, what do we need, oh, hi, Jennifer, okay, we need another case of lightbulbs—any kind, we're going to have to check the storage space at Wal-Mart and Target . . . even Christmas lights would be okay. And also, um, yeah, Jennifer, your dad's—flashlights! Yeah, we can wind Christmas lights around the poles out there to keep the place lit at night, but we—uh—"

"My dad?" Jennifer prompted.

"Right, hang on guys, um, Jennifer, I haven't seen your dad. I know your mom's checking on Bonnie's new baby—premature, poor thing, I don't think her lungs—lighter fluid!" This made Jennifer jump.

Jennifer moved through the lobby, recognizing each of

the faces there. They had become a sort of extended family, including several members who probably wished for a different heritage. Some of them still dropped their eyes when she passed—nurses her mom had worked with for years, EMTs who had come over to the house for barbecues since Jennifer was four. A couple of PAs. Cooks. Physical therapists. An awful lot of them were carefully avoiding eye contact.

Is it because of who and what I am . . . or did they catch a live feed?

The hospital still smelled of antiseptic, blood, and floor wax. It even looked like one, sort of—the place was a mess, yeah, and more lights were burned-out (when they were even turned on) than not.

Still, there were differences anyone would notice at once: staff were scarce; multiple rooms had been converted into "temporary" living quarters; the emergency fire boxes were all emptied of hoses and axes; nobody was asking anyone a damn thing about insurance information; nobody was "Midwestern plump" anymore; and everyone looked exhausted and scared.

Winter's coming again, she thought. *We need a plan.*

But first, we've got to figure out how Skip will react to what Hank has done today.

She heard her mother long before she saw her.

"—dammit, dammit, *dammit*! How am I supposed to treat a preemie without bilirubin lights? Huh?"

"You could try throwing a tantrum," came her father's voice, helping her breathe a sigh of relief as she rounded the corner.

As always (these days, certainly) her mother looked exhausted and . . . well . . . *old*. Though Jennifer didn't like to think about her mom as a, you know, real person and all (gross!), she had always known that Elizabeth Georges was seriously cute. She usually looked in her thirties; today (*and yesterday and last week and last month and*) she looked like she was on the far side of sixty.

"I don't have time for banter," she shot back. She turned back to the man who looked ready for orders—her PA, Michael Donovan. "We're low on ventilators and antibiotics. We've got to decide if baby Marshall here truly needs anything beyond a blanket and a bottle. By the sword of St. George, I *swear*—"

Jennifer raised her eyebrows. That was a rare epithet indeed—one her mother, prior to Big Blue, took care never to repeat in mixed company.

"Basically we're down to freaking kangaroo care!"

Now Jennifer tried to stifle a giggle. Her mom had explained once that in less-developed countries (or in cities that were, say, trapped beneath a dome) the best way for medical professionals to treat premature infants was skin-to-skin contact. And not only from the new moms. People all over town would be pressed into kangaroo-care service: male or female, trained or not, dragon or beaststalker or neither. Lactating or, uh, not.

Jonathan cleared his throat. "I better not keep you too long, Liz. Listen, I scouted those farms you sent me to—the ones to the northwest? There are maybe half a dozen cattle left."

Michael twisted his mouth. "That's maybe enough to feed this hospital population for a couple of weeks. If nobody has seconds."

"Mother fuck," her mom said in quiet despair. Then, "I'm sorry. I didn't mean—thank you so much for looking. It's good news, Jonathan."

"Sure it is. I'll bet Jennifer has more."

They all—both parents and Michael, and possibly even the baby—looked at her. She chewed her tongue, trying to figure out how not to make what she had seen sound even worse than starving to death.

As it turned out, there was no way to do that. So she settled on telling them, no punches pulled, about the repeated hobbling of Tavia Saltin on the bridge in front of Skip and Andi.

Everyone sat down—first Jonathan and Michael, and then Elizabeth, with baby Marshall still in her arms.

"Did anyone see you?" she asked.

"I don't think so. I was in camouflage, circling overhead. No one acted as if they knew or cared I was there."

"That was dangerous, ace."

"I know, Dad." She did know. He might as well have said, *We're stuck under a dome, ace.*

"You say Skip walked away from that?"

"And Andi. But I doubt this is the end of it. Skip doesn't walk away from fights. Not these days, especially. He has something in mind."

Elizabeth handed baby Marshall off to Michael before pounding her forehead with a fist. "Fucking Hank. Fucking Hank. Fucking Hank."

"Liz. You okay?"

"I'm super, honey." Whack! Whack-whack! "This is how I think."

"Maybe it would work better if you could punch Hank instead of yourself."

"Don't tempt me. I can't believe he's provoking arachnids as we head into a second winter. What does he have stockpiled down there under city hall—provisions for eternity? Moronic mama's boy."

"On behalf of mama's boys everywhere," her father said with faux dignity, forcing Jennifer to stifle yet another giggle, "I resent that. And I doubt Hank thinks that far ahead. C'mon, Liz. I know this is bad, but we have to focus. You've got a baby that needs care here. What do you want Michael to do?"

Elizabeth rubbed her eyes and turned to Michael. "Kangaroo care it is. You have first shift. Watch him carefully for symptoms and start an immediate course of antibiotics if you see anything."

As Michael nodded and took the baby out of the room, Jennifer marveled at the deftness with which her father, who not twelve hours ago had been nearly catatonic with pessimism and defeatism, had redirected her mother's despair into positive action.

He really knows her. And she really needs him. No wonder she's willing to resort to bad coffee to keep him going. Hey—I wonder if he does the same thing to me?

Naw. He'd be more subtle. He'd—

As if on cue, he turned to her. "C'mon, ace. Let's you and I go bring those cattle in."

Subtle like a brick to the forehead.

CHAPTER 10
Jennifer

Once the cattle were slaughtered, dressed, carried, and stored in the hospital's walk-in freezer, it was early afternoon. Jonathan suggested a bite to eat (not cattle . . . they'd both lost their stomach for anything more substantial than ramen noodles), and they were back in the air over the town.

I know how to field-dress a full-grown cow. This is a weird thing for a teenage girl who doesn't live in a meat-packing plant to know.

It looked ironically peaceful, as if it had worked out all the violence in its system for the day. Small dots of white and black marked where some robed figures still walked through the streets, but most people were back in street clothes and going about their business.

"Doesn't look like Hank has anything else planned

today," Jennifer called out. *Prob'ly too busy wondering why he's never been admired the way his parents told him he oughta be admired. Looooooser!*

"He's not the one we're worried about. Keep an eye to the east."

"You think Skip and Andi will come back? What's the point? Beaststalkers can assemble quickly. It is part of their essential awesomeness. And according to Mom, city hall is a fortress. It's connected to the police station by an underground firing range, with all kinds of weaponry down there. At least fifty officers are going to be armed and prepared across the entire complex, at all times. Hell—I can see two snipers in the tower right now, trying to figure out if they see us up here."

"I'm sure they can. They must have infrared technology, like we do. Better, since Hank has had access to the town armory for some time."

"So why aren't we picking bullets out of our teeth?"

"Ever try to pick off a moving, virtually invisible target from eight hundred yards through an infrared scope?"

"No," she admitted. "I've gotten behind in homework. And also feeding people who are trapped under a dome. Also, guns give me a rash."

He ignored her lame crack. "Neither have those kids down there. As long as we keep our distance, they'll probably save the ammo."

She looked east, where the trees sprouting from the steep hills were lessening their green and losing their first leaves. "Dad. It's been two years."

"Huh? Big Blue's only been up—oh, you mean for you."

"Yeah. Two years since I learned what I was. Since Skip came to this town. Since I met Catherine, first fought with Susan, then Eddie. I was wondering."

"Wondering what?"

"If I should've done anything different."

He dipped his wings and whistled. "The eternal question. Ace, I don't have the perfect answer for you here."

"One of your half-assed answers will be okay."

"From my own child I gotta take this? Heaven knows I've spent half my life making all sorts of mistakes, as a dragon and a man. All I can tell you is that every single person on this earth, living or dead, has made decisions they regret. No one gets a do-over. Nobody ages backward. And really, even if you did: what do you really think you could change?"

"I could have been more careful around Skip. Maybe it would be different with him, now."

"Ah, there's one where I can reassure you, ace. What hurts Skip is nothing you could fix."

"Why're you so sure?"

"Because of what his mother did to him. Then his father. His parents twisted him beyond anything anyone else could save."

"Hmmph."

"You have to let Skip go, ace. You don't have to hate him. You *do* have to recognize that he's beyond help. Even for the Ancient Furnace," he teased.

"Oh, please, I don't—hey, what's that?"

Changing direction, they both squinted at what was coming over the hill on the highway to the west. At first, Jennifer was convinced the tar was bubbling. After half a minute, she realized something—many somethings—were crawling over the asphalt.

"Skip?"

Jonathan pulled up next to her and hovered with a sigh. "Skip's response."

CHAPTER 11

Jennifer

Jennifer and Jonathan banked lower until they could see greater detail in the swarm that worked its way toward the bridge. It moved slowly but purposefully, seething and clicking.

"They look like drawings," she observed.

"I agree. I don't get it . . ." He dipped down farther, until he was under the bridge's arch. Jennifer looked around nervously for armed patrols, but no one else was near. No sentries? It was as if Hank assumed he could do what he did and suffer no consequence.

Well? Have there been?

She dropped to her father's altitude. The creatures were on the bridge now. They did not climb the beams of the arch, but rather stayed on the road. There was definitely purpose in their movement.

"They're plainly sent to do something. Why send creatures with no thickness?" Jonathan mused. "What could they do? How could they attack or do anything useful if they don't exist in the same space we exist in?"

"Maybe it's temporary," Jennifer guessed. "If they can't attack, they can't be attacked, either. Putting them in two-dimensional space would make for an effective delivery system."

"Delivering what? And where?"

They simultaneously looked at city hall, as the creatures marched under them.

"Oh, crap," she finally said. "We're going to have to save him, aren't we?"

"I'm afraid so, ace. And it's the two of us—no time to get help. One of us disables the guards, the other evacuates the complex."

"I'll disable the guards. You want to save Hank Black-tooth, you do it."

"Good luck."

"Get bent, Dad. Love you."

"Love you, too."

It occurred to Jennifer, as she bolted at the tower atop city hall, that those words had an excellent chance of being the last they ever said to each other.

All because we have to pull their asses out of the fire when they caused the problem in the first place.

Perhaps that's not totally fair, she argued with herself as she dipped below one sniper's shot and flashed to the left to avoid the second. *There must be more than beaststalkers working here, just like there are innocents working at the hospital.*

She flipped into human form as she entered the tower, knocked out the two snipers with the mahogany hilts of her crafted daggers, and tossed their guns out the window she had accessed. *People who come in to work, want to do a good job, and go home to kiss their kids. Families like the family you thought you had two years ago.*

She barely could make out the shape of her father as he approached the tower. He would be counting on her to clear a path, so she got to work.

So for all the janitors and secretaries, she continued to convince herself as she slipped down the tower stairs, *all the network admins and evidence handlers.* A guard positioned on a landing couldn't process the sight of the teenaged girl coming at him until he was knocked out by a roundhouse kick. *We'll do it for them. We'll evacuate them first, as it should be. Of course, they need a reason to leave . . .*

Already back in dragon form, she burst out the stairwell door into the main lobby, a room two stories high, where half a dozen police officers stood guard, three up top and three below. Before they could react, their eyes told them the entire building was beginning to shake and melt. Jennifer added touches to the mass illusion, ones she had picked up from practicing the ancient creeper-dragon skill for the last several months: orange monkeys with elephant ears came shinnying down the grooved columns that dominated the domed chamber, and the stench of sulfur peeled off the elaborately painted plaster walls.

And if Hank Blacktooth manages to get out in all the commotion, she told herself as her invisible father patted her on the back for her fine work and darted off to the mayor's office, *well then . . . no plan is perfect.*

The officers became the best sales force for their plan, ringing the alarm and calling for a general evacuation of the complex. "Earthquake!" went the cry, and Jennifer supposed that was a more efficient if less accurate description than "Earthquake with elephant-eared monkeys!" Very few municipal systems had a specific siren for that.

She gratefully watched dozens of innocent people—exactly the people she had come to save—come swarming from side hallways and stairwells, into the main lobby and out the front and side doors. Off into the lawn they went, to their designated safe zones. Nobody trained for evacuations with more effectiveness than government workers.

In a matter of a few minutes, she saw them all pass before her. Maintaining the illusion required her standing still, and so she did not move as everyone hustled and bustled, even rubbing up against her. She would be visible to them all, she knew—a shining golden form of a dragon, if any of them took enough time to examine her. She didn't want to scare them more than they already were.

Fortunately, very few people on their way out were interested in a harmless statuesque form when everything else was apparently coming down around them.

The one exception was Hank Blacktooth.

"What is the meaning of this?" he was shouting, as an unseen force propelled him out of his second-floor office, down the stairs and onto the lobby floor. "What's happening? Is this an earthquake? This doesn't seem—what's that—YOU!"

The moment he spotted Jennifer, she knew the ruse was up. Fortunately, the last of the workers and beaststalker guards were already out of the building—her father, she realized, had timed this purposefully, since bringing Hank out into the lobby too soon would have ruined everything.

"Hank," she heard him say, "for once in your miserable life, listen to me. We're trying to save you. Give me sixty more seconds of cooperation. If you don't believe me after what you see, you can chop my head off yourself."

"I will do no such—ooof." Hank Blacktooth doubled over, fell down the entryway stairs, and rolled out of the building.

"That's it, Jennifer. We've got to get out of here."

As if to emphasize the point, the black swarm from the bridge began to discolor the walls, seeping in through an infinite number of dimensional cracks. They invaded the first-floor surfaces, then the second floor, then the dome interior . . .

"Out, out, out!" he cried, dragging her with him.

They flew through the darkening doors, over Hank's groaning form, and into the open air as the building behind them began to hum. The creatures covered the exterior as well as the interior. They found every inch of brick, every pane of glass, every bit of wood and plaster, and dug in their appendages. Then the hum turned into a sizzle, and the creatures inflated into thickness. Bodies fattening, their sizzle turned into a whine, then a roar . . .

. . . and then the entire building was consumed by a billion tiny explosions, each one carrying away a small piece of Hank Blacktooth's impregnable fortress, until there was nothing left except a hole in the ground.

CHAPTER 12
Andi

Andi watched Skip, who watched Winoka's city hall disintegrate from the safety of the river cliffs.

"I hope you're happy," she muttered, trying hard not to look at the devastation.

He shook his head and pointed. "They evacuated."

"Whatever. The building's gone. That's what you wanted." She yawned. "You have your revenge." *And it's all . . . so . . . tiresome.*

"I wanted to kill Hank Blacktooth, and the rest of the scum that surrounded my aunt and tortured her."

"Well then, you shouldn't have told the bugs to attack city hall." The moment the comment was out of her mouth, she wished she could stuff it back in.

Skip pretended he didn't hear even though they both knew he did. "How did they know it was coming? There were no guards on the bridge. No one to warn them. I don't understand—"

"Maybe the snipers in the tower—"

He narrowed his eyes and stood up suddenly. "Her. HER. HER!"

Andi knew whom he was pointing at before she even looked. There was only one Her.

"We have more work to do," he hissed, dragging her by the arm back into the woods.

CHAPTER 13
Susan

Susan Elmsmith, would-be roving reporter and (hopefully) future television journalist, sighed and leaned back.

Gautierre's head appeared directly over hers, blocking the autumn sunlight, and he opened his fingers, letting the delightful tidbits drop into her mouth.

"Mmmm. Pez."

"It's not the same as feeding you peeled grapes, I s'pose," he admitted, while Susan crunched. "Grapes being really hard to come by."

"I hate grapes. The seeds get stuck in my teeth."

"Eat seedless ones."

"That's the sinister aspect of all grapes, you foolish boy."

"This ought to be good."

"Even the seedless ones have seeds lurking within.

There you are, trying to enjoy romantic fresh fruit, then the next thing you know there's seeds and all kinds of gunk jammed between your wisdom teeth."

"Wisdom teeth." Gautierre flopped down beside her on the blanket, handing her a pack of Grape Pez. "Huh."

Susan busily shredded the wrapper and popped more candy in her mouth. They were over the border of the town on the south end, taking advantage of the unseasonably warm autumn day.

Eventually, Gautierre had come to see her side of their recent argument. After a face-saving interval of a few days, he had suggested a picnic, and given the limitations of Domeland, she thought he'd done well: Pez, and chocolate chips, and a box of Little Debbie Swiss Cake Rolls, and canned apple pie filling, a bag of mini marshmallows, and room-temperature ginger ale.

Now they were lounging on a pair of sleeping bags zipped together, keeping an eye on the tree line. Gautierre had chosen the spot: the town was at their back, the site of the strange invasion was as far away as anyone could possibly get, they could see an ambush from a mile away, and he had flown over the area first to make sure no one had any nasty surprises planned.

She loved watching him fly, and she had to smile when she remembered his reaction to *her* reaction the first time she'd seen him in dragon form: *Don't let the lavender wings fool you. I'm all man! All weredragon, I mean . . .*

"Wisdom teeth," he now repeated, back to his other body, which was merely that of a ferociously handsome guy. Not many teenagers could pull off long, charcoal black hair woven into three braids, though Gautierre managed handily.

"Uh." She paused in midcrunch. "What?"

"Trying to remember if we've got a dentist anywhere in that hospital."

"Not that I know of. The one me and my dad use knows Hank Blacktooth pretty well. I think he's living pretty close to city hall."

He didn't respond, but she could sense the question: *so what happens if someone needs serious work done? Yet another medical situation we haven't experienced so far but probably will soon. Wisdom teeth, teeth chipped in accidents, root canals . . . it's only a matter of time. So what will we do?*

The answer came, strangely enough, in the voice of Dr. Georges-Scales: *the same thing we do when a pregnant woman has to give birth, or someone gets the flu, or appendicitis. We will make do.*

"Dental stuff isn't supposed to be any big deal," he finally managed. "Growing up in Crescent Valley, it was easy. Dragon physiology is pretty rigorous."

She could see him starting to worry about her again. "I have a perfect dental record," she reminded him. "Teeth like rocks. I've been hoarding floss."

"Hmmm." He didn't smile. "What about other routine stuff? Like having an appendix out."

Ah, that's where this is coming from. He was thinking about a certain poor Mr. Simmons, late of the United States Post Office, former commander of the local American Legion post, and Susan's mailman for the last seven years. Mr. Simmons had been the latest person to die under Big Blue. Jenn's mother couldn't save him in time; his appendix ruptured, and he died of peritonitis.

Death was always scary. Unlike in movies or television, how Mr. Simmons had died was depressingly mundane. It hadn't been sexy or cool or scary—was death ever really that way?—and he hadn't been burned or stabbed; he hadn't died trying to save children or fight for his life. He'd . . . he'd just gotten sick. Didn't feel right standing up.

Sat down. Maybe lay down, after a while. Told a friend to take him to the hospital.

And *died*, before he ever got to sit up or stand up or do anything else, ever again.

It was dumb, but that upset Susan more than anything else. Dragons run amok? Huge spiders jumping around? Overzealous, sword-flinging, jackbooted thugs? She could handle these things. Jennifer Scales had trained her well.

But dying of appendicitis? That was supposed to be nothing. That was supposed to be no big deal.

Also, her gums *had* started bleeding, despite all the flossing, and she was achy and sore almost all the time now. She'd done some research outside her boyfriend's watchful gaze, and was as equally amused and appalled to recognize the early symptoms of scurvy.

Frigging scurvy!

She'd never taken a vitamin supplement in her life (her late mother had been convinced vitamins were a plot by the drug companies to make money on unnecessary crap, so children's chewables were verboten), and by the time she checked out the local supermarkets and drugstores, there were none to be had. As for fresh lemons, oranges, and grapefruit? Forget about it. Even cans of juice concentrate were gone.

She had said nothing of this to Gautierre. Some things weredragons were no good for, and curing scurvy was right up there on the list.

"Maybe we'll go back to the old days," she mused aloud, "and the barber will knock out our rotten teeth and sew up our wounds."

"What?"

"Eh. Pass me more Pez." She wolfed down the sugar pills and chewed defiantly.

At least they were wearing clean clothes. Her gums

might be bleeding excess sugar and Gautierre might have seen every single one of her outfits and she might not remember the last time she had any cheese that wasn't Velveeta (what the hell was "processed cheese food," anyway?) and . . . okay, she was giving serious thought to suggesting it was time for the cats and dogs of the town to be turned into lunch. But dammit, she did laundry every week. Religiously. Possibly laundry *was* her religion now.

"What if we never get out?"

He had been searching the tree line. He looked at her and blinked slowly, like an owl. "We will, though."

"No, come on. What if we don't?"

"We will. I know we will."

"How?" She was genuinely curious; he sounded so certain. "How d'you know?"

"Because I'm not letting the love of my life die under a dome like an ant under a magnifying glass." His calm certainty touched her and, it must be said, frightened her a little.

He looked like a boy, and he acted like a boy, and he kissed and groped and obsessed about sex like a boy. Yet he was more than that. They weren't the same: not the same sex, the same religion, the same political party, or the same under a crescent moon. Yet he was cloven to her, and she felt him in her even when he was miles across town.

"You say the sweetest things."

"Mom."

She sat up so fast the top of her head rapped against his chin. "Boy, did you just get me out of the mood. It's Susan, remember? Sooo-zen."

He'd seized her arms with both hands, stood in one smooth movement (How did he do that? His knees didn't even creak! Who gets up from a sitting position without at least a crackle of cartilage?), and shoved her behind the enormous willow tree they'd been snacking beneath.

"It's Mom."

"I don't see—"

"Quiet."

She hushed, more than a little annoyed. The sky was clear, it was a beautiful day, there wasn't a soul in sight, and there was a can of pie filling right over on the blanket over there with her name on it. The pressure was definitely getting to Gautierre, who was now jumping at shadows and imagining his mother, then manhandling (dragon-handling?) her behind a tree, and—

—and there were a dozen winged shapes on the horizon.

She couldn't get more precise than that. Whether they were dashers or dusters or smashers or crashers (or whatever the hell the classifications were), mattered less than whether they had sworn their lives to Jennifer Scales . . . or Ember Longtail.

These dozen seemed to dance in the air for a bit, doing reconnaissance circles around each other. Then they rose together about a half mile from where Susan and Gautierre hid, and . . .

"Holy *shit*!"

Twelve fireballs crashed into the tree line a few hundred yards away. The blaze was immediate and immense.

"They've seen us! We've got to go!"

Susan followed him without argument, but she wasn't so sure. Surely they would have gotten closer had they discovered enemies on the ground.

She looked longingly at the abandoned picnic site as he dragged her by the hand into a denser copse. More explosions rocked the earth behind them—some closer, some more distant.

"Gautierre, I don't think—"

"Sshh. Hang on."

Biting her lip, she waited for him to figure out what she already had: the destruction was random. That was the *good* news. The *bad* news was, they were sitting in the middle of a heap of kindling.

"Gautierre, we can't stay—"

"I can't fight them, Susan! There are twelve of them— maybe more. It's almost her entire gang! We've got to hold out and wait—"

"You don't wait out a forest fire! Gautierre, dammit, get me out of here!"

He blinked, then nodded, then shifted into dragon shape. Climbing onto his back, she shook her head. *Dr. Georges-Scales is right. Dragons are dreamy and sexy. But they're horrible, horrible planners.*

CHAPTER 14
Susan

"Ember did *what*?"

Susan nodded. She and Gautierre were both resting against the wall near the hospital entrance—him from fatigue (though he tried not to show it, bless him), her from anxiety.

"That makes no sense."

It didn't matter how incredulous Jennifer and Jonathan Scales were. Off to the south, the first wisps of smoke were rising into visibility.

"There's nothing of strategic value there," Jonathan continued. "No buildings. No hideouts—in fact, we were all pretty sure that was where Ember herself kept her gang hidden."

"Defending against an invasion?" Jennifer guessed.

"Possibly. Christopher," he called out to a pizza delivery

boy who had been promoted to emergency team dispatcher. The kid was taking what would have been a cigarette break, back before the last pack was nervously smoked away. "Any word from our scouts on Hank Blacktooth's people? Are they in the southern woods?"

"Haven't heard anything as of fifteen minutes. I'll get back in to check in with the team."

"Thanks." Jonathan turned back to Jennifer. "If it's not Hank, there may be a new threat in town."

"There's a new threat regardless," Susan pointed out. "The forest is on fire!"

"It's far away from any neighborhoods, and there are wetlands in between. If Ember wanted to attack the town, there are more direct ways. She's taken them, in fact." He turned to Jennifer. "Maybe she wants us to waste water fighting it?"

"Mom says water's the one thing we still have in this town, at least as long as the rain keeps falling and the well pumps keep working." Jennifer rubbed her chin. Unlike her father, she chose to be in human form this afternoon. "Maybe she's being a brat. Running drills. Showing her gang who's boss. Y'know. Stumpy-getting-grumpy kind of stuff."

"It could be random," Gautierre suggested, looking at Susan hopefully, since he knew that had been her idea. "She could be trying to get our attention. Distract us."

Jonathan shrugged. "Why would it distract us? It's a fire, but it's far from town. Okay, maybe we've got plenty of water: but it would surprise me if Hank risked the personnel and equipment to go out there. With city hall gone, he's got enough on his hands right now."

"Excuse me," Susan piped up. "As the only representative in this conversation of People Who Aren't Fireproof, I'd like to suggest: Hank Blacktooth will try to put it out.

Hank Blacktooth *should* try to put it out. In fact, if Hank Blacktooth *doesn't* try to put it out, I'll go to the mayor's new office, wherever that may be, and formally complain as a taxpaying resident of this town, and I prob'ly won't be the only one. Don't you guys get it? Don't you watch my blog updates?"

"Well . . ."

"Um . . ."

"I'm sure they're very informative . . ."

They all shrugged, embarrassed.

Susan pointed at Jonathan. "Your own wife was on! She talked about this! And threatened you! Biomass! We're using it for an energy source!"

"And food," Jennifer added thoughtfully.

"So she's burning down what's out there . . . to freeze us?" Jonathan sighed, unconvinced. "She'll have to burn an awful lot of it. Even confined to what's under the dome, there are acres and acres and acres—"

"While we've been talking, she's destroyed at least fifty acres of biomass. Say to be conservative, we've got six thousand acres outside city limits, but still accessible to us."

"How do you know—"

Susan, irritated, waved off Jennifer's question. "*Under Big Blue*, episode 78, 'The Resources that Remain.' Watch the damn blog, ya putz! Anyway, it's less than one percent . . . but it's only been an afternoon. The fire's own momentum will burn down more, before Ember and her cronies even reload. Say this first attack takes out three percent of our biomass. Say they attack every day, and get better at it. Say they hit harder each time, attack the fire equipment when it shows up, and degrade our ability to stop her. By the time January comes . . . are you getting where I'm going with this, or do I haveta break out the hand puppets. Say it with me: by the time January comes . . ."

"We'll only have what's left in town," Jonathan finished for her.

"Hallelujah! He sees the light, Lord."

"She won't dare come into town too many times," Jennifer pointed out. "Look what it cost them, last time. You said yourself, her entire gang is down to a dozen."

"She must have done the same calculation," Gautierre said. "My mother's not stupid. She'll figure we'll turn on each other if we have to compete for what remains within the town."

"That's a bit nihilistic, even for Ember. There are lots of people in town who are no threat to her. She knows that. She's misguided. Not evil." Jonathan looked nervously at Gautierre.

"Okay, Mr. Scales, I don't know what *nihilistic* means, but I have met my boyfriend's mother, right about the moment when she was trying to kill me. Thanks to Gautierre and Jennifer, she missed. But I wouldn't put anything past her. Evil might be a strong word, but mega-bratty-bitch seems to fit."

Gautierre cleared his throat. It was almost painful, all the nervous looks he was getting from the other people in the room. "She's trying to scare us."

"Scaring us isn't the plan. Scaring isn't any fun if you're a sociopathic shriveled-up misfit—sorry, sweetie, but there it is. So now she's deliberately burning down trees. So what if it will be this winter or next, that we need them? We need them! And she's taking them away because it's easy. Because no one will think much about it. Because maybe you're right, Mr. Scales: maybe Hank Blacktooth won't want to risk anything."

Gautierre grabbed her hand. "I agree. I'm sorry, but my mother is too unpredictable, Mr. Scales. Picking random fights isn't working. Waiting for the elements to pick us all off isn't working. Randomly killing off one of Hank's soldiers or a beaststalker caught alone isn't working. Even attacking the hospital in a group isn't working. She's going to continue to adapt."

"Like with the sap in the ears." Now Jennifer was nodding, too.

"So we . . . you guys, I mean . . . you stop her. Right?"

Jonathan gulped. "I don't know what we can do, Susan. And my wife would be the first to point out: we may have other priorities."

"Such as?"

As if on cue, Dr. Georges-Scales came out the nearby hospital entrance. "Jonathan, Christopher was telling me we've got fires out south. What do we know?"

After they told her, they waited for her to respond.

And waited.

And waited.

"Dr. Georges-Scales?"

"Mom?"

"Liz?"

Dr. Georges-Scales chewed her tongue, looked south, shook her head, and went back inside.

Jonathan and Jennifer, shrugging and scratching their heads, went in after her.

"So?" Gautierre looked at Susan quizzically. "What does that mean? We do nothing?"

Susan couldn't stop the chill from traveling up her spine. Even though she'd hated playing second fiddle to Jennifer all these years, she had to admit a certain comfort in knowing that she would take action. So would her father, and her mother . . . there were *some* advantages to being The Loyal Powerless Sidekick, and getting regularly saved was big number one.

To her, she supposed, Jennifer and her family were heroes. Maybe they were even responsible for her own bravery, in places like Hank Blacktooth's office—because she thought about what they might do in such situations.

What if they didn't do anything?

What if it all became too much, and they gave up?

What if the heroes . . . just stopped?

CHAPTER 15
Jennifer

It had been a long time, Jennifer realized, since she had last seen Eddie Blacktooth. She didn't know what was worse—not seeing him or seeing him and being unable to touch him.

Casualty #21 of being in Domeland . . . zero hands-on time with my would-be boyfriend.

He was no more than six feet away, but it might as well have been six million. The blue barrier shimmered between them, casting each of them in an unearthly glow to the other's eyes.

They were not even alone, she grumbled to herself as she imagined holding and kissing him. Her father was here on her side, and on Eddie's side was an even rarer sight: the seraph that had arisen from the dying body of Wendy Blacktooth, Eddie's mother. The enormous angel-warrior

burned with a silent white fire, had only showed up at er-
ratic intervals over the past few months, and never talked
even when it did.

It reminded Jennifer of a huge and annoying conscience,
which reminded them of all the death that had led them to
this point.

Major mood-killer.

Still, perhaps it could be useful now.

"You have to find Skip," she was telling Eddie, yet looking hopefully at the seraph.

"I find him all the time," Eddie snapped. He was in a
mood, which only made Jennifer more anxious. They never
had more than a few moments together; why he acted this
way was inexplicable. Boys: as much a puzzle to the Ancient Furnace as were hieroglyphics.

Well, okay, maybe it was a little bit explicable. He was
soaking wet and shivering, probably as a result of fording
the Mississippi River to their meeting point on the north end
of town without benefit of a bridge. Normally, a boat would
have sufficed; but during the crossing a dragon outside the
barrier sympathetic to Ember Longtail had taken a potshot at
him, and he had been forced to leap into the icy river. The seraph had come to his side shortly afterward to shoo away the
intruder, but apparently it didn't have a clothes dryer handy.

"I'm sorry about that dragon," she told him again.

He wrung out a sleeve, shivering and drippy and crabby.
"I thought Xavier had things under control out here. If he
has rogue dragons running around, I don't know how close
I can get to Skip." He sneezed.

Jennifer put a hand to her mouth and nodded grimly,
thinking: *don't smile. Don't smile.*

"I'm sure it's just the one. Please, Eddie. Won't you
help? If Skip's done this once, he'll almost certainly do it
again."

"Especially since he didn't kill anyone the first time," Jonathan added.

"We don't know what he'll go for next," Jennifer explained. She could see that Eddie was trying to hide his irritation and fear, and possibly the beginnings of a head cold, and she loved him for it. "It could be the hospital, or someone's house, or anywhere . . ."

"Or any*one*."

Jonathan's eyes were fixed beyond Eddie and the seraph, to the northeast and the river. Jennifer followed his gaze, and her heart twisted.

This stream of creatures was thinner and denser than the first. It spilled down the opposite cliffs and over the treetops like a rocket's shadow, moving in an unerring straight line.

For them.

"Eddie," Jennifer whispered, as she heard him gasp, "Jennifer!"

"We've got to get both of you out of here," Jonathan agreed. The seraph turned to him, its cold fire raging, and he spoke directly to it. "Protect him."

"But, Dad, how can it protect him against—"

"Argue another time! Eddie, get moving. To the west. Jennifer, to the east. Make that thing choose. I'll follow the target and do what I can."

Both did as he instructed, but after fifty yards Jennifer stopped.

The seraph wasn't following its ward. Instead, it stomped its foot and cracked the ground.

Jonathan waved it on. "Follow Eddie! Do as I say! If this stays outside the dome, you're the only one who can help him!"

Jennifer looked beyond them, at Eddie. He had stopped as well, and was looking at the oncoming swarm with quizzical panic. It was crossing over the flat current of the Mississippi, too far away yet to be sure which of them it would chase.

Dad's right. I have to get moving. We both have to get moving.

"Eddie, run!" she called out, and turned to do so herself.

She had made it only another thirty yards when a shock wave knocked her off her feet. Scrambling to get up, she realized it had come from the seraph, who had unsheathed its brilliant blue blade.

Not helpful, she steamed. She checked the swarm to see where it was flowing. Only when she saw how close it was—spitting distance from the seraph—did she begin to understand.

It took longer for her father to catch on. "Dammit, you angelic freak, help those kids before—"

It was too late for anyone to do anything, now. The river of death passed over and under the seraph as if it were nothing more than a dead pine trunk. The creatures within splashed through the barrier and pooled around the feet of Jonathan Scales. Before he could think to change form and take to the air, the cloud scrambled up his legs, invaded his face, and darkened his features.

His astonished gray eyes looked at Jennifer for an instant before the entire mass breathed in, and out, and in . . .

. . . and disintegrated, taking his ashes with it.

CHAPTER 16
Jennifer

The funeral of Jonathan Scales did not take place in a cemetery. There were none close enough to the barrier, and Elizabeth decided it would be best to have guests from both inside and outside. The most suitable destination was a potato field northwest of town, which gave everyone involved an excellent view of possible invasion.

Mercifully, there was none. Not that Jennifer would have cared if there had been one. What exactly were they accomplishing, anyway?

They were gathered around a small handful of dirt, within which must have been some of the only ashes Jennifer could recall scooping up in the aftermath of Skip's attack.

She had begged Eddie to help her, senseless to the barrier and everything around it. Beyond that, her memory was shredded by grief. She might have asked for her mother; she might have screamed at Skip to come out of the fucking woods and fight like a man; she might have rubbed some of the dirt cupped in her hand into her face.

She might.

She might have.

She . . .

She had an easier time remembering her grandfather's funeral last year, when several dragons, including her father, had brought the elder's body to the cremation plateau in Crescent Valley. From there, his spirit had traveled to the eternal crescent moon, where it flew in an eternal host. All dead elders received this honor.

But not Dad. He doesn't get that.

It wasn't only because they were trapped here. It was his sacrifice to his daughter, a price of birthright he had paid so that dragons who disliked him would still accept her as the Ancient Furnace. About half a dozen of those dragons were even assembled here today—a pitiful fraction of the total available. No beaststalkers from within the town came to comfort his family, not even the ones his wife and daughter (and he) had worked with every day for the last year.

She chewed her tongue and seethed at the proceedings. Eddie was there, bless him—but he could not even look at her, much less touch her. Ned Brownfoot was saying something, as if it mattered. Susan and Gautierre were here of course, and Catherine. It was good of them to come, she supposed with a sullen internal shrug. For all the good all this would do her father, they could be burying pebbles among the potatoes.

Her mother's arm sought her far shoulder. Jennifer allowed it.

And where were these dragons, she fumed, *when my father died? Xavier and the others—where were they while*

Skip created that swarm? Warm and cozy in Crescent Valley, a place I've protected even though they didn't want me there to begin with?

WHERE WERE THEY? WHY HAVEN'T THEY FOUND SKIP? WHY AREN'T THEY HUNTING THAT LITTLE SHIT NOW?

Her mother's hand felt the tension and began to rub her shoulder. Jennifer shook it off.

I should stop this, right now. End this so-called funeral. I should demand Ned Brownfoot take his fucking Missour-eh accent and sell it somewhere else. I should order Stumpy's uncle over there to gather the Blaze and burn the forests down, until Skip comes screaming out with his eyeballs on fire. I should order Hank Blacktooth and his psychotic legions to focus their rage on the real enemy.

I should lead! So what if some of them die? At least they'll be dying doing something worthwhile, instead of rotting away in this town.

This . . . fucking . . . prison . . . town.

She was stepping forward to say everything she was thinking when she felt her mother seize her shoulder with new urgency.

The burning shape of the seraph approached, the chilled sunrise framing its flames.

She glared at the useless thing. "What's *that* doing here?"

"I don't know, honey."

She wanted no part of it, this thing that had not stopped Skip's swarm from killing her father. It was useless. No, worse than useless: it had inspired a false sense of protection. If it couldn't (or wouldn't) stop anything from hurting her father, how could it stop anything from reaching Eddie? Or her mother? Or herself?

Potatoes under the seraph's footsteps popped, and it

trailed azure steam. The dragons on the far side parted and let it come through the barrier.

"Sweetheart, no." Her mother sensed the revolt inside Jennifer and slipped in front of her. "Let it come."

Her mother's face, an oval of stoic despair, was the only one she didn't despise in that moment. It was the only one she could not deny. Jennifer exhaled and watched the seraph step forward. The air filled with the scent of burning lavender, and all other sound vanished.

It reached a burning hand toward the soil containing her father's remains.

"What is it—"

"Sshh. Wait." Jennifer could see her mother didn't know, either.

"Mom, that's all we've got left of him!"

"Jennifer. Honey. Let it happen." Elizabeth's slender hand came up, and with a surgeon's skill she closed the tears and exclamations of Jennifer's face with soft fingers. "Let him go."

The air around them began to vibrate. They both had to stand back from the resulting heat, and soon so did the others farther away. The seraph wailed, and the crescent moon above trembled. Feeling the soil beneath her harden, Jennifer looked down. It was turning into ice—or was it glass?

The wind changed and began to pull inward, toward the seraph. The vacuum was mild where Jennifer stood—only enough to tug at the ends of her platinum hair. For the seraph, however, it was a deeper force. The angelic figure began to shrink into itself. Its steaming robes, its fiery wings, its sapphire eyes all slowly disappeared into a colorless singularity.

Once the seraph was gone, a shock wave knocked them all flat. By the time they recovered, all that was left of the seraph and the potato field around them was an indigo rain.

It took them a few seconds to realize that it wasn't rain after all—each colored speck was a minute dragon, and they filled the nearby atmosphere.

Neither Jennifer nor Elizabeth could say a word as the indigo spirits ascended, rising like a tide of algae pulled by the inscrutable sliver of moon far above.

CHAPTER 17
Susan

"Good afternoon. It's Day 306, and we have another special edition of *Under Big Blue*—"

"Susan! You can't be serious! Give me that!"

Grunting, she fought to keep the tiny video camera she had hidden from Gautierre. She knew he would act like this—that's why she had slipped the smaller, ultraportable model into her jacket pocket. She could have used a smartphone, but the resolution and memory sucked.

"Gautierre, I swear if you don't let me do this, we are *done*."

He paused, gauging her seriousness. "There's no way my mother will tolerate this. I knew I shouldn't have let you come here."

"You knew what I would do. I'm a reporter, Gautierre."

"You're a teenager!"

"So are you—and you're six months younger than me! What difference does that make? If I can live with the debilitating shame of robbing the cradle, you can let me do this."

He sighed and turned to Catherine, the only other one there. "Help me make her understand."

Their friend, already a dark green trampler, shook her reptilian head. "I'm not getting in the middle of this one, guys. You should figure it out soon, though: it's almost three o'clock. I doubt anyone's going to be late. We won't get that lucky."

"Susan." He shot an edgy glance to both horizons. "Uncle X asked me to come here to help talk with my mother. This is serious stuff. If you poke a camera into her face, she's not going to understand. She's going to think you're mocking her."

"I don't want to ask her any questions. I don't want to talk to her at all."

"So why have the camera?"

Duh! So handsome . . . so brave . . . so, so dumb . . . "To record what happens! To show everyone out there what we're trying to do! I'm going to be real discreet, Gautierre. She'll never know. You have to trust me."

He was still sizing her up when a half-V formation of large dragons appeared to the west. This was Xavier Longtail and several other members of the Blaze.

At the same time, Catherine pointed to the east, within the dome. A solitary winged figure was high above, scouting the surrounding terrain.

"Looks like she trusts us about as much as we trust her."

"I wish Jennifer had come, too," he said.

Susan rolled her eyes. "Ember never would have agreed to show. We don't need Jennifer, babe. You, Catherine, and I are strong enough to handle your mother. If any of her goons show up, we'll fly off."

They kept their eyes on Ember's graceful descent. She dumped the air from her wings gradually, being careful to compensate for the reduction in tail size.

Susan flicked the camera back on, put it into her otherwise empty pocketbook, wedged the purse between her chest and left sleeve, and checked the lens to make sure it lined up with the hole she had cut. It was an old trick of undercover reporters—she'd seen it done on dozens of investigative "gotcha" news shows—but Ember Longtail had little experience of the world beyond Crescent Valley.

They landed simultaneously, Ember Longtail and her uncle Xavier, almost mirror images of each other across the barrier. He nodded curtly as the other Blaze members lined up purposefully behind him. Susan knew a diplomatic show of force when she saw one: Xavier was trying both to show Ember a friendly set of faces and also demonstrate that he had the support of the Blaze.

"Niece."

She nodded back. "Uncle."

"I regret so much time has passed since we last talked."

"The last time we talked, you didn't have anything intelligent to say." She turned to Catherine. "I assume I have you to thank for this meeting?"

Catherine nodded. She had sent alligators all over town, hoping to find Ember or one of the gang.

"You're Winona's granddaughter. The one Glory hobbled."

"I am."

Ember looked her up and down. "You're tough. Our group could use someone like you."

"No thanks. I owe Jennifer and her mother everything. They saved my life, and my dragon self."

Susan winced as Ember scowled. "Fine. Be a lapdog. And you." She was speaking to her son now. "What have they done to you, my dear Gautierre?"

Well, Susan thought, *there's been kissing. Lots and lots of kissing. Oh, the humanity!*

"What lies have they told you, what silly and stupid dreams have they dumped in your head?"

That we should wait? I'm not sure we should wait. Bad enough I'm under Big Blue; do I also have to die a virgin?

"Did they tell you that dragons and their hunters can live in harmony? That all you have to do is hold hands"— she shot a look at Susan here—"and you will attain peace?"

"She's not a beaststalker, Mother. Her name is Susan. She's a good person. I brought her here because I wanted her to meet the mother I loved, growing up."

"I'm the same mother I always was. It's the son who's grown up to be a disappointment." Ember looked Susan up and down, then ignored her.

Aw, come on! I spent almost twenty minutes on my hair, you insensitive bitch!

"You had your friend call the meeting, then. And you invited your great-uncle. Fine. Get on with whatever you have to say to me."

"I assume you know that Jonathan Scales was killed yesterday."

"I'd heard. Who was the lucky beaststalker? I'd be tempted to shake his or her hand."

Susan stirred. Gautierre held out a hand to her and kept his focus on his mother. "It wasn't a beaststalker, Mother."

"Another dragon, then. Even better."

"It wasn't a dragon, either. It was Skip Wilson."

She snorted a plume of smoke. "Skip Wilson? That slight drink of water who came to Crescent Valley with Jennifer Scales last year and insulted the entire Blaze? Wasn't he supposed to turn into a spider someday and crawl under some sort of incredibly narrow rock?"

Xavier acknowledged her sentiment. "He never did look like much, Ember. But he's dangerous, and he appears to have found a virtually unstoppable method of killing whoever he'd like dead."

"Well, he appears to have found a virtually unstoppable method of killing whoever *I'd* like dead, as well. You're not suggesting I help you stop him?"

"That's up to us," Xavier answered, motioning to the Blaze members behind him. "I don't suppose there's much you can do inside there. But it might help your son and his friends to survive if they didn't have to worry about you and your crew firebombing them while we all try to figure out a way through this. If they didn't have to keep Hank from hunting you down, as you burn away the precious resources remaining. If they could count on you as an ally looking for a solution instead of an enemy adding to their problems."

Ember chuckled and raised her head to the sky. "Ah, Uncle. If you could only hear yourself today. Whatever drugs that murderous Georges bitch has fed you, I wouldn't mind a gram or two of, for recreational purposes.

"You want me to make life easier for her, now that her husband's dead? Now that her daughter is in this skinny-ass spider's sights? Now that her legacy of murder is nearly over—you want me to show her mercy?"

"Show your son mercy, then."

"He'll have it. The moment he picks the right side. He

can even bring his boring little whore." Ember winked at Susan and motioned to the purse. "Make sure you don't edit that line out, for your next news report."

Before Gautierre could launch himself at her, she was up in the air and rocketing away.

CHAPTER 18
Jennifer

"Y'know, Mom, I've been sitting here for about forty minutes, waiting for the irony to get a little less thick."

"I hear you." She looked around the basement of police headquarters, which had become the new city hall since Skip Wilson destroyed the old one. "At least we're outside the holding cells and not in them."

Jennifer eyed her watch again. She kept a bland smile on her face; her mother did the same.

"So how's Mrs. Gremmel feeling?"

"Diabetic patient? She's sleeping better since we found a new store of drugs. I don't know how much longer I can keep that going."

"And baby Marshall?"

"Better. By a small miracle, he hasn't needed much in

the way of pharmaceuticals. We keep him warm with kangaroo care."

"God bless the marsupials."

This earned a smile—the first Jennifer had seen on her mother's face since before the funeral. "I suppose I'm at least glad to be away from the hospital for the afternoon. Your father thinks"—she swallowed—"your father thought I've been running myself pretty ragged in there."

"You've been doing awesome things, Mom."

"And now, for a reward, I get to talk to Hank Blacktooth."

Jennifer glanced around the shitty chairs, the dim room, the desk sergeant's desk, now manned by a petite woman with short, carrot-colored hair slicked down like a helmet. Her dark eyes were enormous; she looked more like a child than one of Hank's goons. She was pretending to flip through a fourteen-month-old issue of *Newsweek* while listening to every word. "He'll listen, Mom."

"I hope so," her mother murmured, settling back more comfortably in the hideously uncomfortable plastic chair. "But he's never struck me as the listening type."

Jennifer noticed Carrot Helmet frown at the magazine. *Hank Blacktooth, what a stoop.*

(Stoop (n): abbreviated version of Stupnagel. Origin: an Elmsmithism for "big stupid moron who thinks he's subtle but ain't." *e.g.: Hank Blacktooth was a stoop for making them wait outside his crappy makeshift office.*)

They both knew Hank would agree to her mother's request for a meeting. He would know about her husband's death, and he would see it as (a) an opportunity to learn how to kill a dragon and (b) gloat.

They were okay with that (well, Elizabeth was okay

with that); in return, they hoped to make him aware of the real threat in town.

Just as Gautierre, Susan, and Catherine were trying to talk sense into Ember Longtail across town, so she and her mother were trying to talk sense into Hank.

She hoped they were having more success.

"Maybe I should have gone with them," she mused aloud. "Ember's pretty vicious. It's not like you need me here—you can take on any number of these idiots."

"It's important for you to be here."

"Why? Hank hates me. All I can do is piss him off. Which I'm happy to do, I guess . . ."

Elizabeth held her hand. "It's important for you to be here."

"Oh." *Gulp.* "Sure, Mom. Anything you need."

Carrot Helmet abruptly rose from the desk, marched past the empty holding cells, and disappeared through a door at the end of the room.

Jennifer glanced sideways at her mother, only to see her mother was glancing sideways at *her.* They shared a rare moment of perfect understanding: *freaks!*

"So did Susan tell you she and Gautierre found chickens? Chickens!"

"That *is* good news."

"Feral ones, apparently—"

Her mom laughed.

"I know—but they *are*, they're feral because I guess they escaped from what's-his-name, that really grumpy farmer on the east end of town . . ."

"Max Featherstone. He wouldn't sell, so there's a Chipotle on one side of his field, and a Kentucky Fried Chicken on the other."

"Now *that's* ironic. As Susan would say . . ."

"Oh, the humanity."

"Right. Anyway, they apparently darted off during an Ember attack last year—"

Carrot Helmet was back. "Excuse me—"

Jennifer held up one finger, the way you hold off a waitress so you could finish your menu selection. "Anyway, so a bunch of his hens *and* the rooster took off, and made nests, and now there are feral chickens that don't really belong to anyone, which means they belong to all of us. I bet they'll taste all feral-ey. Mmmm . . ."

Her mom chuckled again. "That's great. We should scoop them up on the way back." Her mom glanced up at the clearly irritated redhead. "What is it, hon?"

"Mayor Blacktooth will be a moment. He apologizes—"

"Oh, is he running late?"

Deep frown. "Anyway, he'll be right with you."

"Thanks. So anyway, honey, not only can you use the eggs for food, but you can grow certain cultures with them, which—"

"Dr. Georges-Scales?"

"Hmmm?" Her mother looked around absently. "Oh, we're fine. We don't need anything to drink."

The redhead's lips were pressed so tightly together, they'd disappeared. "I was going to remind you that you took care of my brother's shoulder surgery. About three years ago."

"Oh? Was he the ATV accident, or the car wreck?"

"ATV."

"Sure. Mike . . . Mike Whittle." Her mother's eyes had gone vague while she tried to remember, then sharpened when she did. "He got out the day before his eighteenth birthday, right? No complications?"

The invisible lips relaxed and reappeared. Dr. Elizabeth Georges-Scales had a computer-like memory for patients, including names and birthdays, and Jenn could see the red-head instantly loosen up. "Yeah, it—it went really good. I mean, you did good. He's, y'know, out there." She gestured vaguely, a gesture they'd all adapted and used to mean Beyond Big Blue.

"I'm glad." Her mother looked the woman up and down. "Is that a catlin?"

She glanced down at her left hip. "Yeah. You won't believe this, it's sort of a family heirloom."

"It's terrific. Jennifer, honey, do you know what those were for?"

"Ear cleaning?"

"Amputations," both women said in unison. "It looks brand-new," her mother continued, not bothering to hide her admiration.

The woman actually *blushed* with pleasure. "Well, we've always kept it—"

"I *said*," Hank's voice boomed out of the far office, sounding vastly irritated, "I can see them now, Chief."

"Vacation's over." Jennifer sighed, standing and stretching.

"Chief?" her mother seemed impressed. "I knew Mike's sister was on the force, but I had no idea how far you'd come. Congratulations."

"Thanks." She raised her voice on the off chance they hadn't heard. "Thanks!"

Jennifer shook her head. *How does Mom do that? Poor Hank, he must know he'll lose this battle eventually. No one wants to follow a tyrant.*

Not when they can pick someone like Mom.

CHAPTER 19
Jennifer

"Sorry to keep you waiting," Hank began. He was sitting behind what was once the police chief's desk. The vanity wall, Jennifer was amused to see, had been stripped of a previous occupant's awards and replaced with his own Salesman of the Month certificates.

"Huh," Jennifer remarked casually as she scanned the wall. "I didn't know you sold propane, and propane accessories."

"I haven't had much time for it lately," he replied, missing the amusement in Jennifer's tone. "I keep them here as a reminder of a better time. A time we might return to, if we can all pitch in together."

It's funny, she told herself. *He tries to sound like a leader, but comes out like . . . well, like Salesman of the Month.*

Elizabeth glanced around, noticing the lack of chairs

beyond Hank's own plush, leather, wheeled office chair. "Hmmm."

"Excuse me." Carrot Helmet had bustled in behind them, carrying the plastic chairs they had used in the hallway. "I remembered I forgot to put chairs in here for your meeting, Mayor Blacktooth."

"I told you I didn't—"

Dr. Georges-Scales beamed a thousand-gigawatt smile at her former patient's sister. "Thank you, Chief."

"Yeah, thanks," Jennifer added, inwardly chortling at the flash of annoyance that creased Hank's face like a fleeting wrinkle. She carefully, slowly, deliberately seated herself with a wriggle and appreciative sigh. "Saaay, this is nice."

"As I was saying, Lizzy," Hank said, glaring at Jennifer, "I'm sorry to keep you waiting. I'm sure you can imagine the demands I've got on my time these days."

"Um? Oh, yes, the burdens of leadership," her mother agreed, pleasantly enough as the police chief left and shut the door behind her. "Say, it's lovely to see you promoting the next generation of peace officers so rapidly."

Hank shrugged. "We've been through three police chiefs since Glory died. I've been forced to rely on younger members of the force."

Her mother gave him a look from beneath her lashes. "Perkier, too."

His cheeks reddened. "So anyhow. What's on your mind, Lizzy?"

"You are aware of my husband's recent death."

He bit his lip, trying for a diplomatic moment. "I had heard. How did he die, exactly?"

"That's why I'm here." Elizabeth sat and pulled her chair right up to Hank's desk. This left Jennifer sitting in the background, which suited everyone fine. Mother had made clear to daughter what her role here would be, and

Jennifer waited for that moment. "He died from the same sort of sorcery that destroyed city hall."

Hank's eyes widened, and Jennifer recognized fear. *Good. He gets that we're all vulnerable.*

"Hank. We've not agreed on very much over the years. Since Glory died, it feels like it's gotten worse."

He coughed. "There have been agreements in principle. You've rendered aid to dozens of my warriors."

"And in return, they've left the hospital alone. This has been a wise policy, Hank. Thank you for that. I wonder if we might come to a deeper agreement."

"Such as?"

"My daughter has arranged for her colleagues in the Blaze to search for Skip Wilson and apprehend him. While they do that, it would help matters a great deal if those you command would . . . tone down."

This elicited a frown. "Tone down?"

"No more provocative rallies. No more hobblings. No more killings. Just protection of the innocent."

"What do you think we've been doing, if not protecting the innocent?" He waved his arms at the walls, and Jennifer didn't know if he was referring to police actions or outstanding customer service in propane-accessory supply. "What do you think it takes, Lizzy?"

"I think it takes less drama than you've inspired."

"You felt the same way about Glory—"

"Don't." Elizabeth took a breath. "Please don't compare yourself to Glory."

"Why shouldn't I?" His tone was petulant now, as if he had been told he couldn't have the shiny lollipop in the candy-store window. "Haven't I led this town during its greatest crisis of the last half century? Haven't I protected thousands of townspeople from the destruction dragons have loosed upon us? Haven't I diverted precious resources toward putting out Ember Longtail's most recent fires—oh, yes, I know what she is up to," he added in response to their expressions of surprise.

"If you know—"

"She wants to starve us out, freeze us out, before this winter is through. We will be ready for her next assault. I will open up this town's armory, and we will spare no sentiment in eliminating her."

Jennifer chewed her tongue. His precise assessment of what Ember was up to disturbed her, because it meant there were things he was doing that were already helpful to them. Did that mean they owed him something?

"Ember Longtail is a small matter, compared to whoever is aiming at both of us from out there. We have to focus, Hank. It's a lesson Glory taught all who followed her."

"Don't patronize me. I know plenty about Glory's lessons."

Sensing the diplomatic effort failing, Elizabeth turned to Jennifer. "Perhaps you should pass on your message, honey."

"Sure, Mom." Jennifer turned to Hank. "Mr. Blacktooth, your son gave me a message for you. He told me to tell you he still misses his mother. He wants you to honor her by working with us to end this conflict. He wants us to work together to build a memorial for her, and for the others who have died here."

"A memorial for Wendy is in the works," Hank said. "As you can imagine, in this time of limited resources, when we have to be in a constant state of readiness, it is difficult to find the staff—"

"I think you may be missing the point of my daughter's message, Hank." To no one's surprise. "Your son wants you to stop what you're doing. He wants you to take a different path."

Hank's features darkened. "I could say very much the same for him."

"If we can't come to peaceful terms within this dome, how on earth are we going to survive? How are we going to stop our common enemy?"

"By common enemy, I presume you mean the arachnids and dragons that infest this corner of Minnesota."

"I *mean*, unstoppable missiles, starvation, and exposure to the elements as we run out of fuel!"

"But not dragons," he said, and neither of them could figure out if he was being ironic. "Look, it's this simple: our goals don't intersect enough. I am fine with your staff continuing to provide medical care to my soldiers, as necessary."

"I'll bet you are," Jennifer said pleasantly.

He ignored her. "In return, we will allow the hospital to operate—"

"I don't need your *permission*," Elizabeth snapped, "to run that hospital." She stood. "I had hoped a year of governing responsibility would have matured you, Hank. But the problem with you was never immaturity. It was, and still is, sociopathy. You are an intractable leech who bleeds everyone and everything around you, all to the goal of feeding a starved ego that never, ever feels full. No matter how bloated you get off of others' misery—Wendy's, Eddie's, this entire town's—you will continue to suck, and suck, and suck. You will be the ruin of us all."

She turned to her daughter. "Did I miss anything?"

Jennifer blinked. "I might have added another 'suck.'"

"Get out of my office!" Hank thundered, rising with a fist in the air and coming around his desk. "Get out of my headquarters! Get out of my town!"

"I will stay in this town, even if the dome disappears someday; and I will go where I please, when I please."

Elizabeth actually stepped forward into Hank's advance, making him stop abruptly.

Jennifer watched, praying he'd try something. Anything. A swing. A sneeze. A seizure.

"My daughter and I will recruit from among your own staff, showing them a different path than the one you've chosen. We will inspire hope where you inspire fear. We will protect the innocent where you torture the helpless. We will do everything we can to render you utterly alone, and when Skip's swarms come for you—and they will, Hank, someday soon, they will, I know it . . . *and you do, too*— you will die, utterly alone, unmourned and unloved. Which is far more than you deserve, you stupid, sorry, pathetic little man."

She all but pushed a stunned Jennifer out into the hall-way and slammed the door behind them. The crash of exactly two upended plastic chairs against the other side of the door made Jennifer flinch. Her mother, however, was already down the hallway.

"Chief Whittle. I have a proposition for you."

CHAPTER 20
Andi

Andi woke up to the rattling of the restaurant's windows, and of the flatware and glassware in the kitchen beyond. She looked out the window and saw fire.

"Skip, wake up!"

He was a heavier sleeper, and it took another two or three fireballs landing in the lawn in front of the Cliffside Restaurant to get him fully awake and paying attention.

When he finally watched a few more land near the building, he collapsed back into bed. "Stop worrying about it. It's a fishing expedition."

"They're fishing awfully close, don't you think?"

"They've done it before." This was technically true. In fact, Tavia had taught them never to stay in one place for too long and to keep all signs of life within hidden from those outside.

"Never this close, or this intense. Skip, they know we're here."

"No way. There are three dozen structures within a half mile of this restaurant. For all they know, we could be in any of them. They're not going to light up the entire cliffside, because they don't really want to hurt anyone. They only want us to reveal ourselves. We need to stay inside. The fires won't even make it to the structure. Trust me."

She looked out the window nervously again. The shrubs that marked the edge of the parking lot were ablaze, but no further fireballs had come.

The chill, wet autumn air slowly extinguished the burning bushes.

A few minutes later, she saw and felt a new cascade of meteors, this one at the convenience store down the street. As with the restaurant, they did not hit the building itself.

Skip's right. She calmed herself down. *They're not destroying structures. They're trying to smoke us out. It's a good thing he kept his head. I would have gotten us into a worse fix. That was stupid of me.*

She lay back down next to him, curled up against his heat, and went back to sleep.

The following morning, Skip was less sanguine about the previous evening's events.

"They have some nerve, coming after us!"

"You did kill one of their own," she reminded him.

"That was personal, between his family and mine. That didn't have to involve these other dragons at all. They're outside the dome, the Scaleses are inside the dome. All they have to do is stay out of my way, and we'll be fine."

"They're not going to stay out of our way, Skip. They're

going to try to protect Jennifer and the others. It's what I would do," she added unconvincingly.

"Then we have to show them that we won't respond to threats. We have to show them they don't have any influence on what we do. In fact, for every night they spend hunting for us, we should be hitting a new target. We'll pick a new one soon." He rubbed his hands and went into the dining room, where their latest art project swirled in a restless pile over the tables, chairs, carpet, and walls. "First, let's deliver this one as planned."

Andi nodded. What else could she say? Skip's arguments made sense; and besides, giving his creatures shape through her music made her feel good. Useful. Loved. Unlike all other sorceries she had ever known, this music did not weaken her, did not cost her anything.

Not anything she could measure, in any case.

CHAPTER 21
Jennifer

Jennifer was coming off shift on the roof when Susan and Gautierre came back from their full-town patrol. She gracefully slipped off his back as he hit the pavement.

"Jenn, the police station! It's under attack!"

"Skip?"

Susan nodded.

"Are they evacuating?"

Her friend could only shrug. The terror on her face was all Jennifer needed.

In a split second she was in the air on blue wings, Gautierre close behind her. They were barely over the treetops when they saw the explosion.

"Cripes!" This blast was fiercer and louder than the one at city hall. *He's getting better at this. The bugs are getting nastier.* Chunks of the building a full mile away landed on the houses below their wings, and they could sense the stench of the green plume that rose from the crater.

"Look for survivors!" she ordered Gautierre.

They found thirteen wounded over the next half hour, with several clearly dead and many dozens more missing. The two of them began turning over rubble and finding more. At first they were the only two who could withstand the poisonous fumes. Then a fire truck arrived and washed most of the reek away, and others could join in.

The ambulances—some real, some makeshift—came quickly and whisked the wounded away to the hospital. Gautierre and she kept at it, still in dragon form, with medics and police officers and townspeople at their side. They found another wounded person, then another.

"Keep digging!" Jennifer ordered them. And they obeyed.

Heavy equipment arrived—there was only one backhoe within the dome, but there were several jackhammers and quite a few trucks to carry the rubble away. In their stronger dragon shapes, Gautierre and she helped them move it all. They unearthed fewer survivors, and more corpses.

Scanning the ruined site after an hour, it occurred to her they might come across Hank Blacktooth. No one had seen him since the explosion.

Did she want him dead, or alive?

Does it matter? He'll die soon enough, the day Skip wants to send a swarm for him and only him. Like he sent one for Dad. What can I do to stop it? Nothing. Xavier can search all he likes—within a month, we could all be dead.

She fought back tears of despair as her wing claws dug furiously. They cut open on sharp edges of rock and steel, and she kept digging through the pain. Voices called out to her, and she kept digging.

Finally, Gautierre put a wing on her and turned her

around. "Jennifer! The police are getting a radio call—it's your mother."

Scrambling out of her pit, she flipped to human and grabbed the radio from a nearby officer. With a double take, she realized it was Chief Whittle—*Carrot Helmet?*—who had a look of concern on her face. She pressed the radio button. "Mom?"

"Honey. Our spotters think another one's coming."

"Where?"

"The hospital."

Jennifer's blood froze. "Mom. Get the fuck out of there."

"We're evacuating. Can you get here? I might need to get in the air, if . . ."

"Sixty seconds." She handed the radio back to the young chief. "I'm going to leave my friend here to help you. You're going to protect him."

"No one's going to touch him, Ms. Scales. You have my word. He's found eighteen trapped survivors and digs faster than the backhoe. Thirty different people have come up to me asking his name, so they can thank him personally."

"Gautierre Longtail."

"I'll pass that along."

"Thanks."

She scrambled into the sky, pressing her wings hard, coming quickly within sight of the hospital and the rolling fields beyond. Her mother was waiting in the parking lot, with several staff bunched around her.

Useless, Jennifer thought tenderly. *They can't protect her. All they can do is get ash blown on them.*

She landed next to them and looked where they were pointing.

"Smaller," Jennifer muttered.

"Big enough," Elizabeth guessed. It was the size of a large dragon—in fact, it held a shape very much like one, trailing wisps as it floated over the vegetation, as if a dragon were melting overhead.

"Turning!" the spotter called out from the roof. "Coming right for us!"

A beaststalker whom Jennifer recognized from the city council—Sarah Sera—tugged at Elizabeth's sleeve. "You or your daughter will be the target. You have to get out of here. You have to get out of here at least five minutes ago."

Elizabeth exhaled. "I don't want to leave—"

"MOM." Jennifer was already spreading her wings. "Get on board."

"Another one!" called out a different spotter, pointing a bit farther to the west. "Coming faster!"

Elizabeth turned to Sarah. "Evacuate the hospital."

"Mom!"

"Use a spread pattern, so it can't hurt too many at once. If—"

"Get on me *now*!"

"If the building is destroyed, take everyone to Smart Bean Foods. Jennifer and I will try to meet you—ack!"

Snarling, Jennifer had grabbed her mother's coat with her teeth and dragged her into the air.

The moment her hind claws left the parking lot, the first shadow changed course to intercept. It was only a few seconds before Jennifer spotted the second one—this one in the shape of a spider, and different from the first in color as well. In fact, Jennifer wasn't sure she could really even call it a shadow . . .

"Honey. I'm slipping out of my jacket. If you could—gah!"

Jennifer snapped her head around quickly enough to deposit her mother on her back. She felt the woman's fingernails embed themselves in her scales.

"That wasn't funny, kid."

"Get on board when I ask, next time. What do you think of these two swarms? They look different from what Skip has sent before."

Elizabeth peered downward. "They're both after us, each in a different shape. The dragon is probably meant for me, the spider for you."

"Aw, that's sweet. I'd hate to have to share. I suppose we should be glad he's not going after the hospital. At least they won't have to evacuate."

"It's a matter of time. Once you and I are gone, Skip's job gets considerably easier."

"Cheery thought. Perhaps we could try to stay alive? For funsies?"

"Head west."

"Over them?"

"We've never seen a swarm jump. I'd rather get out to the farmland on the edge of town. There are fewer people there, so they'll do less damage."

"This doesn't exactly strike me as a survival strategy."

"How long can you stay in the air?"

Jennifer's mind went back to a seemingly endless flight over the seas of Crescent Valley. It was stressful and kind of awful at the time, but now it seemed like a vacation. "At least eight hours. Haven't really ever tried to push it beyond that."

"We have eight hours to come up with a plan, then."

"No problem," Jennifer lied through sharp teeth.

They did not need eight hours. As they crossed over the first shadow, it rose to meet them, and Jennifer at once felt alarm, relief, and irritation.

"Evangelina!"

The shape did not respond aloud, but coalesced into a three-dimensional winged form that cruised by their left flank, momentarily blotting out the sun before it circled back to hover over its companion shape.

Sister. Sister-mother.

"Do you think she and Skip—"

"Friends? Unlikely, given what I saw from her the last time she ran into him."

"Good news, then. And the second one must be Dianna Wilson."

"Pretty odd time to show up."

"Not odd at all. Your father was married to Dianna once, and Evangelina is their daughter."

"So they're here because he's dead? What, they want to bring a pot roast to the after-funeral party?"

"I doubt that."

Jennifer looked suspiciously at the newcomer's tattered black wings, six spindly legs, viciously spiked tail, and shrouded facial features. "Okay, so? He's dead, they're here? How does that make sense?"

"Calm down, honey. We can ask them. If they were going to attack, they would have done it by now. Right?"

"HEY." Jennifer made a beeline for her half-sister. "MY MOTHER AND I WANT TO KNOW WHAT THE HELL YOU'RE DOING HERE."

No time, sister. Another swarm is coming.

"What, are you—is this draw-a-scribble-on-our-home-town day, or some shit?" *How can Skip draw this quickly? It doesn't matter.* "Where is it?"

Mother feels it coming from the bridge. Heading this way.

"Coming for the hospital."

"Evacuate!" Elizabeth called out to the people below. "Get clear of the building!"

Not necessary. Mother and I will handle this.

Evangelina darted off toward the bridge, descending farther and farther until Jennifer was sure she was going to crash. They followed her, as did the spider shadow they now knew to be Dianna Wilson.

Instead of crashing, Evangelina's dragon shape soaked into the surfaces of the trees and structures, becoming a shadow again without losing any speed.

Jennifer saw the oncoming swarm now, a jumbled mess of the same sorts of creatures that had taken away her father, destroyed city hall, and buried townspeople at the police station.

"It's huge—at least triple what he's sent before."

"That can only be for the hospital," her mother deduced.

"How does he do it—how does he make so many, so quickly?"

"The better question is, how are Evangelina and Dianna going to—oh, my."

The hunger never ends it never ends it never ends

Evangelina accelerated toward a swarm that looked ready to consume her—until her shadow swiftly expanded, covering an area ten times that of the swarm. Like a predator fish that had teased its prey with a deceptively small lure, Evangelina opened its maw and consumed the entire swarm whole, seeming to swallow a gulp of the Mississippi River as she did so.

CHAPTER 22
Andi

Andi watched in shock as the shadow of Evangelina Scales—she recognized her right away—dominated the Mississippi River and swept their sorcery out of existence. It was terrifying and beautiful, like the way Skip would sometimes grab her jaw and squeeze while loving her. She felt horribly exposed all of a sudden.

The feeling increased tenfold when she saw the spidery shape of Dianna Wilson flank her daughter. This shadow glowed jade, with each bright eye a different color. All eight were looking right up the cliffs at them, as if they had always known the two of them would be there.

"Mom!" Skip cried out. "MOM?!?!"

Andi grabbed his shoulder. "Skip. Time to go. We can't win this fight."

"Fight? I don't get it. Why is my mom fighting me?"

"Um, maybe because you killed the first love of her life."

"*She* left *him*."

"Yes, she left him. Alive."

"Oh, this is . . . unbelievable. Unbelievable! MOM!?!?" He called down to the river, where the two new shapes hovered in two-dimensional space. "STAY OUT OF THIS! YOU LEFT, REMEMBER? YOU LEFT! LEAVE AGAIN!"

"Skip, we—"

"Yes, I know!" He slapped her hand away. "Heaven forbid anyone stop the great Dianna Wilson from doing whatever the fuck she wants. Fine, let's go."

Incredibly, while Dianna and Evangelina did not pursue them, things actually got worse for Andi and Skip upon their return to the Cliffside.

Six arachnids were waiting for them in the dining area.

"Dear nephew," said one of them, a baboon spider. "You have been failing. The time has come to accept the guidance of your betters."

"Fucking Aunt Tavia," Skip muttered, throwing up his hands. "I hope she died painfully."

CHAPTER 23
Jennifer

They were in the parking lot—everyone from the hospital Jennifer realized, except for a skeleton crew that was taking evacuated patients back inside—when Evangelina and Dianna returned.

They approached Elizabeth first. Dianna shimmered until she was in the form of a woman nearly as tall as the doctor, with jet-black hair that framed a pale, freckled face and spilled down freckled shoulders. Her simple jade gown wrinkled as she bowed to the other woman.

"Dr. Georges-Scales. I've waited a long time to meet you."

Jennifer watched her mother almost faint. "Dianna. I'm afraid I don't know what to say."

"Neither do I, for sure. But I will try by saying, I'm sorry for your loss. Jonathan was an extraordinary man."

"Thank you. I'm sorry, too."

Feeling like she had not so much to do here, Jennifer looked at Evangelina, who had changed into human form at the same time as Dianna. Evangelina was a dark mirror of her half-sister—they shared many of the same facial features as their father, but the older sibling's hair and freckles were distinctly from her mother's side.

"I—I don't know how much time we have," Elizabeth suddenly said. "Thank you for what you've done here. I don't know how you stopped his sorcery, but it probably saved lives. My worry is that Skip may try again."

"Evangelina can consume anything my son produces."

"Are you sure? The last couple have come in rapid succession."

"I am sure, for at least a while." Dianna's eyes were a reassuring cerulean—but Jennifer knew they would change color before long. "Skip has learned how to create servants who in turn can create more servants. A troubling development, to be sure; but we have at least some time to discuss how to stop him permanently."

A murmur went through the crowd, and Jennifer felt a weight lift from her heart that she hadn't realized she had been feeling. *It's over. Dianna can make it all right. She can turn things back to normal, like she did before.*

Elizabeth nodded again, less formally this time. "Thank you again. It's been a long time since we've had a reason to hope for anything in this town."

Dianna looked up at the shimmering shell above. "Yes. I can imagine. Edmund Slider has left quite a legacy."

"I hope it's not presumptuous to ask: is there anything you can do about it?"

The downcast eyes of the sorceress shifted to olive. "Ah, you get right to it. And there, I have less comforting news. I alone cannot reverse what Edmund Slider has done."

The crowd murmured again, less encouragingly now. "But you're Quadrivium," Jennifer pointed out in exasperation. "Like Slider was. In fact, you're more powerful, aren't you? You travel through dimensions. You can't help a single town?"

"Jennifer. They *have* helped this town."

"Jennifer Scales." Dianna's smile returned under indigo eyes, and the warmth in her voice appeared genuine. "I am sorry for your father, but I am so pleased to see you still well."

"I'm not well. Not at all. Let's get to it, please—or did you come empty-handed?"

Evangelina frowned with distaste. Even in human form, she did not use her voice.

Time has passed, Mother—but she's still a bitch. I don't know why you like her.

Jennifer jumped. She'd never get used to telepathy. It was so sudden and intrusive.

"Oh, Evangelina. I don't know why I like her, really. Maybe it's the parts of Jonathan I see in her. Maybe it's her ability to bite off more than she can chew, and swallow it anyway. And maybe it's the fact you *don't* like her that makes her so appealing to me."

"Hello? Standing right here. So you were saying how despite your amazing multidimensional powers, you have no antidote to the sorcery of a dead arachnid."

"Jennifer, please."

"Let them answer, Mom."

"The answer does not lie with us," Dianna said mysteriously. "I can only presume that it lies with you."

"Could you be more precise? We've tried a lot of shit on that wall."

"I have nothing else for you—just my own knowledge of Edmund Slider. He was not the type to leave a town to die, with no way out. He wants something from you. You must give it to him."

"He's dead."

"That's not the point."

"It seems relevant."

"Come, Dr. Georges-Scales. Surely you've seen one or two things that manage to last beyond death."

"The seraph," Elizabeth whispered.

"The what?"

"A protective spirit left by my friend. It sacrificed itself at Jonathan's funeral so that he could move on."

Dianna thought about that. "Edmund enjoyed the idea of self-sacrifice. Has anyone tried to leave the dome since that day?"

"We have scouts attempt every day. They test with their hands, shoot weapons, we've even rolled cars into the thing. The day of Jonathan's funeral, after everyone left that field, I tried to leave myself."

Jennifer scrunched her face. "Mom?"

Elizabeth sighed. "I'm sorry, sweetheart. I couldn't take my eyes off the sky. I wanted to go with him, more than almost anything." She turned back to Dianna. "No matter how hard I tried, or how little, it didn't work."

"Sacrifice could be necessary, but not sufficient."

The doctor's features hardened. "The sacrifices we've made, I would deem *more* than sufficient."

"I don't mean to sound insensitive." Dianna tossed the remark out casually. "I mean that Edmund put up this wall for logical reasons. Everything he did was based in logic."

Jennifer recalled Edmund Slider's geometry classes, and his relentless focus on logic. "Where's the logic in all the suffering?" She surprised herself by asking the question out loud.

"Don't look for the logic in the results. Things happened that he clearly didn't expect. Instead, look for the logic in his goal. What drove Edmund Slider?"

"We don't know, exactly."

"You will have to find out."

Elizabeth rubbed her chin as the crowd absorbed this information. "Okay. The dome has been up for months; it can stay up a bit longer while we figure this out. Meanwhile, we're left with the matter of Skip and the attacks. You imply that your defenses can't hold forever."

"Correct. The sorceries are getting stronger by the day."

"So we need to stop them, the sooner the better."

"Agreed. It is a difficult decision for me, but I am ready to carry out what must be done."

Elizabeth paused. "What did you have in mind?"

Dianna tilted her freckled face. "Why, the only certain solution at our disposal. Death. As Evangelina and I are the only two inside or outside this dome powerful enough to stop a werachnid like this—all due respect to your dragon friends, Jennifer—the task falls to us. We will implement immediately."

"Hold on!" Elizabeth almost grabbed the other woman before thinking better of it. "You're going to resort to murder?"

With black irises, Dianna licked her lips. "I'm not looking forward to this, Dr. Georges-Scales. The responsibility is mine. I don't see another choice."

"I do. We should attempt a diplomatic solution."

"Diplomacy?" Dianna's lips actually curled upward, and a less-than-friendly sparkle shone in her vermilion eyes. "Why, that's absolutely *adorable*."

Oh, here we go.

"My daughter and I will go out there, then; and instead of stopping the problem, we'll begin a fireside chat; you can ask them nicely to stop sending lethal missiles through this prison wall of yours. Since you have absolutely no way to stop them and no leverage of any kind, I'm sure they will unilaterally decide to take up a different hobby, like quilting."

"Anything sounds impossible when you use *that* tone," Jennifer snapped, freshly annoyed because Dianna was right. "So, new plan, okay? Eddie could help. In fact, we were talking about that when—"

"Your bow-toting boyfriend will be the next target," Dianna interrupted.

"He's not—well, maybe in a different set of circumstances, we could—there's really not a lot of dating going on since—"

"It only makes sense," Dianna continued, and Jennifer decided not to notice the older woman's eye-roll. "The first murder was your father, to hurt you. The next will be your *boyfriend*, while you watch helplessly. Whether they tear apart your mother immediately afterward or leave her for later is really a matter of personal style—"

"Never mind Eddie or me," Elizabeth interjected quickly. "We have *you* to stop this. You're our leverage."

So why not stop him now, without the talking part?

Evangelina kicked the dirt and bit her pretty lip.

I told you, Mother. We should not have come here first. They have no power, no place in determining our actions.

"Bye, then!" Jennifer said with faux brightness.

"We came here to pay respect to your father," the sorceress tersely reminded her daughter. "Part of that respect is discussing our next move with his wife and child. The last time you blundered into this dimension and decided to play judge and jury, you caused needless suffering. Let's do better."

Jennifer stirred at being called a child, but did not need the stern look from her own mother to stay quiet.

"Dianna. If you're truly interested in what Jennifer and I think, then I'm asking you and Evangelina to help us do this right. For heaven's sake, Skip is your son. I can't imagine how I would—surely you want to consider alternatives to killing him."

"I'm hoping we don't need to kill *him*." Dianna was almost smiling again. "This sorcery requires two people— one to give the creature life, and another to give them power. Remove his new girlfriend, and all Skip can do is send scribbles your way. For a while, anyhow."

We kill Andeana, then. It will show my half-brother that we are serious.

Evangelina's thought was briskly cheerful: they'd thought up a chore that wouldn't be very hard, and would be helpful to all. Like raking leaves when it was nice out, and you wanted a little exercise anyway.

"We don't need to kill her, do we?" Jennifer turned to Elizabeth. "We could talk to her. That's our leverage. We find a way to talk to her, pull her away from Skip. Andi can't be going along with this willingly. It makes no sense. She's not violent."

"She killed Mayor Seabright." It was hard not to see the anger in the doctor's eyes. "Matricide is violent."

"Yeah, but . . . she was under a sorcery. She had no willpower."

"She has little to begin with," Dianna explained. "That is not how her father created her. She has always been a vessel—first for me to pour knowledge into, and now for Skip to pour his own purpose out of. She's nothing more than a tool. Break the tool, save the town."

"What is she, a faulty screwdriver?" Jennifer hissed. "You don't need to break her. And she's not a tool; she's a human being who can make her own choices."

Choices like, "Don't kill your own mother"?

"Stop pretending to give a shit about anything."
"Jennifer."
"Mom, you can't be seriously considering this! Why is it okay to kill Andi for what she did to Dad but not Skip?

We're agreed, then. We kill them both.

"Why are you here? Why are we pretending to have a conversation like normal people when at least one of us is a proven murderous sociopath?"

"Honestly, pet. You could do more to help." Dianna shook her head and thought a moment. "What if we found Andi and brought her here, alone? You could try to convince her to do . . . whatever it is you think she will do for you."

This is useless.

"That might work," Elizabeth agreed. "We've never considered pulling her away from Skip before, because it seemed impossible. She's devoted to him, and Eddie reports they rotate through lairs unpredictably. Do you think you can find her?"

The answering smile nearly split the sorceress's face open. "My dear Dr. Georges-Scales. I already have. We'll be back momentarily."

CHAPTER 24
Andi

"Skip, you have to talk with them! They've come all this way!"

"I don't need to do any such thing." They were in the kitchen, with only the swinging double doors between them and the six new arrivals. Everyone could hear them, and they both knew it.

"Tavia called them!"

"Tavia's dead."

"They're a critical resource. Skip, it's the natural instinct of our kind to act alone. But we are at our most powerful when we band together—like the Quadrivium did.

"You mean, the Quadrivium that failed?"

"Don't be immature about this. You could learn from these people. Half of them were thought dead by Tavia herself."

"Terrific. I can learn how to play dead."

"There's more to it than that."

"What—I can learn how to keep secrets? How to be supercautious? How to lay intricate traps that take decades to unfold? Who gives a shit about any of that? What good does it do?"

"You don't know until you ask. They're willing to help. To teach."

"No, Andi. They're not here to help or teach. They're here to take over. To control. Like my father *had* to control, and Tavia and Edmund after him."

"Are you kidding? Tavia and Edmund did so much for you. They protected you. They gave you precious time."

"I didn't need their protection or time!" Skip kicked a boiling pot off the lower rack. It skidded and slammed into a pile of lids, all of which dumped onto the linoleum. "I can handle what's out there on my own!"

"Your mother? Your half-sister? Get real, Skip. You were as scared as I've ever seen you when they appeared on the Mississippi."

"They won't be able to stop what I have in mind."

"What's that?"

Before he could answer, the shadows from under the racks and appliances converged on Andi and seized her. She let out a shriek of alarm as the ground collapsed under her feet, eroding her thickness and distributing her across a single plane. It was petrifying feeling, not least because she had no idea how to move. It turned out not to matter— whatever shadows had trapped her here pulled her away.

His startled gaze followed her. *"Andi!"*

Skip, help me. I don't want to . . .

CHAPTER 25
Andi

". . . leave you."

Andi stirred, opened her eyes, and started. In Skip's place were the four people on the earth she least wanted to be with.

"Relax," said the second wife of the late Jonathan Scales. "You're in Winoka Hospital."

"My mother decided not to amputate," added the younger daughter of the late Jonathan Scales.

"She has convinced us to try diplomacy," explained the first wife of the late Jonathan Scales.

It won't work. They'll see that. Then you'll die.

"Evangelina." Andi nodded through a cold sweat. "Dianna. Jennifer. Dr. Georges-Scales." It was quiet. The door was open. Andi was not restrained, and she wondered how many guards were out in the hallway.

We don't need guards in the hallway.

"Stay out of my head," she snapped, sitting up in the bed. She began thinking of a discordant tune, anything to throw off the telepaths in the room. They probably wanted information, and she would not give it to them so easily. "Why did you kidnap me?"

"Don't see it as a kidnapping," Dianna replied. "See it as an invitation. Even a rescue, if you like."

"Rescue. That's funny, coming from the woman who raised me in an inescapable void for over a decade." Andi's forearms began to itch, but she refused to scratch them here.

"The rescue was my idea," Elizabeth said without a smile. Andi examined the woman; it was her first good look up close at the rangy blonde who had provided leadership for this town after Andi's assassination of Glory. *Focus* and *polite* were the first two words that came to mind. *Dangerous* was the next one.

"Can we get you water? Dianna tells me interdimensional travel can dehydrate certain tissues."

"Sure."

Elizabeth motioned to Jennifer, who stalled, then rolled her eyes and headed for the corner sink.

"You've been living on the edge of town for some time," the doctor noticed, taking the fabric of Andi's jeans between two fingers. "Why don't you tell us your story?"

"My story? You know my story, Dr. Georges-Scales. I'm the offspring of Esteban de la Corona, a man so self-involved he abandoned his daughter and called himself The Crown, and Glorianna Seabright, a woman so self-involved she gave up on motherhood so she could keep killing her enemies.

"Instead of parents, I had Dianna here as a sort of dark nurse. Based on her track record with Evangelina and Skip, you can imagine what that was like for me. Once I was properly trained, she and her two incredibly well adjusted colleagues, Otto and Edmund, put my musical talents to work on the Quadrivium's attempt at universe-shifting. Your own daughter put a stop to that, and I hitched a ride back to this world. I've been liking it okay, though I have to admit it was more fun when schools and restaurants were open. Now, there's no reason to come into this town."

"Perhaps you could help us with that."

"Thanks, Jennifer." She took a gulp of the water, watching the girl's expression over the rim. There wasn't much hate visible for what had happened to her father; perhaps she was hiding it. "I don't think I can be much help, Dr. Georges-Scales."

"You knew Edmund Slider."

"No better than you did."

"Surely he must have told you and Skip something about this barrier, before he put it up."

"We were as surprised as all of you when he created it. We had no idea what he would do—what he did, for Skip. Skip didn't want him to. He even tried to stop him that night."

"Why didn't he?"

Andi paused. She had slipped into a conversation—or been slipped into one. Polite and dangerous, indeed. "I don't see the point in discussing this further."

"Andi, please!" Jennifer cried out in exasperation. "You know Mr. Slider didn't want this! He was a teacher, he liked his students, he wouldn't want all of us and our families to die!"

"Maybe just Glory?" This was Dianna, her voice seeping under Jennifer's harsh plea like oil under rocks.

"Of course he wanted Glory to die. But she's dead, and the wall is still up. I don't know anything else!"

Elizabeth massaged the bridge of her own nose. "Jennifer, you were on the right path. Mr. Slider wanted more than dead people. He cared for things. He cared about his students. He probably cared a great deal about Skip, too. He wanted to protect him." She looked up at Andi. "Right?"

"I guess."

"So if Edmund wished to put up a barrier that would protect Skip, he'd want it to last. That suggests multiple conditions before it would come down."

"Glory's death could be one of those."

"Yes, Dianna. We've established that as a possibility. But it also suggests that Skip may need to reach a certain age or accomplish something, before the dome will fall."

Andi tried to sit very still.

"Can you think of what that might be, Andi?"

Several moments passed. Andi wanted to say something, but couldn't. Was the doctor right? Skip had said he had "something in mind." If so . . . would the barrier protect him anymore?

And even if it did, how could they stop his mother and sister? Did the barrier even matter anymore?

Her forearms began to itch madly.

Can we kill her now?

"*No one* is going to kill her." The doctor sighed. "She been through enough. And this universe hasn't been as kind to you as you'd like me to believe, Andi. You can't tell me life with Skip has been ideal."

Jennifer snorted. Andi shot the girl a look. "It hasn't been so bad."

"Really? He's a good match for you? Because I had a higher opinion of you than that."

The comment stung. Andi didn't know why Jennifer's opinion mattered, but it did. Maybe it was because Jennifer had shown her kindness in both universes. Maybe it was because the girl had stood up for herself, even when she was utterly alone. Could she do that? Could she stand to be alone?

"Have you thought about what he's doing?" Dr. Georges-Scales took Andi's wrist lightly in her hand, feeling for a pulse and timing it. "You know he's killed people in this town." Now she grabbed a blood-pressure cuff from the nearby table, rolled up Andi's sleeve, and attached the cuff to her upper arm. "Not only my husband. Dozens of others, buried under the rubble of the police station." *Squick, squick, squick,* she pumped the cuff. "Soon it will be hundreds, under more ruins. I doubt Edmund Slider ever wanted that."

"You had something to do with those murders, Andi. You've been helping my son."

"Please, Dianna. I can handle this. Andi, I would imagine the sorcery that you and Skip generate together makes you feel special." She released the cuff and pulled out her stethoscope. Pressing the metal end on the girl's chest, she listened briefly. Then she put the scope away and pulled out a flashlight and tongue depressor. "Say 'ah,' dear."

"Aaahh."

"Thank you. It can be easier to feel special like that, when you don't see the consequences of your actions."

"Nnnnn?"

"Yes indeed." The flashlight went in one ear, then the

other. "Perhaps you could stay with us a few hours. You could visit with some of the patients we've brought back from the police-station site." In a flash, a rubber hammer was out and bumping the girl's knees. *Poomp*, her feet kicked out. "If you like, we could take you down to the site itself."

If you like, we could bury you there.

"Fucking. Interrupt her. *Again*." Jennifer had a hand on one of her sheathed daggers, and a glare for her half-sister.

Amateur.

"Shit-chomper."
"Children."
Andi wondered how lethal the doctor could be with that small, rubber mallet.

"How'm I doing?" she asked.

The doctor considered her. "Your pulse is a bit low, but within normal limits for beaststalker adolescents. Your blood pressure is higher than I'd like, but I don't have much to offer you here in the way of medicine. Try picking up more fruits and vegetables from the grocery store north of town, drink low-fat milk, and skip the salty prepared foods. Reflexes are good, as I'd expect from someone with your genetics. Your left ear has a wax buildup, and what I saw in your mouth suggests you don't floss, though you must brush your teeth since your breath is passable, and no teeth are falling out. It's good in some ways, I suppose, to have a boyfriend you're trying to stay attractive for. Overall, physically, you're keeping it together."

"Holy crap, you say a lot between the lines."

"Stay with us. Help us figure this dome out. Help us rebuild this town into what you remember. We can change the world, starting right here."

"Change the world"? I'm going to vomit.

Jennifer drew both blades. "Go play a card game. Maul a trailer truck. Suck the life out of a blue whale. Go do something—*anything*—*anywhere else*!"

Come with me, and we'll play together.

"Blades down, Jennifer!" and "Evangelina, enough!" came out simultaneously. Both young women snarled and backed down.

The doctor turned back to Andi. "What do you say?"

"Dr. Georges-Scales, I've never had anyone worry over me over fifteen years, the way you've worried over me in fifteen minutes."

"There's a lot going on in there I'm worried about." A finger went to Andi's temple.

"I'm okay, Dr. Georges-Scales. I like Skip. He's good to me. He makes me feel special, powerful."

"Does he?"

"Yeah. He scares a lot of people, I know. Maybe he scares you because you can't control him. Not like I'll bet you can control everyone else."

Dr. Georges-Scales widened her eyes at the mild shot. She motioned to the other three. "Does this look like a crowd I can control?"

Andi felt a smile try to crease her face. A wave of guilt smashed her insides, and she shook her head so hard the room teetered. "I've got to go, Dr. Georges-Scales. I appreciate what you're trying to do for me, but—"

"Don't say you appreciate it if you're going to blow it off. Say what you mean."

"Okay. What I mean is, I'm sticking with Skip. He loves me. I love him."

"He loves you. You love him." Dianna licked her lips and looked carefully at the doctor. "You realize what a horrific cliché you sound, dear."

"Yes. The cliché of the teenager nobody ever listens to or believes."

"Oh, give me just a *small* break . . ."

"Dianna, if you'll let me—"

"No, with all due respect we've tried it your way, Dr. Georges-Scales. You've gotten a fine blood-pressure reading on Jonathan's murderer here, but you haven't gotten much else to show for it . . ."

Andi closed her eyes and began to hum. It was time to go. This place was perilous—not because of Evangelina or Jennifer, or even the great Dianna Wilson.

It was because of Dr. Georges-Scales, and the sweet care she had shown Andi. She knew she didn't deserve it. She didn't feel comfortable with it. She didn't know why someone would do that, unless they were trying to get something from you. At least she knew what Skip wanted from her. That was easy. Dr. Georges-Scales was hard.

She didn't want hard anymore.

The hum rose in volume and pitch. Another note rang, and another and three more, and soon her throat was unleashing a chorus through closed lips.

"What is she—"

She's going to escape. We must kill her, now!

"NO!" Andi opened her eyes in time to see the doctor tackle the changing, darkening shape of Evangelina to the floor. A cart crashed against the wall, and Jennifer gasped. There wasn't much time—soon Evangelina would slip away from the grab and capture Andi again.

The window overlooking the parking lot melted gently from the vibrations and crept down the flowered wallpaper. She found an air current outside, listened to its melody, and sang harmony. Astonished, it swept into the room and carried her away. Only the voice of Dianna Wilson could keep up.

"Andeana Corona Marsabio, you tell my son I am not through with him yet!"

CHAPTER 26
Jennifer

"Oh, mighty and benevolent Ancient Furnace—"

"Ah, geez, don't start up with that."

"I, the humblest of your many subjects—"

"I don't have *subjects*, and you damn well know it, Goat."

"—beseech thee to aid me into confronting mine own blood for the sake of peace."

The Ancient Furnace snorted and banked left. She and Gautierre weren't scheduled for patrol tonight, but she'd been restless and had volunteered. Anything was better than listening for another wailing alarm.

Then Susan's boyfriend had tagged along, jumping off the roof and shifting to dragon form in midair; within seconds his powerful wings had brought him abreast of her.

That was when things started to get weird(er).

"Gautierre, will you kindly cut the crap? And speak English?"

"Okay." He turned serious. "I want to talk sense into my mother."

"Who *doesn't* have mother issues in this town?"

"I think there's an eight-year-old on the edge of town who has two daddies."

"Brilliant. Look, I will gladly help you find and confront Ember Longtail, anytime you're available. But only if you never call me the Ancient Furnace ever again."

"Agreed, Elderly Heating System."

"You and Susan really deserve each other."

"Ah! Speaking of the light of my life—"

"No. Let's focus on the purity of your revenge, on how major a smackdown we're gonna give your—"

"I love her, and we've been talking about sex."

Jennifer dropped thirty feet in about a second and a half, nearly crashing into a tree. "Yerrrgg," she managed, spitting oak leaves. She stole a look behind; the poor tree was still shaking like it'd been hit by a gale. "What about me, or about any of the talks we've had in the short year we've known each other, indicates to you that I have *any* interest in talking about this, ya goob?"

"Oh, come on. Girls talk about everything. Pretend I'm a girl."

"Okay. You're a girl dating my best friend. Oh, wait— you just made it worse. How about we pretend you're a mute instead?"

He laughed, swooped close, and managed to clumsily brush the large clump of leaves that had been sticking to one of Jennifer's wing claws. "Wow, you're going to be spitting toothpicks for a week."

"A small price to pay on patrol, I s'pose. So let's focus on what we're supposed to be doing—confronting your mom—as opposed to what you'd like to be doing, which is violating my sweet and innocent best friend."

"Violating? There's no romance in your soul, Decrepit Blast Kiln."

"Yeah, my soul's all crowded with survival instinct and foraging for food."

"Do you think if Susan and I do it, I'd be taking advantage, because I'm bigger and stronger and faster? And also because she's really supergrateful I saved her life?"

"Ah, geez . . ."

"Maybe she's not really in love with me, maybe she's just happy she isn't dead, and that would be how she wants to express it. Isn't making love the ultimate expression of the thirst for life? I read that somewhere, once."

I don't think I've ever wanted to get ambushed more than right now. Come on, Ember, would you please show up and try to kill me already?

"Yes, she could love me as a physical expression of gratitude. Like sending a thank-you note!" he enthused. "Except naked. What if I do something weird and dragony while we're doing it for the first time? If I set her on fire by accident, that would be so weird and . . . weird. Did your father ever do that to your mother?"

"My father and my mother *never touched each other.*"

"Oh, how we all wish that were true." This new voice was older, more feminine, nastier . . . and came with an extra surprise.

A hind claw ripped through Jennifer's wing as the black, streaking form of Ember Longtail dropped like a meteor from an incredible height. *A meteor strike,* Jennifer realized. *Without the landing or explosion. Tricky.*

Before either teenager could adjust to the ambush, she was ascending again, the peach markings under her wings flashing as she pumped harder and harder, until she had rammed into her son.

"Ooomph!"

"Fool!" she spat. "You've gotten weak. You've lost your training. You depend on this hybrid freak to protect you."

"Also, he talks too much about sex." Jennifer was relieved to see Gautierre looked okay—Ember was not trying to kill him. *Yet.*

For Jennifer, however, she would show no such restraint. Nor would the half dozen others who abruptly rose from the treetops to surround them.

Flying too low, Jennifer chastised herself. *Classic mistake.* She banked high, avoiding a cascade of sparks as three different dashers tried to pin her with their tails.

"Your gang's getting slow, Stumpy."

They were chasing each other up the river, from south to north along the east edge of town. Jennifer could see the downtown area in the distance—the fire department, the post office, the western abutment of the bridge, the remains of city hall. Beaststalkers would have spotters in all of those locations, and more.

As she was trying to gauge the distance and likelihood of a rifle shot, she heard five or six gunshots.

One of Ember's gang—an indigo dasher who didn't look all that different from Jennifer's father—took a bullet in the throat and fell hundreds of feet to the ground.

"Snipers!" Ember called out. "Spread out, ascend, and find them!"

It was good advice—at least the first two parts—and both Jennifer and Gautierre took it. From a much higher holding pattern, they could be reasonably certain no rifle could touch them.

That's why the surface-to-air missiles were such a surprise.

Four of them streaked from nondescript buildings on the south end of downtown. *Portables,* Jennifer guessed. *More surprises from the armory Hank inherited from Mayor Glory Seabright.*

Two missiles converged on a careless sea-green dasher who had been flying too low. What was left of her splattered over a fifty-yard radius of streetscape.

The third missile came for Ember, and the fourth for Gautierre.

They both tried banking out of the way, but the missiles changed course.

Infrared homing, Jennifer realized. *Awesome.*

Up and up the two Longtails went, the guided rockets in pursuit.

Someone's got to take out those rockets, before they fire again.

She descended to a height of a few hundred feet until she could make out some of the figures on the rooftops. There were a dozen of them—four pairs of portable SAM operators, who were in the process of reloading; and three snipers; and Hank Blacktooth.

"Hank!" she called out. "Call off your brownshirt brigade! We're trying a diplomatic solution with these dragons."

Seeing him motion to his snipers, she camouflaged herself to cloudy sky and dumped the air from her wings. Their shots were way off.

Hank raised a black, wicked-looking rifle to his shoulder. Jennifer wasn't a gun expert; she had no idea what that thing would shoot—armor-piercing rounds, or rattlesnakes, or hydrogen bombs.

She started to scramble back, only to be clipped by the racing form of Gautierre. The bump cost her in altitude, but ended up saving her life, since the heat-seeking missile was still tracking him only thirty or forty yards behind. Both soared overhead, followed closely by Ember and her own dedicated missile.

It was immediately clear that they were returning the missiles to sender, by finishing a large circle and flying low over the rooftops. Inevitably, the missile's guidance system would try to keep up with a sharp bank downward—and hit whatever was closest.

Clever. Suicidal, but clever.

Hank, seeing the dual threat approach, aimed and fired at the near dasher.

The powerful rifle blasted a hole in the young dasher's wing.

"Gautierre!" Jennifer and Ember both cried out. His trajectory suffered immediately, and he crashed through a third-story window of the four-story building Hank and the others were standing on. The missile followed shortly afterward, exploding on impact with the brick side of the building. Beaststalkers stumbled and rolled on the roof.

Ember accelerated, hissing. She passed over them, roaring an inferno that bathed the entire rooftop. Then she dropped, leading the missile to do the same right behind her—on top of the beaststalkers' burning heads.

Shaken by the sudden violence and loss, Jennifer fled. The last she saw of Hank Blacktooth, the self-proclaimed mayor of Winoka was screaming in midair, limbs withering and flaming, as he tumbled from the rooftop and came to an end on the pavement below.

CHAPTER 27
Susan

It wasn't true. It absolutely wasn't. It was a trick, or a practical joke, or a mistake, or a bad dream, or a secret hidden message that meant something else, anything else, but did not, did *not* mean Gautierre was dead.

If Gautierre was dead, it meant that all the books and movies and stories were wrong. If he was dead, it meant that anyone could die beneath this stupid dirty grimy dome. She could, Jenn could, anybody could.

If he was dead, what did that leave for her? What did that *mean* for her?

The other deaths to date—Glory Seabright, Winona Brandfire, even Jonathan Scales—were sad, a shame, a bummer, too bad, so sad, but they were—what was the word?

They were *abstract*. They were sad like it was sad to

read about an earthquake in Chile. If Chile was your best friend's father. Even with a relationship that close, there was life to return to: school and work and friends and fun and Gautierre and none of that because he was dead, it wasn't abstract at all, it was extremely *real*, extremely concrete and unshakeable: the boy who had risked his life for her, who thought she was beautiful and smart and cool, the boy who could have picked anyone, the boy who picked her and thought she was cooler than Jennifer, that boy was *dead*; he wasn't a boy anymore, he was *abstract*.

She had walked and walked, running out of the hospital when Jennifer told her the news, her sick stupid eyes big in her sad long face. She'd said something about Hank Blacktooth, how Ember killed him for killing her son and the boy had died a hero and blah-blah-blah and do-si-do and she'd run away from those sad eyes, run until a stitch in her side forced her to jog, then to trot, then to walk fast, then just to walk.

Now she was in a quiet part of town, deserted and boring, a part she'd never had any interest in before—not really convenient to anything Winoka needed, not near the hospital or a gutted drugstore or a water supply. Sure, before Big Blue came, these were nice apartments, but all they offered now was the view.

The view of the willow. The tree beneath which Gautierre, when he wasn't abstract, when he wasn't dead, had fed her Pez and teased her for not trusting grapes. It was far away from the building, but still clearly visible, along with some of the random destruction Ember and her gang had visited upon the far reaches of this town.

Rudduddudaduddudadud

The faint, familiar, clipped whirring sound broke her train of thought. She had fled the hospital and been so upset about her abstract boyfriend, she'd barely noticed the thing that was new, the old thing that was new: the helicopters.

Pre Big Blue: not such a big deal. They'd occasionally fly over, usually traffic or news copters circling to get closer to the Twin Cities. Sort of a "ho, hum, there's the WTCN traffic chopper, lost its way again" situation.

But now: more and more often they could be spotted (and heard) outside the dome. And they were never news choppers; nope, those were Army Hueys, each and every one.

She didn't like to look at them, even before the abstract thing had happened. They reminded her of her father, which reminded her that he had done nothing to contact her and, very likely, nothing to help her.

And who wanted to be reminded of *that* when you were stuck under a dome and the whole world was apparently adopting a wait-and-see attitude toward you and all your friends?

How could they watch and wait? How could they not try to contact them? Heck, holding up a damn sign to the window would have been something. But no . . . nothing. They did nothing.

So: under the best of bad circumstances (to wit: the day of the picnic) it made her feel weird to hear and see the choppers.

Today, though. Today that sound was wretched, it was the sound of failure and loss and fathers who were waiting and seeing instead of caring and trying.

It was the sound of people who didn't give a tin shit that a wonderful weredragon named Gautierre had been brave and strong, and had gotten his ass handed to him as a reward.

"Nope. I'm done. That's it. I am *out*. Tilt. Overload." She paused. Nature had no reaction to that; there wasn't even a lone bird chirping. Winoka was silent around her, and at last she knew what that meant, what it had always meant: Winoka would be her tomb. She just wasn't smart enough to lie down and be dead.

"At least you're out, Gautierre," she said. Then, "Screw everything." She forced her feet to resume their trudge.

CHAPTER 28
Susan

"Susan? Hello?" Jennifer rapped on the door . . . for some reason, since Gautierre died, Susan had holed up in one of the empty apartments in the complex directly across from the abandoned radio station.

Before Big Blue, these "2 BR, 1½ BA" townhomes would have rented for a brisk $1,800 a month, utilities not included. The radio station wasn't the draw for renters who weren't Susan; the draw was the river view, and the new construction, and the ice-cream shop less than two blocks away.

Jennifer had no idea why Susan would have left dozens of other spots to stay, by herself, in a part of town that wasn't convenient to the hospital, the train, or the grain elevators.

Hell, the only thing this place did have was that nice

river view right beside the big willow tree where she and Gautierre had seen Ember—

Oh. Right.

"Susan?"

"For cripe's sake." The door was yanked open. "What?"

"Yeesh."

"I'm aware," her best friend retorted, "of how I look."

"Um. If you say so."

Susan looked wrecked. Jennifer had no idea when she'd last washed her hair, which was floppy, more stringy than curly, an unattractive length, shiny with grease, and needed a trim in the worst way. Not to mention deep-conditioning treatments.

Her skin was blotchy and uneven, too pale in some spots, flaring with acne in others. The circles beneath her eyes were enormous and dark; she'd lost at least eight or nine pounds, and Susan hadn't needed to lose an ounce. Shit, these days in Domeland, nobody needed to lose weight.

"You look like you can't find your heroin dealer."

"Well," she replied, turning and walking away, "I can't."

Jennifer followed, closing the door, and followed her into the living room. Her friend had done nothing to make this apartment a home; it was furnished—it had been the model apartment—but looked like a page in a catalog, not someone's refuge.

All she'd done was bring in a sleeping bag, a backpack, and two rolls of toilet paper. No books. No knickknacks.

"Um." *How have you been? Nope. How's it going? Uh-uh. So what's new? Definitely not.*

Under Big Blue was no place for irreverent small talk.

"How awful is it?" she finally asked.

"Pretty damn awful." Susan sighed, and flopped down on her sleeping bag.

"Yeah. I figured."

"What do you want, Jenn?"

"Me?"

Susan snorted. "Please. You're not here to check on me. You need something."

"Maybe it's both," she replied, stung.

"It's not. You've remembered I exist because someone—probably your mom—has an updated plan of attack, and someone—probably your mom—has realized I can play a tiny, stupid part in it. And lo, the Ancient Furnace approacheth."

"There's no need to be unreasonably nasty," Jenn said nervously. She knew Susan wanted her to be embarrassed and guilty. But she fought against it.

Dammit, she'd had a fistfight with her mother over this exact thing. *Time to step up, Jennifer. Stop being a baby, Jennifer. Why aren't you there for me, Jennifer. Get back to work, Jennifer. Save the world, Jennifer. Raise the dead, Jennifer. Help Susan mourn Gautierre, Jennifer. Don't think about your EXTREMELY DEAD DAD, Jennifer.*

She felt dull heat in her palms and looked; she had clenched her fists so hard, her fingernails had cut the skin.

I am doing the best I can, Winoka, thank you very much, and if that doesn't leave time to stroke people, that is too damned bad.

"Are you okay?" Susan asked. "You look weird."

"I'm fine." She practically strangled on the lie and abruptly was tired of the whole thing. "Yeah, I'm busted. I am not fine. I am the polar opposite of fine. And we need your help."

"With what?"

Jennifer stared. "Seriously?"

"What's wrong now?" Susan was unrolling the toilet paper, which was two-ply. She was separating it, making two piles of one-ply. Waste not, want not. "You know, specifically."

"Well, specifically, my dad's dead, my mom's dead on her feet, Skip's trying to kill us all, so then we'd all be dead, and we need to get the word out to the world, which is pretending we're dead."

"Why?"

"What?"

"Why? You think they don't know? Everybody knows. My father probably knows, for all the good that's done me, or anybody." She shrugged. "We're screwed. We haven't got the sense to lie down and stop kicking. It always takes longer for the dumb ones to clue in."

"Anyway," Jennifer continued, determined not to strangle Susan . . . not yet. "Anyway, we need you to do another broadcast. Several, in fact. If they see—if they hear—"

"What? We'll be saved? The National Guard will show up on horseback and save the day? Even you're not that arrogant." She paused, then asked, seeming honestly curious, "Are you?"

"Susan, I love you, but will you please knock it off? You think you're the only one hurting? Have you seen my dead dad around anywhere lately? Hmm? You think I don't want to curl up on a smelly sleeping bag and turn two-ply T.P. into one-ply?"

Susan shrugged. That maddened Jennifer more than anything else. She wouldn't even get mad . . . didn't care enough to so much as raise her voice. It was like yelling at a store mannequin.

"So that's it?" she yelled.

"Yup."

"You're out. You won't help."

"Nope."

"Because you're *sad*."

"Because the cost is too high, and it pretty much always has been. Find another tool, Jenn. I'm done."

"You're *not* a—"

"Don't even bother. I'm the screwdriver in the Ancient Furnace's Toolbox of Life . . . or I was, anyway."

"That's the worst metaphor I've ever heard."

"Don't care. Run along, why don't you. Make a couple of boys fall in love with you or fix a parallel universe or find out about a weird half-sibling or roast a couple of neighborhood cats with your weird sparky smelly breath." Her eyes turned hard. "Make your way through life, dodging every bullet and arrow while those around you get killed. Come through unscathed, while everyone around you feels pain."

"That's not fair, Susan—"

"And do it outside, please, because I've got zero interest in continuing this conversation."

Jennifer wasn't sure if she was numb or shocked. "What about you?"

"People like me? What you and your mother call 'the innocents,' in your clueless, patronizing way? Why, that's easy. We'll die." Susan looked forty years old, which scared Jennifer more than anything else that had happened since she'd knocked on the door. "Gautierre and your dad. They're the lucky ones, y'know."

Jennifer turned, began to leave, paused, booted Susan's backpack into the dining room, and kicked the door open on her way out.

"We've got all *kinds* of toilet paper at the hospital!" she yelled, before slamming the door behind her.

CHAPTER 29
Jennifer

Too much talk. We should go kill them now.

Jennifer rubbed her forehead. An Evangelina-sized migraine was forming behind her eyes. "Color me astonished. Psycho-Beast, here, wants to strew death like I salt french fries." *Mmmm. French fries. When was the last time . . . ?*

At what point does the chatter end, with you?

"We're getting nowhere," Elizabeth said.
"Then it must be Tuesday."
They were where people seemed to always end up: the hospital roof. Jennifer wasn't sure why—it wasn't exactly supersafe. The view, perhaps.
"I do think," Dianna said, resplendent in a jade T-shirt

and black leggings liberated from the Wal-Mart, "we've given your approach enough time, Elizabeth. It's time to change tactics."

"What—kill them?"

"At least one of them. Andi, Skip—perhaps it doesn't matter which."

"You are so cavalier with other people's lives. Have you ever read a history book? People kill people, and more people kill more people to prove that killing people was a bad idea. It's called escalation, Dianna, and nobody wins."

"Except those who wrote the history book."

Her mother sighed and looked at the sky.

"Hey, Ms. Wilson," Jennifer called out. "It's not that I wouldn't love to see Skip choking to death on his entrails. Frankly, the thought makes me tingle all over. I'm just not sure what I get out of the deal. It won't bring down Big Blue. It won't make a new herd of cattle appear. It won't make a bunch of—of—I dunno, antibiotic-type thingies like—like—"

"Doxycycline," her mother said helpfully. "Latamoxef. Cefoperazone."

"Right, those. It's not like they'll suddenly appear in orange bottles stuffed with cotton balls. So what's the point?"

"The point, silly child, is that he is the enemy, and he is trying to kill you. The most certain way to make sure that does not happen is to kill him first."

"*Do unto others, before they do unto you.* That's your motto, isn't it, Dianna?" Elizabeth's tone dripped with contempt.

"It has worked for me so far."

"Sure it has. You abandoned Jonathan, after all—you hurt him, before he could hurt you. You stuffed your child"—

she motioned to Evangelina—"into a dark hole rather than face the consequences of your actions with him. Years later you ditched Otto before he could consume you—though I can't say I blame you entirely for that. Then you left Skip, before he could grow old enough to leave you. You led the Quadrivium's sorcery to change the world into something that suited you better, before the world could change you into something that might fit better—and then you called a halt to the whole thing and undid your whole creation rather than risk what Jennifer might do to it. Then you disappeared into some really thin piece of paper, or wherever the hell you've been with Evangelina, teaching her the same lessons you've taught Andi: avoid what you can, disdain and kill what you can't."

Dianna's lips pressed harder and harder throughout this speech, until Jennifer was certain they would split apart into mandibles. "I was wondering when you would stop being diplomatic with me, *Doctor*, and start being honest."

"You want this honest doctor's opinion? I'm grateful you left Jonathan. I can't imagine what he would have turned into had you kept your claws in him through early adulthood. At least he died an honorable man."

"And you'll die an honorable woman, is that right? And your daughter—she'll die an honorable girl? And you'll all be dead, and everyone will honor you and feel sorry that they didn't *listen harder* and *care more*?"

"It's so touching that you'd rather we all lived, and acted more despicable. Like you."

"I'd rather *Jonathan* lived. You and your daughter can go to hell."

"Whoa, hey." Jennifer raised her hands. "Why all the sudden hate? Don't tell me you're still bitter that I fucked up your stupid Arachno-Land."

"Jennifer, let me explain. Dianna doesn't hate you because you disturbed the Quadrivium's plot. She hates you because you represent the child she and Jonathan *could* have had, if she hadn't run. If she hadn't been so weak. If she had maintained a shred of responsibility, and dignity, and respect for her own offspring. Instead, she ended up with the wreck of an excuse of a thing you see festering over there."

I feel like I should take that personally.

"Dearest, most exalted, most honorable Elizabeth Georges, daughter of such hallowed lineage!" Dianna raised her arms to the sky in mock homage. "What astute words you speak! Tell us, can we come lick the morsels of wisdom from your palms, like dogs before a goddess? Can we, from such a humble ritual, learn to be a hint more like you—the self-righteous, insecure, overbearing perfectionist who can't stand the thought that her dead husband ever loved another woman? I mean, what was his problem, right? Not waiting for you, instead going off at age sixteen and fucking some cheap spider-tart, when your virginal aura of perfection must have been so damn visible and obvious from hundreds of miles away, even at an early age? And then, only when I was done with him, did he bother to look around and settle for you. Settle for your quaint, homespun philosophy of peace and self-loathing. Settle for a daughter who didn't have the guts to pull the trigger and kill a ruined, dangerous child like Skip when she had the chance. Several chances, in fact. How much blood is on her hands, because she didn't stop him? How much blood is on yours? How much more will you let spill?"

"Sounds like you wish you'd done it yourself," Jennifer shot back. "So why didn't you? What, after you ditched

Evangelina, you ran out of extradimensional holes to stuff your kids into?"

A black fog covered Evangelina. Jennifer drew her blades. *Yes.* This time, there were no parents interested in stopping them.

You will be excellent practice for when we kill brother and his whore.

Dianna reached out and slapped Elizabeth.

Elizabeth's head snapped to the left ninety degrees, but she was already grinning as she faced forward again.

Then she giggled.

What giggling giggling why?

Jennifer lowered her blades. "I was thinking the same thing."

Dianna stared at her adversary, irises burning crimson. "How dare you laugh at me?"

"Well, because it's all so ridiculous!" Elizabeth pulled out her sword and flung it off the roof; they heard it clatter on the asphalt below. "You don't want this! You don't want to hurt me at all!"

"Um, Mom. She seriously looks like she wants to hurt you."

The doctor could not stop smiling. "Okay, sure, so we have Dianna Wilson here, Sorceress Extraordinaire, Traveler of All Dimensions, Warper of Worlds. She's less than a foot away from me, and what does she do? She slaps me. She doesn't immolate me with a blink of an eye, or point her wand at me and blast me with a bolt of lightning—"

"We don't use wands," Dianna interjected through clenched teeth.

"She doesn't use any one of what must be three dozen lethal sorceries at her disposal. She reaches out with a flimsy hand and whacks me across the face. Slaps me. Slaps me—she might as well pull my hair and call me a poopyhead! She slaps me like a grade-schooler, Jennifer. Why would she do that? Why?"

It did look ineffective and pointless, Mother. No one can die from slapping. Or hair-pulling.

"Seriously, Jennifer. Why?"

Jennifer rubbed her eyes. "Well, Mom, it sounds like you have a pretty good idea already. Clearly, my rabid half-sister is curious. Why don't you share?"

"*Because she doesn't want to fight me.* Fighting me—I mean, seriously fighting me—would risk killing me. And she knows Jonathan wouldn't want that. Doesn't she?"

Dianna stared at her.

Elizabeth leaned in closer and yelled in the other woman's face. "*Doesn't she?*"

"I'm pretty sure he wouldn't want you spitting on her nose, either, Mom."

"See, she can talk tough all she wants about taking action and going out there and killing people. And if your father were alive and tried to argue with her, she could ignore him and go off and do whatever she wanted, free of conscience. Heaven knows she's done what she pleased until now. But she can't, anymore. Because he's dead. And you can't argue with a dead person."

Then soon, she won't be arguing with you, either.

Before anyone else could react, Dianna had her hand out at the advancing form of her daughter. "Stay *back*, Evangelina."

"Yeah, doggie. Stay. Good doggie."

"You can't argue with a dead person," Elizabeth continued, "because the only voice they have left, is the one in your head. The one that won't hold back, won't lie, won't sugarcoat the truth. Dianna here knows *exactly* what Jonathan would want her to do. And because she still loves him, in her twisted, warped way, she's going to do it."

"Again, Mom—are you sure? Because back when she was calling you a self-loathing, overbearing perfectionist, it sounded like she was on a different course."

"She needed to say her piece. I needed to say mine."

Dianna exhaled. "You're done, then."

"Almost." Elizabeth wheeled around and slugged Dianna across the jaw. The sorceress dropped like a rock.

"That's how we learned to slap someone in grade school, here in Winoka."

The sorceress groaned and rolled halfway over. Elizabeth crouched down and pulled a clump of her beautiful, jet-black hair.

"See, it's foreplay like that right there, Dianna, which helped Jonathan to get over you. My bed was like a boxing ring, in the best possible way. The love of your life couldn't wait to go fifteen rounds with me—more, when he could get it. Why, there were weeks we nearly starved to death because we couldn't bear to stop touching each other. If he hadn't changed during the crescent moons, we would have ended up with nutritional deficiencies."

"Okay, Mom. Now you're hurting *me*."

The doctor whispered harshly. "No one asked you to come to this town, Dianna. You don't like the leadership, don't let the dome hit you on the ass on the way out."

She let the head drop, stood up, stepped over the prone form of Dianna Wilson, passed the stunned shadow of

Evangelina, and headed for the stairwell. Jennifer followed her, glancing back long enough to point to her eyes, then the two of them, then the sky.

"Um. I guess our watch shift is over. You guys got next."

CHAPTER 30
Jennifer

The next morning, Evangelina and Dianna were gone.

No one had seen them leave, and Jennifer feared the worst. Or was it the best?

"Do you think they've gone to kill Andi and Skip?"

"I don't know," her mother answered over a breakfast of highly artificially flavored toaster pastries. "I don't think so."

"Well, if they're gone, what are we going to do the next time Skip sends another swarm?"

"Evacuate, like we did last time."

"And then?"

It took a few seconds for Elizabeth to stop chewing. "Jennifer, I don't have all the answers."

"You sounded pretty sure of yourself yesterday when you were pissing all over your KO."

"Cute. If you're done haranguing your mother, I'd like you to take Catherine and Susan and do a townwide patrol. Spend some time in town. Get Susan to do a blog. See if we can rally a few more to help us."

"Susan doesn't want to do a blog."

"How do you know?"

"I asked. She's still down on Gautierre."

"She needs to pick herself up."

"Try telling her that."

"You try telling her that. She's your friend."

"What's the point?" she snapped. "No one listens to me. Or you. Not Susan, not Ember, not what's left of Hank's army, not Evangelina or Dianna, not Andi, and certainly not Skip!"

Elizabeth's calm did not give way. "You're suggesting we give up."

"I'm suggesting the two of us can't do it all!"

"We have others."

"What others? A few dozen nursing assistants? What are we going to do—sling bedpans at these people? Mom, it's time to give up. We're not doing anything useful—"

"Don't you dare." Elizabeth actually reached across the cafeteria table and clenched her daughter's hair, ignoring the startled yelp. "Don't you dare dishonor him like this. I do not care how hard this gets for you. He sacrificed his afterlife for you. People are depending—on *you*. You have a responsibility. You will see it through."

"Ow, Mom, my hair—"

"Preferably without whining."

Without looking away, Jennifer reached up carefully and disentangled her mother's fingers from her locks. Elizabeth relented, but her face retained its hardness.

"You're a bitch."

Her mother blinked slowly, like an owl. "You're soft."

"Well, I'd rather be soft than—"

"You mean, you'd rather be selfish than take responsibility."

Jennifer kicked back her chair and stood. "Oh, *here* we go. I've been taking responsibility for the last two years! I became the fucking Ancient Furnace when I didn't want to. My reward for that dumb-ass stunt was I got to watch Grandpa die, and then found and fought his murderer when no one else could. Remember? Or were you too busy working at the hospital and giving patients more attention than you ever gave me?"

This made Elizabeth stand. Jennifer sucked in breath and resumed the attack. She knew it was being unreasonable. Who cared? It was entirely possible she had never, ever been this angry at her mother.

"Take responsibility? *Take responsibility?* I woke up in a whole other universe and took responsibility for changing it *back*. Changing *you* back, and raising Dad from the dead.

"Then I took responsibility for facing down dragons and beaststalkers the night this damn dome went up. I've done everything you've asked, every time, and I'm sick of it! I'm done! I'm through! Fuck you and your responsibility! And fuck you for throwing Dad in my face!"

Elizabeth punched her.

Bent over, Jennifer held her jaw. Several silent moments passed as she considered her options.

Finally, she chose one. "Cripes, Mom. You and hitting people lately."

"There are more thick skulls out there than usual." Her mother grimaced and massaged her knuckles. "If it makes you feel better, it's possible I've jammed my index finger. With Dianna, it was simply rejuvenating."

"You're quite the superironic pacifist."

"You're still talking, aren't you?"

"Well, maybe you'll want to find a sledgehammer and shut me up."

"Tempting." Her mother's grim-but-cool expression wavered; her lips trembled. "Oh, boy, if your dad could see me now." A lone tear slid down her mother's cheek.

"He would understand, Mom." The near-killing rage that had swept over her had evaporated the moment the tear made its appearance. The rage was gone, and all that remained was dull embarrassment, and sorrow.

Her mother took a deep, steadying breath. "Ever since Dianna came back, I've felt more and more empty inside. The loss of your father—it sounds strange, Jennifer, but I had always wished for a second child."

Jennifer said nothing. They both knew that had been a physical impossibility for Elizabeth, since Jennifer's birth.

"So he dies. It was so much easier to avoid the truth when he was alive. And then here comes Dianna, with Jonathan's other child. And then here you are, growing up so fast . . ." She choked back a sob. "I'll be alone soon, Jennifer. Either because you die like him, or you succeed brilliantly and leave me behind."

"I'm not going to leave you, Mom."

"Don't be daft. Of course you will. You'll be an adult someday. You're not going to want to live in my house forever."

"You won't be alone. I won't allow it."

"You'll have no say in the matter. It doesn't matter; right now, we're all living under this . . . this . . ." She waved at the dome, then wiped the tears from her face. "I'm sorry I suggested you don't take responsibility, honey. Of course you do. I want you—I *need* you to keep taking responsibility. I can't do this alone, any more than you can. We have to stay together, focused on the same goal."

"Okay. Um. What is the goal again?"

"Protection of the innocent. Healing of the sick and wounded. Negotiations toward peace."

"Right. I knew that. That's it, huh?"

"No. Also, we have to figure *that* out."

Jennifer looked out the window where Elizabeth was pointing and groaned. A two-hundred-foot-high wall of mist was billowing over the neighborhoods to the west. It shimmered with unnatural silver menace, and its tendrils swirled around houses and trees before the glistening bulk swallowed them whole.

"What do you make of it?"

"I have no idea, Mom. How can it possibly be good? Cripes, my jaw still hurts . . ."

"We should find Dianna."

"Wow. You must really be worried, if you—"

"Find Dianna please, honey."

There was no need. Dianna and Evangelina had already appeared in the parking lot outside. From the concerned look on the face of the sorceress, Jennifer already knew they would have little help to offer.

As they walked to the exit, they thought through the possibilities. "Ember?"

"Doubtful. There's mist outside the wall as well." Elizabeth pointed to the south, where the barrier was shrouded in this strange weather.

"Skip?"

"Possibly. It's coming from a new direction, though. His attacks have come mainly from the northeast." They were outside now and close to the other two.

"He can go wherever he likes, Mom. And don't forget about Andi."

"Andeana's power flows from the music inside her," Dianna interjected. She closed her eyes. "There is no music inside this mist. It's a different sound altogether. Something . . . dragon?" One eye opened with an inquisitive brow.

Jennifer shrugged. "I've never heard of one of us doing anything like this. If it were Xavier, he would have told us."

Not if he allied with his niece, after all.

"He's not going to do that." But Jennifer felt something fall inside. What if Xavier had been holding back? What if Ember had finally convinced him that the destruction of the town was the golden opportunity his vengeful heart sought?

She burns half the town, and her uncle drowns whatever's left.

Evangelina sounded bored:

The answers are coming soon enough. It's headed this way.

As it neared, a thunderhead with a long snout formed before the front like a figurehead on the prow of a ship. It took an unmistakable bearing—straight toward them, gaining speed.

Elizabeth took a subtle step closer and clutched her daughter's hand. "My, my," she murmured. "We are the popular girls this week, aren't we."

"What do we do, Mom?"

"No idea. You, Dianna?"

"It's dragon . . ."

"So you've said. Yet this is hardly going to care about a bullet, or a sword. Do you have anything more helpful?"

"Wait. I hear it more clearly now. It's water . . ."

"Really." Elizabeth dropped Jennifer's hand and hissed.

"You've traveled through dozens of dimensions to come back here and tell me that mist is water. Wow. Just how stupid *was* my husband, at age fifteen, for you to impress him?"

Dianna shot back an unkind smirk. "I meant, the dragon. The dragon is water."

"What do you mean, the dragon is water? How can a dragon be . . ." Jennifer trailed off. The leading shape twisted and unfolded two wings, each the size of an aircraft carrier. The appendages curled around the hospital, and a gentle rain began to fall upon them. From deep within the mist, a roll of gentle thunder began to speak.

We've come far, ancient girl, since we met at the
    sea;
Destiny's tides pull at us, we yearn for the sea.

What you left behind does not drown or drift away,
Oceans stay faithful, though you live far from the sea.

"I know that voice." Jennifer felt a thrill as she burst into dragon shape. *"I know that voice!"*

What you left behind does not drown or drift away,
Oceans stay faithful, though you live far from the sea.

"Sonakshi! Oh, wow. Even with the poetry, you are the best damn thing to happen here in a year. The last time I saw you, you had tentacles. How did you get through the dome?"

Is there a place in this world where rain does not
    fall?
Is there a place that denies the seeds of the sea?

From water we are born, to water we return,
We pass through such magic as do fish through the
*   sea.*

"Of course," Dianna mused. "In the form of mist, they're weather. Weather can pass through the dome. Edmund created it so. I'm sure he had no idea . . ."

"Weather can—" Jennifer's brow furrowed. "And tell me, Sonakshi. You've been able to whip through magical walls for . . . how long exactly?"

Time flows like the current that warms and sustains
*   us;*
Our ways, like the waves, are as ancient as the sea.

"So, longer than a few months. Um. How do I say this without sounding slobberingly ungrateful—*where have you been?*"

Do not tell the ocean when it may rise and fall,
Tides may be quick or slow, like the beasts of the
*   sea.*

"Great. Slow tides. Okay, well, I'm still really happy to see you! Um . . . how many of you are in there?"

Sonakshi, like the ocean, can only be one.
But my friends are plentiful as fish in the sea.

The massive wings flexed, and suddenly the raindrops grew larger and faster. Jennifer felt like dancing—*help is here! Help is finally here! We're going to figure this out! We're going to stop Skip! We're going to beat this dome! We're going to find out if blue really can be the new black!*

After all, she could do anything any other dragon could do . . . *and if there are dragons that can pass through the dome . . .*

The rain kept falling.

I have to get them to teach me what they can do. Once I can pass through the barrier, I can lead them—not a few dozen, but an army of dragons as big as a rainstorm! No one can stop that, not even Skip!

Oh, Skip, you are gonna pay and pay and pay . . . it'll almost be worth losing Dad and everything else to see the look on your face when my new friends and I rearrange your guts for you.

The rain kept falling.

At the point when they all considered going inside to avoid the sheets of water, the skies began to clear and thousands of shapes began splashing down next to them. In an instant, each one became as solid as any other dragon Jennifer had ever seen. They filled the parking lot and the yards and fields beyond, each one a true-blooded dragon with gray and dull green or dull blue markings, each one bound to the Ancient Furnace through loyalty . . .

. . . and each one less than a foot long, inclusive of the tail.

"Wha?" Jennifer exclaimed.

"Huh," Elizabeth added.

"My." Dianna snickered.

CHAPTER 31
Andi

"You're back here with the birds?"

"Sorcery requires sacrifice, Andi."

Andi tried to hide her disgust, but it was hard. The birds were her least favorite part. "Dianna taught me that the sacrifice must come from within."

"Was that before or after she fucked everyone else over to get the universe she wanted?"

She didn't have an answer to that, so she averted her eyes from the blood and feathers and took in the weather outside the office window. "Getting pretty dark out over town."

"Go check it out, if you want."

"You don't want to come? It might be important."

"You don't want to go alone, take an aunt or uncle. I've got plenty to spare." He picked up a butcher knife and pointed back toward the restaurant's main room. "All they've done since they got here is mumble and disapprove of everything we're doing. See if you can get them to do something useful instead."

"You know they'll say no."

"They are pretty fucking ungrateful, aren't they?"

Upon their arrival, the six remaining brothers and sisters of Tavia and Otto Saltin had claimed the most comfortable parts of the restaurant for themselves, started gorging on food Skip and Andi had been storing away for months . . . and didn't even acknowledge the fact that since they'd come into Skip's presence, they had been able to keep their crescent-moon shape . . . even though it was a new moon.

If Dr. Georges-Scales is right, and Edmund Slider set up that wall to last as long as Skip needs it . . . then that wall won't be up for much longer.

"Maybe we should move somewhere else."

He carefully sliced a new part of the bird open. "Tempting, but we were here first. I'm thinking we'll come to a new understanding soon enough."

"They creep me out."

"It's not the eight-legs thing, I hope."

"Funny. No, it's their attitude. They're too—" *Like your father,* she was going to finish, but realized how that would come out. "They don't appreciate what you do for them. Won't you come with me instead?"

"Geez, Andi. It's late afternoon in autumn, and you're concerned that it's getting dark." He twisted the knife through some of the entrails. "Could you check the thermostat? It's getting a little warm in here. I'll bet they turned it up again."

She hesitated. "Your aunt always thought that ornithromancy was a bit . . . outdated."

"It's a proven technique since the pyramids. My mom

taught it to me. Over the past few months, I've added a few touches."

"And who'd know better how to improvise on a grotesque, millennia-old technique than a teenaged boy?"

"Joke if you want, but you know full well we'd never have been able to create so many creatures for our swarms if I hadn't looked at a few birds to unlock quicker ways to create them." He picked up a strand of intestine and brought it up to the light so he could examine it more clearly. "The trick is to look for possibilities instead of certainties. Tavia was a musician like you. Music works like math and logic, clear and certain. To do this right, you have to be willing to try new things."

"You don't know anything about music, then. Musicians improvise and take risks all the time."

This finally got him to turn. "Andi, if you'd been listening to popular music for the last twenty years, you'd know how ridiculous and hollow that sounds."

"So what? I don't know about risk? I don't know about improvisation?"

He turned back to his entrails. "You know it when you see it. You follow others fine—my mom, the Quadrivium, me. And you obviously contribute. But you don't create or lead much of anything yourself. You don't know about trailblazing. Flying to new heights. Playing with fire."

Andi stomped her foot. "Sounds like you miss a certain teenaged dragon."

Skip snorted. "Miss her? I haven't aimed at her yet."

"Whatever. You want to play with dead-bird guts, stay here. I'm going to check on the town."

Oh, crap.

Andi didn't know whether to feel terror at what she was

seeing, or pride in being here to see it without her obnox-
ious, patronizing prick of a boyfriend.

The roiling maelstrom pushing through the near edge
of Edmund Slider's barrier made no sound. Two hundred
feet high, the wall of mist set the Mississippi swirling as it
touched the muddy waters.

Not a storm. Not random. And coming up the hill.

For us.

The mass shimmered and shook and vibrated and shone
with unnatural silver menace, churning and flowing around
the trees below her and stretching even higher into the
sky. Then the glistening vastness had gulped it all, shutting off her view of the town, and the river, and the barrier
altogether.

She turned and ran.

Dianna, she thought. *It has to be Dianna.*

Only she had never seen Dianna do anything like
this. *Evangelina?* Possibly—she didn't really know that
twisted spawn too well. She seemed more like a brute-
force sort of threat than a fancy-towering-wall-of-mist
sort of threat.

Jennifer Scales. The thought shook her, even though it
made no sense. If Jennifer had a trick up her sleeve, she
would have played it long ago.

*Unless killing her father unleashed something, removed
all restraint.*

As she crossed the highway and neared the Cliffside
Restaurant, she spared a look back at the mist. Its tendrils
were already visible again, and they curled around the stars
as if capturing them before blotting them out.

"Skip," she called out even though he was too far to
hear. "Skip!"

By the time she reached the restaurant doors, the Saltin
siblings—all six of them—were at the windows, looking

outward. They were in arachnid form of course, thanks to Skip.

And thank goodness for that—we're going to need their best powers for what's coming our way.

"Can you tell what it is?" she asked them. "Is it Dianna Wilson?"

The brown recluse wrinkled her mandibles. "This does not smell like sorcery. It smells like . . . like . . ."

"Like dragon," one of the two sun spiders hissed.

"How can that be?" the other asked. "No dragon can do this!"

"Jennifer Scales might be able to."

The recluse backed away from the window and spat. "The dragon-stalker girl? That makes no sense. She'd have attacked long before now. Waiting a year suggests planning. Dragons do not plan."

"That's a fascinating theory, Auntie . . ." Skip snapped his fingers as he entered the dining room from the office. "Auntie-whatever-your-name-is. 'Dragons are dumb, they can't plan, we're supersmart, rah rah rah.' I think my dad thought the same thing, before she and her mom kicked his ass."

"Show your elders more respect," ordered the thick-legged baboon spider.

"Bite me, Uncle Ugly." He examined the scene out the window alongside them. "Look, guys—it doesn't matter what it is. What matters is Andi here has given us time to pull together and fight it. Thanks, Andi." He flashed her a charming smile, and she forgot how upset she had been with him in the Dead Bird Office.

"So what do we do?"

The elders laughed at her question. "What do we do," repeated the spindly harvester among them. "We fortify!

We weather the storm, wait for it to pass, learn from it, and counterattack when the time is right. On our terms."

"Arachnid Tactics 101," Skip said. His gaze remained outside. "I doubt it will work here. Whatever that mist is, it knows us. Which means it knows arachnids. Which means it knows we will want to hide. Better to fight it, test its strength, and learn something more useful than how to duck. Andi, I've got two swarms ready. You want to send them?"

"Sure."

"Great. If the rest of you can stand with us, we can focus on the center of the weather front—there's a shape forming there, if you look—"

He was talking to an empty room, except for Andi and her sad smile.

"They left right after your 'Arachnid Tactics 101' remark. I don't think they like you very much."

"Probably why we never had Thanksgiving dinner all these years. Fuck it—we don't need 'em. Get outside, learn what you can, and have a song ready. I'll be there with the swarms in sixty seconds."

He headed for the basement. Soothed by his confidence, she went back through the flung-open doors and faced the massive front.

It was approaching the highway, and the trees on the other side sparkled with moisture. There was a sound she could hear now—a pattern of hisses not unlike rain smacking a sidewalk in summer. She closed her eyes—then opened them nervously, then forced them closed again—and listened for the music.

There it was—rhythmic, ancient, deep. Familiar and exotic at the same time, she found she could almost hum along . . . but not quite.

What the hell is this?

It was making a new melody now, something dissonant. A piece was breaking off, a rogue line of tiny notes . . . now another, in harmony with the first . . . and another . . . and another dozen . . . the volume was reaching painful levels.

Her eyes opened, and she gasped.

"Skip, hurry!"

He was beside her in an instant, and she could feel the swarms following. "Go, go, go!" He hollered over the rising wind.

Voice cracking at first, she sang. Only the thousands of two-dimensional creatures passing under her feet could hear or understand the words. As each particle of swarm touched her, it began to glow with new power. Her song became stronger, and the creatures more agitated. More raced by to touch her and share in the power she offered.

"Take them out!" Skip ordered, and the smoldering multitude flowed from her and spread across the damp grass.

What faced them on the highway was now an army of miniature dragons. Andi would have thought them almost cute, if it weren't for two things: (a) she had heard their song, and (b) they were gathered in the shadow of what was left of the mist—an enormous dragonlike thing, with wings more vast than buildings.

The insect swarms rushed at them, their glow intensifying. Andi knew they would explode quickly and violently—*perhaps we should get inside,* she thought, judging the distance. She tugged at Skip's sleeve.

The moment the first creatures touched the pavement, the dragon army lifted as one, clearing the nearby treetops and letting the colors of the sunset briefly through. Being as close as they could get and still trapped in two dimensions, the insectoids mindlessly triggered, blasting each other apart. The explosion was indeed impressive, and Andi felt the heat of it as the shock wave reached them. Small chunks of pavement sailed by their heads and cracked the glass of the dining-room windows. They staggered backward, into the restaurant.

Then the entire mass of dragon flesh and misty weather lowered itself, unharmed, onto the broken highway and extinguished the sunset again.

She was terrified and thrilled. *We can't stop them!*

"Shit." Skip grabbed her hand. "Got any other tunes to try?"

She clasped his hand in both of hers and began a new melody. Her songs were not usually this strident, but she knew she needed something rapid and strong. Skip jumped at the electricity coming through her grasp, then he understood.

The poison she created in him was potent enough to mottle his skin green. He smiled at her and began to change.

He chose a plated scorpion form, fifteen feet from pincers to stinger. Viscous goo dripped from his armaments, and his mandibles sizzled.

"Go get 'em, tiger."

He charged them, scuttling faster than a cheetah could race. A new song came from Andi now—not of poison like the last one, but of speed and power.

The throng scattered above his head at first, adopting the same tactic it had with the explosive swarms. This did not work for long, as Skip began spitting a hail of projectiles from his deformed mandibles. A dozen of them fell screaming, their faces and eyes smoking with corrosive fluid.

A voice, deep and mysterious, dropped upon them like unhappy rain.

Unnatural child, your ways are out of balance.
We must cleanse you now, with the fire of the seas.

Andi had only known dragons who could breathe fire. What happened next therefore astonished her—and certainly surprised Skip.

The cloud of dragons lowered again, and a thousand jets of steam blasted his exoskeleton. Skip screamed and scuttled back. The boiling gloom followed him, and Andi suddenly realized that she was in everyone's path.

"Get inside, get inside, get down, get down, get down!"

She did what he said, diving into the restaurant and scrambling across the dining-room floor on all fours. He skittered in behind her, and the ferocious hiss followed.

The large windows burst, making Andi scream. She dragged Skip through the kitchen doors. The wooden furniture in the dining room was warping, and dozens of the tiny dragons were fluttering in, unharmed by their own breath. Their flashing silver eyes tracked her like a formation of sharks locking in on prey.

They hunt like this, she realized. *Deep in the ocean. They heat the surrounding water, cook whatever they find— schools of fish, sea monsters, whatever—and serve it up right there.*

Skip was back in human form, gasping. Ovals of boiled skin were sloughing off his arms and face. She could heal him—but only if they survived.

We need to leave.

She rushed him through the kitchen and into the back pantry. Three or four of the dragons were right behind them, knocking into pots with their wings and slapping utensils off the counter in their frenzy.

"Andi, there are no windows in this room! We're trapped."

"Hush. Hold that shut." Kicking the door closed behind them, she breathed deeply, pressed her hands against a bare spot of wall, and hummed.

Skip dragged down plastic shelves of canned goods and piled bags of flour on top of that. The knob turned, and he grunted with the effort to twist it back and lock it. The hollow metal door shuddered with the weight of several slams. Steam leaked under the door onto Skip's ankles, and he screamed.

Hang on, baby. She hummed, pressing her fingers into the cement. The solid wall gave way, and a portal opened. It was nothing much—a tiny bit of folded space that still belonged to this universe. It would not last forever since she had borrowed it from elsewhere, and elsewhere would need it back before long. But right now, it would have to do.

The steam stopped, and a cooler, sparkling formation of vapor was slipping through the door.

"Skip, now!"

She squeezed his fingers and drew him into the New Space. It snapped shut behind them, leaving them safe in darkness.

They stayed there as long as Andi felt they could, perhaps an hour and a half. She had let the space float—no sense in trying to enter the same room they had left, since the dragons (if they had any brains at all) would be waiting there for them. By the time they exited, they were an hour's or so walk deeper into the woods behind the restaurant.

They climbed the nearest tree together, until they were high enough to see the restaurant and surrounding buildings, about five miles away.

The weather had brightened slightly, though the sun had lowered itself farther since their escape. Specks of dragon hovered loosely around the massive mist dragon as it lumbered through the woods immediately surrounding the restaurant. They were still searching.

"It won't take long," she whispered to Skip. "Even if Dianna's not helping them, it won't be difficult for them to find us again."

"Mom's not with them," Skip grumbled back. "Why would she risk herself?"

"Still. I can't keep making voids for us to slip into. That sorcery took a lot out of me." She could still feel her heart pumping hard. "We should get moving." Anything to put as much distance between themselves and *their*selves as possible.

"I can't believe it." He was gritting his teeth as he looked at them. "These things may actually bitch things up for me."

She stroked his hand. "They won't have the element of surprise next time. C'mon. We've—"

"I've got to counterattack."

?!?

"What I saw in the birds convinced me I could succeed," he continued. "I thought I might have a few weeks to prepare everything. I don't. I don't have a few days. Maybe a few hours."

"Skip—"

"Don't try to argue with me, Andi. Did you see that gigantic flock of aqua worms? I need all the power I can get! I need everything I can yank from anybody who's not me, and I need it right now."

"But the ritual—"

"Is my only chance. It'll tie me to the moon." He looked to the skies; the new moon was invisible, but he knew where it would be hanging. "And once I have the moon . . ."

"But we don't even know if it will work!"

"It'll work. As long as I can find my uncles and aunts . . . it'll work."

"What, you *want* their help now?"

"Andi, my love. I can't do it without them. Can you communicate with them, get a message to them, wherever they ran off to?"

Her eyelids softly closed. "Each of them still has a song. They've scattered. I can get them together again. Where do you want to meet?"

He thought quickly and pointed. "The abandoned convenience store about two miles down the road."

She had no better plan and nowhere else to go. "Okay, love. Whatever you say."

"That's my girl."

CHAPTER 32
Andi

"Outrageous!" shrieked the baboon spider.

"Impossible!" thundered the brown recluse.

"Ridiculous!" added the slender harvester.

"Dangerous!" intoned the twin sun spiders.

"Just like your father," hissed the last, a yellowed scorpion, whose stinger hung heavy over its bulbous back. "All anger, all ego. His poor planning sacrificed rigor for showmanship. Lack of rigor leads to inefficient traps. Inefficient traps lead to wasted poison. Poison is life. You have no respect for any of this."

Skip's jaw twitched.

Andi bit her lip and slid an arm under her sleeve to massage the tracks from her most recent cuts. "I don't think it's about anger or ego or respect," she said. "I think Tavia wanted Skip to have your guidance. Let's be more constructive. What help can you offer?"

"None."

"Skip, maybe—"

"No, Andi. The answer is none."

"Please, Skip. Tavia wanted—"

"Aunt Tavia is dead for a reason. I didn't ask her for help, I didn't ask her rotten and cowardly brothers and sisters for their advice, and this meeting is over. Almost."

Through the muttering and mandible-grinding of the creatures assembled closely around them in the abandoned convenience store, Andi wondered aloud, "What do you mean, 'almost'?"

Skip suddenly relaxed, as though he had reached a decision. "I mean, that even though I didn't ask for her help, I'm glad she tried. In fact, it's for the best."

The brown recluse twitched. "How so?"

"I haven't been completely honest with all of you. I mean, I do plan to ascend and become our kind's greatest. And I do plan to poison the moon, to make that happen. I shouldn't have made you think this would be a proposal review or decision council."

"What is it, then?" snapped the scorpion.

"More like a breakfast meeting."

They had no time to take in what he meant. Even as he rose tall on two extended legs, his other six were fully formed and twice the length of any of them, each tipped with a spear-like tarsus. By the time the adults gasped at his sheer size— *no one can possibly morph that large!*—the six jagged limbs came down and made the linoleum floor shudder. Each was a skewer, with a kabob gasping and wriggling at the end.

"SKIP!"

"Quiet, Andi. This is the most important part." The enormous arachnid—Andi couldn't say for certain if it was a true species or something out of Skip's own imagination—minced on its hindmost legs quickly, holding high the dying relatives on its way to the back room. "Could you grab the door to the refrigeration corridor?"

"What's in the—ah, geez, you're going to stuff them all in there? That's gross. And weird. Skip, these are your uncles! Your aunts! Not TV dinners!" Andi nearly threw up as she took in the sight of them all, abdomens spasming and eyes bulging, hanging off their nephew's limbs. "You've killed them!"

"Not quite yet. I need their blood fresh, and I can't weave fast enough to keep them alive with this much blood loss. Also, I want to soak up what's on the floor. Every drop will help. You'll thank me later."

At his impatient hiss, she opened up the walk-in door. "At least keep them away from the milk. Skip, how is this going to help you poison the moon?"

"I had insight, during my research."

"You mean your bird-flaying."

"These idiots only know one way to get it done. It generally involves eighty years of the sorcerer traveling through sixteen different dimensions and damning himself at the end. Boring and worse . . . not exactly enjoyable. But I found a faster, better way." He flicked the bleeding creatures off each tarsus, letting them collapse over each other in the middle of the slick floor. Vapor seethed from his mandibles as he turned from them and faced Andi. "Quick. Easy. Brilliant. Good thing Aunt Tavia thought I was an ignorant ass who needed help."

"Yeah, that'll learn her." She managed not to shudder. "Skip, I don't understand."

"I can reach the moon with the blood of enough arachnids. Finding our own kind is tough enough nowadays—

Tavia seemed to think we might even be the last—but being the helpful person she is, she tracked down these recluses and brought them here. Well, one recluse, anyway." He snickered, waving a back leg at the brown spider. "Get it, Andi. *Recluse?*"

Which is more horrifying—the insanity, or the puns? She gulped. "Yeah, nifty gag. So you need their blood—to do what, exactly?"

"To weave into the soil. What arises will poison the moon in my favor. It won't matter if we're the last arachnids on earth—what will rain down from the sky will be all the replenishment our kind needs."

"Huh. So. How many do you need?"

"I've got seven already."

"There's only six there."

"I have Mr. Slider wrapped up in a chest freezer in the basement of one of the nearby houses. The night he died, I told Tavia I'd bury him. I didn't say where."

"Ugh, Skip! He's been dead for nearly a year! How fresh can his blood be?"

"I'll average it out. I figure the blood of a living arachnid, mixed with his, should work fine."

"So you have seven. One of them's dead. You say you need to mix living blood, and you're out of arachnids . . . unless you've resurrected Aunt Tavia and have her stuffed back there somewhere as well."

"No. It would have been ideal to use her, too. But with her gone, I really only have one option to get the number I need."

The air near the freezer suddenly seemed frostier to Andi. She took a step back. "Skip. How many arachnids do you need for this ritual?"

His head lowered, his front legs began to pull him out of the freezer . . . and all eight inscrutable eyes fixed on her.

CHAPTER 33
Andi

Andi sucked in air again, a violent and painful act.

Plink, plunk. Plink, plunk. Plinkplunk, plinkplunk. Plink, plunk.

It was dark and chill, wherever she was. She was leaning up against a cement wall. She couldn't move her spread and slightly bent limbs, and the rattling of chains suggested she should not bother to try. A wet rag was taped into her mouth.

Her arms felt heavy, something was tickling them, and they hurt.

Plinkplunk, plink, plunk.

She let out a low hum, then another. She built one note upon the other, and the music made her throat glow faintly. What she glimpsed made her choke, shutting off the light.

Swarms of round black ticks clung to each arm. A few

of them moved, but most were feeding from her flesh—
from her smooth underarms, her bony elbows, her wriggling fingertips, and most of all from the forearm welts she
had inflicted upon herself.

Those that had swollen to full size were dropping off
into large buckets lined up by her feet. The buckets were
about a third full with a thick, crimson, boiling mixture.
New ticks crawling up the wall quickly replaced them.

It felt like all her innards were roiling and clenching at
once. Her skin crawled—literally! It felt like a greasy fist
was clenching her throat; she had never been so frightened,
or repelled.

She swooned in her chains and tried not to retch into her
gag. *This is what you get for sticking with him. This is what
you deserve, for turning Jennifer down.*

Plink, plink, plunk, plinkplunk.

For a few minutes, she let herself hang from her wrists,
bile rising from her gut, swaying back and forth.

*Let it be done. What else can I hope for? You win, Skip.
You win.*

The answer came from an unseen source. It was a voice
from her past, from a life she barely lived, in a moment
even before her birth—her mother, strong and vibrant,
holding her in her womb, standing up for herself:

*You won nothing! You don't test me! You don't control me!
You don't tell me what I can and cannot do! Screw you!*

SCREW YOU!

Her skin began to tingle all over—not from the sensa-
tion of tiny arachnids crawling, but from something within.
Something was unwinding. Was it her intestines, her lungs,
her arteries? It felt like it was everywhere. It . . . it wasn't a
scary feeling, exactly.

I've felt this before, she realized. *On the bridge. With
Mother, before I killed her.*

You've failed, came her father's voice.

Screw you, her mother replied.

I'm not just a sorceress born in the dark, raised in the dark, and left to die in the dark. I'm the daughter of the most powerful beaststalker to ever walk the earth. She wouldn't just hang here. She wouldn't let a slob like Skip bleed her slowly. She would control her own destiny.

Her torso unfolded, and four new arms appeared, unrestrained, each holding a dagger.

And it would start with a weapon or four.

Once she had cut off the gag and scraped the ticks off each arm, it was a matter of finding the right melody to unlock the chains . . . and then a quick stumble up the cellar stairs. It was a house, she recognized, between the convenience store and the restaurant. One of the first they had occupied.

Probably the same one he stored Mr. Slider in.

She wasn't sure if she wanted Skip to be here for a fatal confrontation, or to escape unseen. In any case, he was nowhere to be found, and she did not wait for him. She was sick and weak, having left most of her blood in pails.

In the pails he set out for her blood. *Oh, you bastard,* she thought, crashing and reeling through the room, intent on flight.

Get to Libby, her mother's voice told her. *Libby can save you.*

She burst out the back door of the restaurant and into the woods, toward the blue dome in the distance.

I'll help them now. Jennifer, her mother, all of them. They'll heal me and make me strong again. Then we'll stop Skip together.

If anyone can.

CHAPTER 34
Jennifer

Jennifer ground her teeth. *This isn't supposed to be hard anymore!*

"Better focus," advised one tiny dragon with watery scales.

"Eyes closed," suggested another.

"But not too tightly," added another. "You need the tears."

"Don't try to disappear," a fourth reminded her. "Try to *dissipate*."

"Breathe quickly."

"Crouch down a little."

"Become moist."

"All right, all right, all right!" *Become moist?* Their recent help against Skip notwithstanding, Jennifer felt like punting these runts into the dome wall and seeing if they'd bounce back.

This was the basic lurker skill. Basic! Lurkers were dragons. She was the Ancient Furnace. Whatever any dragon could do . . .

"Can you do it yet?" came Catherine's voice. She was coming out of the hospital into the parking lot, holding a packet of Perk-E Turk-E Jerk-E.

Jennifer growled. "Don't you have a watch shift to start up on the roof?"

"You kidding? Who needs a watch when you've got three thousand misty dragon-midgets here in the parking lot? Ember would be nuts to attack here now."

"First, in case you haven't caught up with current events, Ember *is* nuts. Second, we're going to try another attack soon. Sonakshi and I agree—they can't stay hidden forever." She motioned up to the mist creature who hovered like a cumulonimbus above the hospital. "So they'll be leaving again within the hour."

"Why not have them stay out there—didn't they say they'd almost gotten to Skip and Andi?"

Jennifer felt a thrill of irritation. "Because *I* should be leading them. They're my responsibility. This whole situation is my responsibility."

"That seems a bit much."

"If you don't understand, I can't explain it."

"You're surly because you're getting shown up by the Tuna Brigade." Catherine held her hands up defensively as a murmur of discontent washed through the sea of lurkers. "Hey, joking, guys! I'm a big fan. You smell great."

"Why don't you go on a supply run? Or practice your whomping? Or drown yourself in the Mississippi?"

Catherine gave an easy grin as she looked east, toward the river. "You kidding? It's way too cold—what the— Jennifer!"

Staring where her trampler friend was pointing, Jennifer

still took several seconds to process what she was seeing. Out of the forested cliffs across the river to the northeast, a shape was rising. At first, she thought it was the cliff itself heaving—but when several appendages appeared and rubbed away the clinging vegetation, she realized it was something else.

"Skip's behind this, isn't he?"

"Hard to imagine anyone else."

The colossal eight-legged form expanded, pulling back onto its hind legs and lifting its other appendages high. Its earthen tones brightened into a sickening lime hue, and its abdomen stretched to cartoonish proportions.

"It's going to attack!" one of the lurkers called out. This inspired alarm among its brethren, who offered helpful input such as "Spread out!" and "Brace yourselves!" even as Jennifer saw that this creature had no interest in the town of Winoka. In fact, she wasn't completely sure it was a creature at all.

Whatever it was, it was reaching for the moon.

Impossible, she told herself: but she knew it immediately to be true. Even under a new moon, Jennifer always felt the subtle tug of the invisible satellite, and her heart always pointed like a compass to its location. This arachnid—this sorcery, this thing—was intercepting her connection. Up, up it rose into the indigo, so high that Jennifer felt like a gnat at the base of a tidal wave.

Tidal wave. The words hit Jennifer hard. She turned to Catherine.

"Skip has found a way to stop the lurkers."

As if pulled out of hiding by her son's sorcery, Dianna Wilson appeared at the hospital entrance. She was not looking at the unfathomably long spider-sorcery, nor at the place in the sky where Jennifer knew the dark side of the moon to be. She did not have to; she kept her gaze on the crowd of dragons before her.

"You are all in great danger," she told them. "The end has begun."

"I know," Jennifer replied. "Once Skip destroys the moon, anything that depends on the tides . . ."

Dianna shook her head with a sad smile. "You don't understand. Skip isn't going to *destroy* the moon. He's going to *become* it."

They were all in the parking lot—the sea-scented lurkers with Sonakshi looming over them, and Jennifer and her mother, and the dragons and beaststalkers and everyone else who lived at the hospital. Everyone, Jennifer noticed, except Evangelina.

Where is she?

It didn't matter, right now. Dianna was talking.

"The end as our kind knows it," she was explaining, "is not about death or judgment. It is about—"

"Blood?" Jennifer guessed.

Dianna looked at her evenly.

"Because you guys seem to care an awful lot about blood. I'm just sayin'."

"It is," the sorceress continued without breaking the younger's gaze, "about poison."

Jennifer snapped her fingers. "Poison!"

"I'll bet blood still plays a part," Catherine muttered with glum helpfulness.

"Poison is about change," Dianna continued. "Instead of death or life, we worship the change that poison represents—what it forces upon our prey and the rest of nature. And there is no prey like the satellite that has danced over us since the dawn of time."

"And the moon is important why—because of the tides?"

Elizabeth guessed, as Jennifer had. "Will he dominate the seas, once he captures the moon?"

"Shifting the seas, and the creatures that live off them, is only the start. The Poison Moon is—"

"Full of poison?"

"Jennifer, honey."

"Oh, come on. Like that would surprise *anyone*."

"The Poison Moon is the ultimate weapon and fortress in one," Dianna explained patiently. "Once this ritual is complete, Skip will exist in two places at once: here on earth, and within the moon. We could destroy his body here, and still he would exist. From an impregnable position, Skip could do as he pleased: throw the seas into chaos, break off mountain-sized pieces of the moon and hurl them at us, seed smaller chunks with whatever creatures he saw fit to create and sow the earth with millions of them."

He will change all below, yet resist change himself
His power will draw from the moon, which pulls the
seas.

"Great. Thanks for the iambic armagedda-meter, Misty. It was a real contribution."

"The moon has more than military value. It is a portal— *the* portal—into all the universes where arachnids, dragons, beaststalkers, and every other power you know exists. A few you don't, as well. Once he controls the moon, he controls that portal—and he can spread his dominion into those universes."

"The Quadrivium tried that once," Jennifer pointed out. "I stopped you."

Dianna could not hide a patronizing smile. "Jennifer, darling, *I* stopped us. You advanced a loud opinion and caused a whirlwind of trouble, which gave us an opportunity to reconsider our goals and methods."

"Still."

"It doesn't matter—it will do you no good to travel from one universe to the next if Skip spoils them all. The Poison Moon is something the Quadrivium never contemplated—the costs of performing the sorcery were too high to us, personally."

"What costs?"

"Basically, the sorcerer has to endure endless, immortal pain."

"Yeah, but there's probably a drawback, too, right?" When a pained silence was her only response, Jennifer muttered, "We're somewhat levity-free today, I see."

"The Poison Moon becomes weapon, fortress, portal . . . and hell. Since only the most powerful among us could even contemplate the sorcery, the idea of someone willing to pay such a price seems incredible."

"Yet Skip is willing to pay it." Elizabeth looked back at the spider-sorcery. "Why?"

"Because it's Skip," Catherine and Jennifer said in perfectly eerie unison.

Her mom was shaking her head. "There's more here than that . . . is it possible he doesn't understand the cost?"

"Or maybe he truly is insane," Catherine guessed.

"Either is possible," Dianna answered. "But the most likely explanation is that Skip has divined an alternative way to start the sorcery. Instead of damning himself, perhaps he discovered a way to damn others."

Jennifer's heart fell. "Andi."

"A reasonable guess."

"Right up his genetic alley, to make others pay the price."

Dianna ignored that comment. "We can't know for sure

what price Skip paid. If all the secrets of this sorcery were known, it would doubtless have been tried before. By The Crown, if no one else."

"I know how we can find out. We can go over there and kick his ass."

Dianna, confused, turned to Elizabeth. "Does she listen any more carefully to you than she listens to me?"

"I wish."

"Cute, Mom. Look, I know you said he's going to be immortal and all—but can't we stop this sorcery before that thing reaches the moon?"

"*We* can't do any such thing, honey. We're stuck in this dome."

"Not after I learn how to self-vaporize—"

"No time for lessons," Dianna chided her. "Those who can go, should go. It is time to face this threat down. No more diplomacy." This last was directed at Elizabeth, who did not react.

"Okay, so they go." Jennifer motioned at the water dragons and Sonakshi. "We'll get Xavier and the dragons outside to join this time. And you. What about Evangelina . . . where the hell is she, anyway?"

The sorceress shifted uncomfortably. "I will find my daughter and join the battle as quickly as possible."

"Whoa, whoa, whoa . . . you don't know where she is?"

"At least things aren't getting complicated," was Elizabeth's dry comment. "You two showed up and started talking about how we have to stop Skip. Now the time is here. And she's where—trying out the new city trail system?"

"She's likely feeding."

"Likely? It was your turn to watch her! It's *always* your turn to watch her!" Jennifer shook her head. "I feel like I shouldn't want the answer to this, but: feeding on what, exactly?"

"Or whom?" Elizabeth added.

"Not important."

"Well, if you say so . . . then it must be incredibly important."

Dianna ignored her. "Sonakshi—you should take your people to the Cliffside Restaurant." She pointed. "It is not far from where that thing originated, and where its hind legs are still anchored. Jennifer will send along the others, and we'll not be long in joining you. Hurry, please—once the bridge to the moon is complete, stopping Skip becomes far more difficult. Probably impossible."

She turned to Jennifer and Elizabeth. "The rest of the world is also in danger. You might want to tell them that."

CHAPTER 35
Andi

Andi was having considerable trouble staying upright when the gigantic sorcery erupted a short distance away.

Against her own better judgment, she had taken a short rest—maybe an hour—once she was a few hundred yards into the woods. She couldn't help herself—by her best guess, she had lost at least two pints of blood. Maybe three. Wasn't four lethal?

Whatever. She had to rest, even if Skip was chasing her. And as it turned out, he didn't find her.

Maybe he didn't need to, she reflected as she watched the giant spider reach for the heavens. *Maybe he already had enough blood from me, and he decided to start the ritual with what he had.*

The Poison Moon. Oh, how could he? Driven, yes. Selfish, yes. Filled with hate, yes. But this . . . the times they talked about it . . . the times *he* talked about it . . .

A fact she didn't know she had bubbled up in her mind: Skip had always been the one to initiate discussions about the Poison Moon.

Skip always liked to touch her, to love her
(love he doesn't know love and neither do I)
after they'd talked about it. After he'd talked about it.

She had never thought.

She never thought he had the power. Or the drive. Not for *that*. It was love talk.

She had found the path down the steep slopes to where the bridge vaulted from the eastern shore, when she saw the mist roiling within the dome.

They're coming for him already. She stretched her head up at the spider-sorcery. *Good. I hope they're not too late.*

She briefly considered ways in which she might assist them—could she help them locate Skip? (No, and Dianna probably had that covered.) Could she fight alongside them? (Not without keeling over.) Give them advice? (Not without wasting their valuable time.)

No, there was nothing to do but continue toward the town. She would beg Jennifer and Dr. Georges-Scales for mercy, gratefully receive aid, and then rejoin whatever battle was still in progress. If she was too late for that last, then she would work with her new allies to bring the dome down. Sure, Slider's sorcery was powerful—but she was Quadrivium as well, and with the right song, maybe she could unlock this barrier's secrets . . .

"Freeze!"

CHAPTER 36
Andi

Andi froze. She was pretty sure she placed the voice right, but she didn't know if this was good or bad news. Or possibly an aural hallucination based on blood loss.

"Eddie?"

"Don't turn your head! Face front! I've got an arrow pointed right at the back of your skull—you know I could hit you from ten times this distance!"

"I do know, and stop shouting. It's killing my poor head." She raised her arms and stared ahead into the empty woods. "Eddie, I'm giving myself up. Skip tried to kill me. He's gone insane. I want to help Jennifer now."

"You've had your chance for months."

"For heaven's sake, Eddie. Look at that thing." Without turning, she pointed back and to the right. "Which threat do you think is the real one—me, or *that*?"

"I can't do anything about that. I can do something about you, though."

"Fine. Escort me to the barrier. Hand me off to the town sentries. I won't resist."

"Escorting you anywhere seems a whole lot more difficult than releasing this bowstring."

"Please don't." Her vision began to cloud again—freaking blood loss!—and she stumbled. "Eddie. Cripes. I need a hospital. Please."

Wherever he was—he sounded like he was in an elevated position, perhaps in a tree—he hesitated. "You look pretty damn white."

"Normally, I'd take that as an insult on my father's behalf." Her jaws almost split from an enormous yawn. Slowly, she dropped to one knee as an alternative to keeling over. "Eddie—escort me to the bridge, or carry me, or shoot me, or leave me to die."

She heard him sigh, then the sounds of tree bark crumbling. "I'm dying for you to be tricking me into some sort of trap."

"No trick. No trap."

"Right. If there's two things arachnids hate, it's tricks and traps."

She shook her head, partly to disagree and partly to unseat the spots that had settled in her peripheral vision. "I'm not just arachnid, Eddie. I'm beaststalker—like you. Glorianna Seabright was my mother. Your mother was a beaststalker, too."

"*Don't* talk about my mother."

"Okay. So, how about this weather? Looking pretty misty." She motioned toward the mob of water dragons rolling over the river, through the dome.

"Yeah, they're back. I liked what they did the first time. I suppose your boyfriend has a new plan, though."

She shrugged, not having the strength for any more words. *He sure does have a plan. Wait until you see it.*

He was directly behind her now; even his careful steps made noise on the first fallen September leaves. She imagined him with arrow cocked once more. Perhaps the bow was put away, and he had blades ready. It didn't matter. She only wanted to get to the bridge.

He slid an arm under her and lifted her to her feet. "Let's go."

As they descended the slope, the mist came up to greet them. Andi wondered whether this thundercloud of draconic fury would recognize her, envelop her, try to destroy her. Did they know Eddie? What would they make of her surrender?

And why did any of it matter to her, even now?

It turned out, they did not care. The broad wings of their obvious leader passed overhead with little more than a distant rumble of meteorological irritation, and the ghostly shapes of thousands of small, winged lizards weaved through the birch and oak as if their haunted forms knew every branch and bush on the riverside.

"Skip will have his hands full," Eddie muttered. Andi knew he was weighing whether he ought to join the invasion force. Plainly, she was no threat to him. Why escort her?

As if in answer, she lost her footing and stumbled away from him. Her head slammed the earth, less than a foot from a moss-covered rock. Dizziness overwhelmed her, and she spat bile.

"Geez, Andi. Here." He knelt and lifted her again.

"I'll be all right once I get off my feet," she mumbled.

"You *are* off your feet, Andi." His determination to aid her overpowered her desire to support herself, and she let her body melt into his arms. He carried her, one long arm behind her shoulders and the other under her knees. Though her head lolled back, she could still take in his serious, sparrowlike features.

"You smell like you could use a shower," she observed.

"Yeah, well, you stink like blood."

That got her laughing and coughing. "I can see what Jennifer likes about you."

He did not respond. She found the travel jarring since the way was steep, and he was descending quickly. Beyond his head, she could see the mist lift. In its place, at least three dozen large dragons were in half-V formations.

"Xavier Longtail," she slurred to no one in particular.

"How much time do they have?"

"I dunno. The Poison Moon—I didn't even think it would work . . ."

"He's come a long way since he coldcocked me in the Mall of America parking lot."

"So have you." She thought of the arrows he'd been placing near them for months. "Tell the truth—you could have killed us long ago. Right?"

She felt the lift of his shrug. "I guess. I'm not a killer, Andi. I wanted you guys to feel a slice of the fear Jennifer and the others are coping with, every day. I didn't want you to get comfortable. I wanted you to think. To listen."

"I should have listened better."

"Yeah, well, maybe I should have shot better. When I was aiming at him," he hastened to add.

"It's okay," she groggily reassured him. "Not mad."

They reached the highway, and the aging arch of the bridge loomed to the west. Now that they were out of the trees, they had a clearer view of the dragons that were closing in on the root of the sorcery. The Cliffside Restaurant and other nearby buildings were out of view, and Andi imagined Skip sitting on the roof as he sometimes did. Would he stay out in the open, to watch his sorcery progress? Would he fear the dragons at all?

How powerful was he?

Missiles of fire began to rain down to the east—Xavier's dragons had begun their attack. Eddie paused and turned to watch, and Andi signaled that he could let her down.

"You can walk into town from here?"

"Eddie." She held his arm. "Don't go up there. I don't think—"

"You're right, Andi. I could have stopped this. I didn't realize how dangerous Skip was. I should have had the killer instinct."

Poor boy, she thought. *What he means is, he should have been more like Skip. Poor, poor boy.*

"I should have been a beaststalker, like my dad always wanted me to be."

"Your mom wouldn't want you up there. It's suicide."

He didn't chastise her this time for bringing up his mother. Nor did he show any sign that she had convinced him. "I'm going up there. The sentries can see us. With Dad dead, they'll be taking orders from Dr. Georges-Scales. They won't let a girl die. They'll know you need a hospital."

"Carry me farther. I'm getting faint again. It's so far away."

"Nice try. I'm—"

A piercing shriek blasted the atmosphere, knocking them both to the ground. When Andi looked back up, the enormous spider was no longer there. Instead, where there was once an uninterrupted expanse of afternoon blue, now appeared a dim, smoldering disc of jade.

"I thought it was a new moon," Eddie observed.

"It is." She could barely hear herself, she was so afraid to speak.

"So why can we see it?"

"Because we'll always see it, for as long as we last. Even the dark side."

"What does it mean?"

Up the highway, over the hill where the Cliffside would be, a collective roar went up. Thousands of streaks of vapor retreated from the fray, pulled away from the earth and toward the moon. Once they were high above the treetops, the gases turned ugly green and dissipated completely. The massive cloud that was Sonakshi collapsed into a chaotic emerald whorl, which came screaming down the road at them.

Eddie pushed her into the ditch and fell on top of her. Moments later, the Sonakshi-twister blasted by, cut a path down the eastern bank, and splashed with an unmistakable death rattle into the chilled river.

Immediately, the waters of the Mississippi began running green, as if sweeping away the corrupted spirit that had inexplicably drowned there.

A few seconds later, winged forms began dropping from the sky. Most crashed into trees, groaning. It was an awful, screaming, thumping hail.

A few yards away from Andi and Eddie, the enormous shape of Xavier Longtail slammed into the pavement with a sickening crack. His golden eyes stared blankly at them from beneath a bleeding skull, and poisoned vapors trailed from his black nostrils.

CHAPTER 37
Susan

"Susan! Open this door or I'll boot it off the hinges!"

Nothing. Susan's new digs were still weird, still isolated, and still had that view of the big dumb willow tree under which she and Gautierre had had that stupid picnic.

"Susan! I know you're in there! You're always in there!" *And why,* Jennifer wondered, *am I knocking? What's she going to do, call a cop? What's a little breaking and entering to my reputation?*

"The neighborhood," her friend observed, opening the door, "is really going to hell."

"Tell me." Jennifer pushed past her and walked into the boo-hoo-Gautierre's-dead digs. The scene was almost exactly as it was the last time.

Same stale smell. Same stupid sleeping bag. Same battered backpack. No toilet-paper rolls, but two Kleenex boxes.

"Gah, it smells like a wolverine's butt in here."

"That's nice," Susan replied. "Who's dead now?"

Jennifer paused, and Susan bit the inside of her cheek. *Shit. Maybe her mom.* "Well. Um. Nobody you were close to, anyway."

Good. Not her mom. Susan let the resentment swell back up.

"Listen, I—"

"Need my help."

"Yeah. Because I—"

"Don't remember a single thing about the last conversation we had in this room."

"That's not—"

"Going to change a thing. Nothing has changed, Jenn. Except I'm in dire need of highlights. But who cares? It's not like there's anyone to look pretty for." She paused. "Did I tell you I lost a tooth? Woke up and found it in the sleeping bag, like I was seven again, and hoping to get a buck from the Tooth Fairy. I'm getting scurvy. Isn't that hilarious?"

"Hilarious isn't the first word springing to mind." Susan looked as bad as Jennifer had ever seen her, except maybe the circles under her eyes were bigger and darker. And scurvy? Losing teeth? Ye gods. For the first time, she hoped her friend was just in a funk and not losing her sanity.

How much more can she take? Jennifer wondered. *Who's dead now . . . ?* That was getting to be the question of the day. Fight and get stomped, or just get stomped, but sometimes it was hard, really very hard, and maybe getting stomped wasn't so bad.

At least, she could understand why Susan would find that a less awful alternative, even if she couldn't let her friend give in to it, not for one more day or one more hour. "Why didn't you come see my mom, dumb-ass? She—"

"Is overworked and saving lives on about forty seconds of sleep a night."

"Yes, but for you—"

"She'd drop everything, and another life would be endangered, and for what? To tell me I need to eat grapefruit? I'm aware, Jenn."

"Susan, I'm not going to argue with you. I am in full agreement: everything sucks, all the time. But we have to pull together on this."

"As opposed to everything we've done for months? In case you haven't noticed, Jenn, none of it worked. Nothing at all works. We. Are going. To die. In here. And it would be really great if you would go away and let me rot in peace. Go away, Jenn. And take your bad news with you."

"Susan. I so don't have time for this."

"Run along, then. You—hey. Hey!"

Her oldest friend, her finest friend, her very best friend, had taken her by the shoulders and lifted her until they were eye to eye and nose to nose. "You are going to help me, Susan, if I have to yank out all your other teeth to get you to do it. Pull your head out of your ass, stop sniveling about a boy—"

"Hey!"

"—and look at the goddamned moon! Skip is going to kill *everybody*, is that penetrating through that thick self-involved selfish pissing and moaning sniveling poor me poor me crybaby skull of yours?"

"Your shrill penetrating voice is the only thing getting through my thick skull."

"I need you, dumb-ass! Get your *thumb* out of your *rear* and *help me*."

There was a long silence as the two friends eyeballed each other.

"Your breath," Susan said at last, "is unbelievably bad."

"Toothpaste is gone. Mouthwash is reserved for certain medicinal purposes."

Both girls almost started to laugh, remembered they were furious at each other, and deepened their frowns instead.

"This is about Skip, then."

Jennifer nodded. "Dianna told my mom and me. It's this completely horrible thing called the Poison Moon."

"Why is it always something like the 'poison moon'? Why not ever the Kitten-and-Ball-o-Yarn Moon, or the Cotton-Candy-Sprinkled-with-Marshmallow-Bits Murder Plot?"

"Seriously." Jennifer explained what Dianna had told all of them.

"So come on. I need you."

"All right. Unclench your hands from my fragile shoulders before you snap me in half like a damn wishbone."

Jennifer felt blood rush to her face. The entire time she'd been running down Poison Moon 101 for Susan, they'd been nose to nose as Jennifer clutched her shoulders like they were anchors. "Uh. Sorry."

"I'll admit you have a point—that green moon is a total bummer." Susan rubbed her shoulders. "But why do a broadcast on it? Surely, the world has seen it. It's, uh, the moon."

"They don't know why it's green. They don't know that the cause is lurking out there . . . where they can reach him. They don't know what it all means."

"Huh. Okay. *That*, I'll tell the world about. Why should I be the only one hideously depressed and waiting for death's sweet embrace." She paused, her eyes narrowing. "Skip deserves to have his ass kicked for choosing green. Also, I've decided, someone should do something nice for you. Since. You know."

"Okay."

"He told Gautierre to look after me. Even before the night Big Blue went up. I guess your dad saw something there, even before either of us did."

Jennifer told herself she would not cry, she would not. But she blessed and loved Susan, and would forever, if only because Susan, too, had loved the man Jennifer loved best. "I, um, I forgot about your thing with green."

Susan had worn a grass green jumper to school on the first day of fourth grade, had earned the name Grass Ass, and had been unable to shake said nickname for years. This resulted in a poisonous hatred of all things green, even salad, or twenty-dollar bills. Or poison moons.

"I'm glad you're talking like an actual person instead of a weird scurvy robot."

"Says the girl who shook me like a damn maraca to get her way. And if you go *near* my backpack again, I'll tell your mom about the time you ate all the raspberries off the neighbor's bushes and blamed my parakeets."

"Don't talk about those parakeets. I loathed them. Do you know how many times they pooped on me?"

"Not enough times, is how many. And I'll talk about them, Ms. Ancient Furnace. And you'll listen. That's my price for broadcasting source information about *la luna verde*."

"And don't be showing off with Spanish all the time. I could have taken Spanish. I could have! I just had this dumb Ancient Furnace thing to do instead."

"Buenos dias, los Estados Unidos! Me llamo Susan Elmsmith, y me amiga Jennifer es un estupida puta . . ."

CHAPTER 38
Susan

Welcome to day eight zillion in Under Big Blue, *where things seem to get suckier and suckier.*

Susan had found it was comforting to write web logs in her head. And the weirder things got, the more she wrote.

So she was writing a lot.

It was weird being back in the hospital. Actually, it was weird to be on the hospital roof—Jennifer seemed to like lurking up there, and Susan liked being able to see all around. It should have been nerve-wracking, all that space, but it was comforting instead.

"You would not even believe the ridiculous conversations that have taken place at this hospital lately," Jennifer was saying, resting on her forearms and looking over the parking lot. "Slapping, whore-insulting, sex comparisons, dragon-slugging . . ."

"Sounds like I came back just in time."

Without looking around, Jennifer reached out and squeezed Susan's hand. "You did."

Susan smiled. "I guess I didn't handle Gautierre's death very well."

Jennifer turned to look at her. Her eyes were very big. "Who said you were s'posed to? He was one of the few nice things about being stuck in here; think I can't relate to that? I'd give anything to be stuck under this shitheap with Eddie." She paused. "When Gautierre died, holing up across town by yourself seemed pretty sane to me. It's just, everyone needed you, is all. I needed you to know that." A short pause, then she added, in a tear-choked voice unlike any Susan had heard from this, her oldest and dearest friend, "I needed you so bad."

Susan said nothing. Another nice thing about friendship: often, you didn't have to.

She rubbed her friend's back, and they both pretended Jennifer wasn't crying bitter, angry tears.

CHAPTER 39
Susan

"Okay, well, that was embarrassing and pointless."

"Feel better, though, doncha?"

"Irrelevant!" the Ancient Furnace proclaimed, furtively wiping her wet cheeks on the sleeve of her denim jacket. "Also, I had something in my eye."

"Yeah, like tear ducts pulling overtime."

"I loathe everything about you," said the Ancient Furnace, "so much. In fact—whoa."

"Hmmm?" Susan raised her head. Jennifer was staring, almost *leaning*, forward. She looked like an English setter on point, eyeing a flock of delicious grouse. "What?"

"Something nutty-nut-flavored this way comes."

It was Evangelina flying—more like lurching—toward the roof. When she got close enough, she simply gave up and crashed.

"Dr. Georges-Scales!" Susan screamed, running toward the exit door. She yanked it open and screamed into the cement throat of the stairway, "Dr. Georges-Scales, come quick, come quick, get up here *now!*"

She ran back to help, knowing there wasn't a damn thing she could do—she had zero medical skills.

"Aw, geez, Evangelina, you're all—" Jennifer was covered in her sister's blood. "Lie still, you're being all thrashy."

Got them dead they're dead almost all of them so hungry almost all full so dead so very dead

"Tell your story later," Jennifer snapped. She seemed to be looking for the right wound to apply pressure to. There was a depressing array to choose from. "Preferably outside my head."

Stop trying to save me.

"Mom! Mom, get up here!"

She can't help almost dead almost full almost all of them are gone now and you can do the rest sister you could finish the job if you're hungry enough yes you can

"Mom!"

I needed to feed needed to feed Mother let me go so I could feed

"So that's where you've been—feeding off Ember's gang? Helpful, I suppose. But Mom's going to be pissed at you. And her."

Owww that hurts.

"I have to apply pressure, or you'll bleed to death before the angry surgeon gets here."

You are kind. Stupid, but kind.

"High praise," Jennifer muttered, trying to hold her sister's guts in one place.

It will be the death of you.

"Thanks for the tender moment. Susan, see if you can stop that spurting over there." Rubbing her hands over the black, gleaming scales, Susan found a spouting wound, clapped both hands over it, and leaned with all of her 137 pounds. A year ago, she would have been holding her vomit down. Now it was all too normal, save the creature herself.

Your friend is proud that she doesn't have to vomit.

"We're all proud of her for that. Stop squirming. Also, stay out of our heads."

Susan shared Jennfier's view on telepathy: it was so creepy to hear someone else in your brain.

You. Sister's friend. You mourned the boy I saw the boy alive they hurt him but not after I killed them all almost all of them dead but a few alive the boy you mourn.

The rush of words confused Susan, but she heard *boy* and *alive* just fine.

"What?"

"Are you talking about Gautierre?" Jennifer, in her surprise, loosened her grip and got an arterial spray in her eyes for her trouble. "He's—ack, your blood is the worst! Who has black blood? Honestly!"

"Is he alive?" Susan pressed. "Gautierre Longtail, my boyfriend—he's alive?"

I said so. Sister, stop trying to save me.

"Move!" someone said, and it seemed to Susan that about a hundred people had rushed to the roof with Dr. Georges-Scales. "Get me some light! Hand me that—no, the other one. Be still, Evangelina."

Easier and easier not to move almost dead they are almost all dead

A nurse pulled Susan back, and she stumbled. Then the medical personnel closed ranks, and Susan couldn't see Evangelina anymore. But she could sure hear her—and talk to her.

Where is he? she asked.

Where the water stinks.

How many left?

Three. Maybe four. Only the stump-tail is healthy enough to fight.

Is he okay?

He so wants to die.

That was enough for Susan, she backed away from the flurry of activity, slipped into the stairwell, and took the stairs down three at a time.

CHAPTER 40
Susan

Alive.

Gautierre was alive.

She—Susan Elmsmith, would-be TV journalist and dateless wonder, Prisoner of Big Blue and much-put-upon best friend of the Ancient Furnace—had been mourning a live boyfriend.

What a colossal waste of time! Also: he had a lot of nerve letting his sorry self get captured by the likes of that horrible, psychotic, pseudomaternal *thing*, Ember Longtail.

Once she realized exactly what Jenn's crazy-spooky half-sister had been saying, Susan had immediately gotten down from the roof, made her way through the lobby (mentally marveling that shock had stiffened her limbs, so she marched like a run-down robot), and headed home. Not her latest apartment, but her actual house.

She hadn't been there in over a year, and it certainly had seen better days: a white, two-story "3 BR, 2 BA" Cape-Cod-style house with yellow shutters. The lawn was an ugly yellow, almost sidewalk-to-sidewalk dandelion remains. It was a good thing her dad must be spending most of his time at the air base; otherwise, he'd weep bitter tears to see the state his lawn had come to.

Yes, Dad, you're better off outside Big Blue. We'd all be battling bad guys and trying not to croak under a freakin' poison moon, while you'd be raiding hardware stores for cases of Weed Git Out.

Back when the last winter had approached, she'd been here to raid the pantry and haul away anything that could be used for food or medicine or split ends—the baby aspirin she'd outgrown a decade ago, the can of Nacho Cheese Soup that dated back to her dead mother's precancer days.

Nothing from the basement, though.

Nothing from the reloading bench.

At the time, it had made sense. Reloads weren't as safe as regular ammo. With the odds stacked as they were after Big Blue arrived and plenty of new ammo available at the time, she hadn't wanted to add to their troubles by supplying scared green kids with ammo that might or might not work. But things were different now.

Everyone else had their own fish to fry, what with stopping Skip and fixing the moon, so no one would be available to stop her or talk her out of this. Talk her out of it? Chances were nobody'd even notice she was gone. Which would be intensely irritating 99.9 percent of the time, but not so much right now.

She was an innocent, a normie. Not the heroine. Good for a humorous quip, or a pithy observation.

"Now, good for Sucky Sundays." She hurried into the backyard toward the gazebo, where a spare key had been hidden longer than she'd been alive. Even now, she thought of the key before a more expedient solution, like a brick through the dining-room picture window. "I cannot believe those Sucky Sundays are gonna save my boyfriend's life."

The basement, always gloomy and gross, was even more so after so long unattended. As she came down the steps she could hear mice scurrying. Mice. Prob'ly be reduced to trapping and eating them if they couldn't get out of Big Blue anytime soon. Mice Surprise. Filet de Mice. Mice on a shingle. *Yergh.*

She tried the light switch at the door—nothing. Blown fuse, probably. She rummaged through her backpack, hauled out the flashlight, flicked it on, and left the bag open as she approached the reloading bench.

Even here there was dust and dirt everywhere. Dad would have a nervous breakdown if he could see it. She flicked the beam over the reloading press, the trays, a stack of empty ammo boxes, then trained it on what she had come for—well, on *some* of the things she had come for.

She checked a couple of the boxes to be sure. Dear Old Dad was as methodical as he was distant, and everything was as expected.

She began raking the boxes into her open backpack.

CHAPTER 41
Susan

Susan pulled her scooter up to the entrance of the sewage-treatment plant. She hadn't exactly been shocked to hear from Evangelina that Ember's gang were holed up in the sewers beneath Winoka.

If movies and books have taught us anything, she told herself as she pulled the keys out of the ignition, *it's that villains are drawn to dank underground caverns and, let's not forget, the smell of shit.*

She popped the kickstand so the scooter could stand. Strangely, she felt optimistic about her chances here to-night. In fact, she began to wish she'd trimmed her bangs before setting out. And possibly shaved her armpits.

Readjusting her backpack, she walked into the main building of the treatment plant. It wasn't locked—why would it be? Nobody knew they were holed up in there except supercreepy Evangelina (and *she* sure hadn't been talking . . . they'd had to *drag* all this crap out of her!).

As she had expected, there wasn't anyone in the office area . . . too small and confined a space for three or four dragons to whomp around in. Also, their tails would probably knock over the copier and the file cabinet.

She'd tried to imagine where Gautierre would be held in such a place. Not primary or secondary treatment; too much crashy-bangy equipment. Not tertiary and certainly not odor removal (*thank you, eighth-grade science report*).

No, pretreatment was the place to start. It was fairly close, it wasn't especially complicated or noisy, and, for funsies, Gautierre could suffer in a smelly prison.

Her time in Big Blue had given Susan new insight into weredragons: they were regular people who could occasionally fly and belch fire. That was it. That was all there was to them. Even Jennifer Scales.

Big Blue had wiped away a lot of her awe. It wasn't hard to be enchanted and thrilled by something so magical and fairy-tale-esque as dragons when they were rare and flashed by every hundred years; but when you saw them be crabby and careless, or make dumb decisions based on fatigue or too much caffeine, or get pissy when things didn't go their way (which had all the charm of watching someone blow their nose), it got harder to stay impressed.

So she was cautious, sure, and careful, yep, but mostly she was annoyed at Ember's intransigence and the cost everyone around her had to pay for it. Susan had learned better in kindergarten.

What did it say for the rest of Domeland if the grown-ups were acting like selfish teenagers, and the teenagers had to be the adults?

CHAPTER 42
Jennifer

Patrol choppers darted back and forth like large, metallic, noisy, armed dragonflies. Jennifer watched them work.

She assumed they were working; it was hard to imagine that sort of activity would be recreation for anyone. They were showing in greater numbers, especially since Skip's superspider had jumped for the moon.

Nothing gets military attention like space invasions. Who'd have thought the invasion would be in the other direction?

She knew nothing of military helicopters other than the fact that there were lots of them on the air base where Susan's father worked. *Wait. Is it an Air Force base, or an Army base? Can you call an Army base an air base, or do they get offended? What does Susan's dad do, anyway? Small-arms instructor? Fire-support specialist? Flight of-*

ficer? Signals coordinator? Intelligence officer? Which of those involved helicopters, if any? Would he come talk to us if he could? If so, why haven't we seen him? She knew none of this. Not knowing made her nervous, and tired.

Speaking of tired, Jennifer's mom was still inside the hospital, performing miracles on Evangelina while Dianna kept a watch on the moon. And what will watching the moon get us, she had wanted to ask—but for once, she wasn't feeling the snark. Instead, she had gone for a long walk.

She was thinking of discussing the helicopters with her mother. Naturally she didn't want to bug her overworked, exhausted, emotionally numb, widowed mother unless it was critically important. This might qualify. Would her mother know any more about helicopters than Jennifer?

It looked like patrolling. There were always at least three darting back and forth along the fringes of Big Blue. They did not hover, did not flash lights, certainly didn't fire anything.

No, they were probably watching, no more, no less. They were careful to make sure there were always at least three, and sometimes (near dusk, and again near dawn, she had noticed), there were as many as six.

The random recollection that her father was dead hit her again. No reason. She sighed and supposed this was her brain's way of trying to process that he was dead, in the midst of a crisis that would not give her any real amount of time to grieve. The lack of true grieving was an awful disservice to her father's memory. It was draining the life and will and strength from his widow and filling his daughter with resentment.

She couldn't recognize anyone in the helicopters, but she granted she was too far away to get a better look. All she could see were helmets and sunglasses.

Was Susan's father flying one of them? Had he sent them? Was this his way of helping? Or did he have nothing to do with them? In which case: was that good, or bad?

Susan's dad was a distant schmuck, a man who seemed to think the loss of his wife was far greater than a daughter's loss of her mother. He had turned mourning into self-absorption; Jennifer had never liked him.

But still: maybe he was helping.

And maybe not.

Susan would know; she'd have a good guess, anyway, and might even know who some of the other chopper pilots were. If nothing else, she'd have some hilariously sarcastic comment. This would cheer Jennifer up, if only for a few minutes.

But Susan wasn't here—not since Evangelina got back. She wasn't anywhere around the hospital and hadn't done any blogs or newscasts. For all Jennifer knew, she was holing up in her odd-smelling apartment. Probably upset that there was nothing she could do for her boyfriend, or really anyone she cared about.

Poor Susan. You have no idea. You're better off staying put in bed. You don't want the responsibilities Mom and I have. At least you're safe, wherever you are.

CHAPTER 43
Susan

Susan moved through the building quietly, thinking about reloads and their hazards. Homemade ammunition had a long and noble history . . . and her father was tight-assed enough that everything he made at his reloading bench would probably work all right. It had always seemed to her a lot more work, for not much in the way of savings, but such things appealed to her father's nature.

So she'd checked them over an hour ago before leaving the house. Now she thought about stealth: she was wearing comfortable, quiet tennis shoes with her jeans and black sweatshirt.

She thought about her surroundings: everything was operational. This was weird, since Ember and her gang seemed the sort to kill anyone who might be coming in here for maintenance. Maybe they had just moved to this

place; or maybe they let folks come in and out to help pre-
serve their secret. Who goes looking for the villain in a
well-maintained public facility?

*You mean, public facilities like city hall and the police
department, under Hank Blacktooth?*

Focus, Susan.

Her plan was simple, based on the fact that she knew
Ember Longtail to be a crummy hag with no imagination
and a shrinking circle of friends. She would conduct her
search, using her knowledge of Ember's attack patterns
(dusk and dawn) to visit the place when she would be most
certain guards would be at their fewest.

She thought briefly of the moon phase—*new moon,* she
reminded herself. *It's okay. You've thought this through.*
She wondered if Gautierre would still have his moon elm
leaf, or if Ember would have taken it from him. It didn't
matter to Susan's plan, so she stopped thinking about it.

She passed through another corridor, and found herself
in the pretreatment section of the building. She was zero-
ing in on the part of the plant she was reasonably certain
Gautierre was being held against his will.

If he was being held against his will.

Oh, don't start.

Except. Ember was his mother. A nasty shrill icky hag-
like mother, but still. Susan, motherless too long, wondered
if Gautierre could really stand against her. What wouldn't
Susan do to have her mother back? Hide in a sewage-
treatment plant? Do a few bad things? Tell the Scales family to screw off?

Fool someone into thinking she loved them?

Maybe he wasn't a prisoner at all. Maybe he was a
guest. Maybe he had been a plant the entire time and faked
his own death to escape back to his mother. Maybe he
wouldn't be happy to see her. Maybe he'd hurt her.

Not even if someone stuck a gun in his ear, she decided. It was a momentary weakness, brought on by stress and aggravation. Also by the sight of two of Ember's people, curled up inside the door right next to each other like kittens. Except for the leathery scales, and the enormous teeth, and the wings. *Maybe not kittens.*

Their heads rose at the same time; she felt the force of their gazes. She was better at reading dragon expressions than she'd been, say, eighteen months ago. She was pretty sure they were surprised. Which was an improvement over homicidally pissed.

"Hello. My name's Susan; I'm here for Gautierre."

They looked at each other, then back at her. The one on the left had dull, copper-colored scales shading to a muddy brown on the wings—spoke in a hushed baritone. "Uh— you're not a beaststalker. Right?"

She straightened her back. "I'm a reporter."

The coloring of the two dragons seemed unusual . . . muddy, almost vague browns and mustard yellows and faded coppers.

Sick. They looked sick!

"Are you guys okay?"

They harrumphed, which momentarily made Susan feel stupid. Then resentful: what, she was supposed to be a dragon doctor? They were heaps of scaled lethargy.

"You're not out attacking anyone. I thought you guys were going to burn down the forest."

One of them shrugged. Susan had a brainstorm.

"But you're living on the run," she guessed. She stepped toward them, suddenly far less afraid of them. "Not much to eat, at a sewage plant. Easy game is disappearing. You're burning the wildlife to a crisp. Ember has you starving yourselves."

"You might want to keep your distance, dear," said the one on the left with a raspy female voice. But her gums were bleeding, and Susan knew she was hitting the mark.

"If Ember has you starving yourselves, then you have to be wondering if you've made the right choice."

"Actually," said the other dragon in a croaking male tone, "I was wondering how you'd taste."

"That's disgusting," said the female. "Look at yourself, Gary. You're on the verge of cannibalism."

"Ain't a cannibal if she ain't a dragon."

"That sounds too much like the bitch that got us into this."

"Yes, she *is* a bitch," Susan interjected, seizing the momentum and taking another step forward. "A big, stumpy bitch whose own fabulous son hates her. I'm here for him. Why do you care? You could go to Winoka Hospital."

"They'd kill us," said Gary.

"Not if you walked in calmly."

"They'll recognize us, even looking this sick. We've attacked that hospital ten times."

Susan shrugged. "So take off the moon leaves." They were visible, hanging off their throats on necklaces of woven fabric.

The female dragon snorted. "You think we're stupid? They'll kill us the moment they figure out who we are. Even easier, if we're not in dragon form."

"Look—do it, don't do it, I don't care. I just want to know if you're going to let me by so I can help my boyfriend. Does Ember have you guarding him, or are you simply resting someplace inconvenient?"

Gary snorted; more smoke curled from his nostrils. He got up and started to walk away. "I can sleep anywhere around here. Makes no fuckin' difference to me."

"Me, neither," said the female, following him. "But, honey, if you mean to leave with Ember's boy . . ." She tactfully trailed off.

"I'll have to kill her," Susan finished flatly. "No worries. I've got it covered."

"Have fun getting roasted."

"That's the spirit." Their carelessness made a bit more sense if they expected her to die anyway. *Who wants to keep murdering while you're dying?* she asked herself. The answer came quickly: *Ember Longtail, that's who.*

She put her hand on the door and braced herself.

CHAPTER 44
Susan

Gautierre was in the next room, a tall, dank space that would have seemed chilly in July heat because of the sweating concrete walls, the cement floor, the lack of windows . . . it really was the next best thing to a cell, and here Gautierre was on a cot in the middle of it, rather undramatically. Except for an atrocious smell, he was alone.

"Susan!"

"In the nick of time, I see. Geez, you're hardly even cute anymore, Gautierre. There's a nifty new invention; it's called a hairbrush."

He looked around wildly. "Are you okay? Who else is here? Jennifer? Her mom? Where are they? What's their plan?"

He really did look dreadful. Ember had, as Susan expected, taken his silver moon elm leaf away, so he was human, and thin, and white-faced. His glorious dark hair was matted; his trio of braids, usually so neat and tidy, were clusters of tangles.

He wasn't tied or chained or restrained in any way, but his arm was in a sling, and his chest and face were marked with scorch marks and bruises. Susan figured with the duo of dragons in the room behind her, his mother was probably in the room beyond. He couldn't get past them as a human, so ropes were unnecessary.

"It's just me," she said, taking off her backpack and rummaging inside. "Everyone else is off saving us from the Poison Moon."

"The what?"

"Try to keep up. We've got to go. If your mother tries to stop us, I'll have to kill her. I won't mind doing it—look at what she's done to you!—but let's be honest: killing a potential in-law is bad for a relationship. Plus, I'm hungry, and my scooter's low on gas."

"I don't care about my mother, you're right about what she—Susan, I can't believe you came alone! You nitwit; what were you thinking? When I'm done being thrilled to see you, I'm going to strangle you."

"You won't get the chance," Ember said, abruptly entering the room—the doors had been removed, Susan figured, for that reason.

Susan never stopped being amazed at how quietly dragons could move, even though they weighed anywhere from three to eight hundred pounds. And Ember looked, Susan was thrilled to see, almost as bad as her son. Wasted. Thin. Brittle. Ugly.

"Oh, good. You're here. So, I'm rescuing your son."

"What?" Ember seemed a little taken aback. Possibly because Susan wasn't sobbing with fear. "What are you up to? What are you, the distraction? Does that disgusting mother-daughter duo you hang out with think you can distract me while they invade my lair and kill my gang?"

"What gang—the two depressed, starving creatures who loped away when I asked politely?"

The dasher hissed, and Susan remembered she would have little time if the fire came. Right now, her only hope . . . was the hope this woman held out for her own son.

"Gautierre, I think your mother doesn't believe I'm good enough for you."

"The first smart thing I've heard you say." Ember sucked in breath. Her sides bulged, revealing some pallor in her own normally sharp coloring, and she coughed up phlegm and steam.

Susan didn't want to wait for anything worse. She pulled the Coke bottle out of her pack.

Gasoline, of course, was far too precious to be wasted on something silly like a Molotov . . . she had known at the house she'd have to go with the turpentine in the garage. She'd also grabbed a box of sugar from the kitchen; there were no egg whites to be had, and no time to cut a tire into strips. Sugar was an acceptable thickening agent.

She'd also yanked her dad's glass cutter from the tool bench and scored the Coke bottles with crisscrossing lines, for a better explosion. Her dad hadn't taught her that one; she had read it in a book.

Finally, she had scored extra tampons from her bottom dresser drawer. Tampons make excellent fuses.

"Uh . . . Ember?

"Behold, I am a former Girl Scout, and the daughter of a military man who *really* wanted a son." She flicked a lighter, lit the tampon string, and tossed the bottle between Ember's feet. Both the dragon and her son were frozen in astonishment, so she pulled Gautierre behind a steel railing. "Hear me roar."

The explosion was gratifying. Glass burst everywhere, and flaming gunk stuck to all possible surfaces, mostly Ember. The sugar fused the liquid to her target, and obligingly produced choking clouds of smoke. Much better than straight turpentine, though the smell would have to be washed out of her hair.

Sucky Sundays . . . her dad had dragged her on a number of weekend survival trips, soothing her mother with "it's a camping trip, hon, it's father-daughter time." She hadn't been able to look at a roasting wienie without irritation since. But she hadn't ratted him out. Sure, she grew to loathe sleeping rough, and positively despised finding wood ticks on herself almost every Sunday in the summertime, but learning how to shoot was fun . . . and so was blowing up dead trees.

She had assumed for years that this was an unusual upbringing, but look around her! Growing scales and picking off sheep was more normal? Maybe, maybe not. She'd have to be out in the wider world, on her own, for at least five years before she'd know for sure how weird she was.

"Uh . . . Susan . . ."

"Stupid girl!" Ember sounded triumphantly surprised, even as the smoke made her cough and the flames stayed vibrant all over her wings, torso, and belly. There were no burns on her. Even the moon leaf around her neck, on a metal chain, seemed unaffected by the heat. "You're fighting a dragon . . . with fire?!"

Gautierre sighed. "It was a good try, babe," he said sadly. "You should run now. I'll hold her off as long as I can. I love you—"

"Get out of the way, idiot." She clutched his shoulder and yanked backward. She then pulled out the two-liter ginger-ale bottle, and threw it at Ember's neck. The head was too risky—Ember might have ducked, and the ginger-ale bottle would have sailed over her head. Too low, and it wouldn't do what she had brought it for. But the neck was perfect: the plastic bottle ruptured from the impact and heat, and a new liquid doused Ember.

She stopped chortling and began to scream.

"Acid bomb," Susan explained to Gautierre, pulling the sawed-off shotgun from beneath her baggy sweatshirt. She was careful; it was extremely powerful and extremely illegal. If her dad heard she was using one, she could kiss television and computer games good-bye for at least a month. It was loaded, of course. She flicked off the safety.

"Fuck a duck!" was her stunned boyfriend's contribution to the altercation.

"Well, I needed something in case those other two dragons wouldn't move. Turns out I can still use it here, to put her out of her misery."

The necklace and leaf around Ember's neck began to smolder, and then melt. Then it fell off.

"Say hello to the new moon, bitch."

Ember kept screaming, then . . .

. . . abruptly lost her dragon shape.

What was left of Ember Longtail—burning skin, yellowed teeth, noise and rage and fire—crawled toward them, swearing to kill them both.

What a waste she has been, Susan told herself. *Of lives. Of time. Of everything. Poor Gautierre.*

She gently raised one hand and covered her boyfriend's eyes. With the other, she leveled the shotgun.

CHAPTER 45
Jennifer

"All right. That's that. We're not waiting another minute. Another nanosecond."

Her mother shook her head, but Dianna, at least, was on board. Jennifer felt like marking the day somehow.

Assuming she survived it. Jennifer had a fleeting thought, more a flash than anything, there and gone again: *If I get killed today, I don't think Mom will be able to take it. Not both of us in the same month.*

But if I stay, I'm dooming us all.

"Dianna's right." Hearing the words come out of her mouth was *so* surreal. "Let's get it d—whoa."

They had been having this discussion outside the hospital, so they were all in perfect position to observe the battered minivan (tastefully painted Serial Killer Green) come roaring up the street and screeching to a halt about four feet from their little group.

Her mother sighed—this would be some sort of medical disaster. A mass onset of rickets, maybe. Or the bubonic plague—the way things had been going, a plague seemed uncomplicated and boring.

She didn't recognize the vehicle, but that meant nothing. Here under Big Blue, if you needed to drive somewhere, and you didn't have a car, you poked around town until you found one with gas. It was amazing how many people kept spare car keys in those little black metal boxes that stuck to the underside of the driver-side door.

Three doors—driver, and both back doors—shot open, and several people seemed to boil out: Catherine had been driving, and Susan rushed to the other side of the van to help her boyfriend out.

"Susan, geez!" Susan looked grim, bordering on defiant. She had what looked like burned sugar and turpentine stains all over her; she had a backpack stuffed with foul-smelling stuff; she was pulling Gautierre-in-a-sling along with one hand; and in the other—

"Is that a sawed-off shotgun?"

"Gautierre needs help, Dr. Georges-Scales."

"I can see that." Gautierre looked and smelled even more awful than Susan. Elizabeth motioned to a nurse, who escorted the couple inside.

Jennifer turned to Catherine, who appeared in better shape, though all the time under Big Blue, along with the trauma she had suffered and the intense physical therapy still left her gaunt. "What the hell happened here? How did you rescue Gautierre?"

"I didn't. Susan did. I picked them up on the way back. September's a bit cold for a scooter."

"Aren't you the one who drove your grandmother's Ford Mustang convertible with the top down in November?"

"Those were better days. And it was a Ford Mustang, Jennifer. I'd drive that thing upside down in January, if I could."

"Touché. Well, you have good timing. We could use your help if you're fit for battle."

"I'm not clearing her for fighting," Elizabeth protested.

"So she goes against medical advice. Catherine, we're about to go remove Skip's head from his shoulders. And possibly play soccer with his head."

"You might want to rethink that plan," Catherine warned. She had slammed her door shut and stepped around to pull the passenger-side door open.

"There's not a single thing you can say or do to make me rethink that plan. This is overdue by about fourteen months."

Catherine bent into the vehicle, pulled up, and carried Andi over to the small group.

"We are rethinking the plan!" Jennifer shouted. "Everyone, gather round! We are rethinking this plan!"

"What is she doing here? How did you get her here?"

"The answer to both questions is, Eddie rescued her and got her as far as the bridge sentries. I was there with them, and I borrowed one of their cars to bring her back. Right before we picked up Susan and Gautierre."

"Andi." Elizabeth took the girl from Catherine's arms. "Andi, stay with me. Stay with me, or you'll die."

"Okay," the girl said tiredly. Jennifer wanted to feel rage, but the sorceress was like a dried-up shell or a doll left out in the rain. Dried blood streaked down her arms.

"Andi!" Elizabeth ran inside with her, taking her to the first emergency bed she saw. The others followed, Dianna bringing up the rear. "Catherine, clear off that bed. Jennifer, get my bag from behind the admittance desk—I'm going to need the last of the dopamine."

"No way, Mom! You can't give the last of *anything* to . . . to her! She refused to help us when we needed her! And she's going to die anyway!"

Elizabeth turned, and Jennifer was certain another swing was coming. *"Don't you dare second-guess my medical decisions! Get the bag."*

Jennifer got the bag.

"Thank you. Catherine, put that pillow under her head. Then find a nurse—I need someone who can run an IV wide open; I need fluids and electrolytes, and transfusions. Dianna, come next to me and hand me what I need."

Silently, the sorceress moved closer and laid her slender hands on the bag.

"There's a white plastic bottle in there with a few blue round pills left. Take out the pills and put them in my hand."

Elizabeth did not even look behind her, she continued to peer into Andi's pupils and check her pulse with one hand, while holding the other one out. Clearly, she trusted Dianna to find the right medicine and deposit it there without argument. Which Dianna did.

"I'm sorry," Andi murmured, after Elizabeth gave her the pills. They couldn't tell whom she was talking to. "I should have left him when you gave me the chance."

"You loved him," Dianna answered. "I was no older than you when I fell in love."

"It's my fault."

"Sssshhhh. I can't check your pulse with you moving and talking, dear. Dianna—the syringes, and the bottle with the clear liquid. Yep, that one. Andi, I'm going to give you something for the pain . . ."

It won't work.

Elizabeth turned to the next bed, where the delicate human shape of Jennifer's half-sister lay recovering. "Evangelina, if you can't say anything helpful . . ."

Sister-mother. You are wasting your medicine.

"Darling, please." Dianna sighed. "If you're strong enough to argue with Dr. Georges-Scales, you're strong enough to get up and help us fight your half-brother."

I am. I am recovering well. I can leave soon with you. Will you listen to me now, Mother? Will you tell her? She is still wasting her medicine on this one.

"Why?"

She doesn't want to kill the pain. She never has.

They all stared at the neat, even scars down Andi's forearms. Andi lifted her head but could not keep it up.

"I want to go back . . ."

"Are you crazy?" Jennifer spat. "Skip will kill you!"

"No. Not Skip. I want to go way back . . . way back, when it was dark. When I could sing and make light. Do you remember, Dianna?" Andi's head lolled so she could smile at the sorceress. "Remember the sunrise song?"

Dianna's fingers whitened around the edges of the medical bag. "Yes. I remember."

Andi's lilting voice filled the room:

> *Eyes open, eyes open,*
> *Where are you? Where are you?*

There you are, shining star!
Look at you! Look at you!

Andi blinked up at Elizabeth. "I'm sorry I killed your husband."

The doctor stopped what she was doing, clenched her eyes and fists, and pressed down on the mattress. "I forgive you."

A broad smile lifted the girl's cheeks. A bloody tear welled and tricked toward her left ear. "You're going to be the first one out. I just know it."

She began to laugh, an easy and carefree melody that filled the room. Before she could complete it, she died.

CHAPTER 46
Jennifer

By the time Dianna and Evangelina came to the bridge a couple of hours later, Skip was waiting for them, alone on the other side. The suddenly chilly air around had caused a fog to settle along the river, and droplets began to sparkle as they crystallized on the cold pavement. Off to the east, the carcass of Xavier Longtail was still visible.

He looked at both of them. "Are you here to kill me, Mom? Or will your favorite child try to do it for you?"

Brother. You feel strong.

There was admiration in the words, but no fear. "Stronger than you."

Time enough to find out.

"Francis." Dianna looked around in despair—at the chaos under the barrier, the ruins of two buildings not far away, the green haze above. "Look at what you've done here. You have to stop."

"You've been spending too much time with the Scales family, Mom. You're no diplomat. Let's get on with it."

Dianna glanced at her daughter.

Yes, Mother.

Immediately, the creature's black corona expanded, and the powerful figure of Evangelina sprang through the barrier.

Skip waved his right hand clockwise, and she veered off the bridge and careened into the river far below. "You're going to find the laws of gravity have some difficulty applying consistently near me, Evanga-loser. The closer the crescent moon comes"—he glanced up at the sky—"the more power I gain over the forces of nature.

"How about you, Mom? You have anything you'd like to try?"

The human form of Dianna dissipated, leaving a play of bright hues—greens and oranges and yellows. The colors fell to the asphalt and crept toward him without thickness, slipping through the barrier where it met the bridge.

"What's your plan—you're going to watercolor me to death? Ugh, you know, I don't care. Let me end this right here." With a twirl of his finger, a void burned a circle around Dianna's display. Try as it might, the two-dimensional form could not pass out of the ring. Nor could she revert to three-dimensional form.

"That's your own little world I've created there for you, Mom. Like a moon hanging still in the sky, you're going to stay there. For once, you're going to *stay.*"

Evangelina had emerged from the water and was approaching from his blind side with more care than before. He turned as if to face her, then paused at a whistling sound from a third direction. In a flash, he was something else—an arachnid, if anyone could call it that, twenty feet of silver and vermilion streaks, with eight jointed and plated appendages. Each was tipped by a hairy, starfishlike claw. One of those claws caught something out of the air—an arrow—and the creature faced the woods to the south. An octet of yellow eyes focused on one large oak.

"Eddie, I saw you two hours ago when you helped Andi escape. You could do with a bit more imagination. But I do appreciate the arrow." A spinneret threw up a long thread of silk, which Skip looped around two of his arms. A third knocked the arrow, and a fourth aimed it into the gloom surrounding Evangelina. The missile flew.

AAAAAAAAAAIIIIIIIIIIIIIEEEEEEEEEEEEEEE

"Not bad for a guy who never took an archery course!" Skip reverted to his human form, tongue licking a loopy grin. "C'mon, Eddie! Toss me another one, and I'll hit 'er again!

"A shame Jennifer can't join us," he told the crippled Evangelina, the helpless Dianna, and the unseen Eddie. "How convenient for her that she never found a way out. She doesn't have to face me—she and her mother can send their pals, and if *you* die, what do they care? Have they bothered to mourn Xavier Longtail? Any funeral in there for Eddie's dad? Cripes, the ceremony for Mr. Scales was, what, five minutes in a potato field? Five minutes more than Mr. Blacktooth got, anyway.

"And I'll bet Jennifer didn't even think twice when a thousand or so of her new best friends got on the wrong side of my tidal sorcery. That's a whole misty subspecies, folks. *Gone*. And her buddy Susan didn't even do a blog entry on it." He glared into the foggy woods where Eddie was, and pointed at the river. What might have been tears—of frustration, or regret—welled in his eyes. "They came to help her, Eddie. Like you come to help her. I don't blame you. *I* tried to help her, more than once. And she never gave a crap." He kicked at the sparkling pavement. "She won't care about you, either, no matter how hard I make you bleed. And I will make you bleed, Eddie. You'll bleed, and you'll hurt, and she won't care. Did she care about a single one of those water balloons with wings? Did she even *bother* to learn their powers, try to join them, and risk her own life alongside theirs? *I killed every single one of those watery motherfuckers, and—*"

"Missed one."

A patch of fog behind him gathered instantaneously into the shape of the Ancient Furnace. A sparkling wing claw came up and grazed him on the back of the neck, as she breathed vapor over his spine. Ice crinkled his skin too rapidly for him to act. An expression of surprise froze on his face, and his arms hung in midair.

"It's the weirdest thing," she explained as she shifted from dragon to human. "Every lurker knows how to self-vaporize. It's like riding a bicycle, for them. It was so hard for me to figure out that bicycle. In fact, I didn't have it down until about twenty minutes ago.

"But the elder skill, the one that's supposed to be *hard* to learn"—she flicked an ice chunk off his nose—"well, I got the hang of that right away. Only needed to see Sonakshi demonstrate it once in the hospital parking lot. Maybe it's the winter weather that made it so easy to pull the last bit of heat out of the water within you."

The circular void around Dianna disappeared. Evangelina managed to straighten herself after reaching into her corona with a spindly claw, extracting the arrow from wherever it hit, and tossing it into the river behind her. An oak tree to the south rustled with the sounds of a teenaged boy scrambling down. Jennifer found herself exhaling a breath she hadn't thought she'd been holding.

"The air smells fresher out here," she observed. She lifted the collar of her jacket. "Colder, too. You might be like this for a while, Skip. Though I only need long enough to shove these into your heart." Two daggers appeared before Skip's glazed brown irises. "What do you think? Can all the poison in the world thaw you in time to save your own ass?"

Dianna and Evangelina advanced. Neither of them made a move to stop her.

"End of monologue. Good-bye, Skip. Fuck you for killing my father."

"NO, JENNIFER!"

Jennifer sighed and rested the points of the blades against Skip's stiff breastbone. "Mom. He deserves this."

"I forgive him. I forgive him, and I want to help him."

This got her daughter to look up. "Mom! How could you! He killed Dad! He killed all those other people! He even killed Andi, who at least said she was sorry! He's not sorry."

Elizabeth bit her lip and looked at her through the barrier, a world away. "Jennifer, don't you get it? This is our chance to destroy the dome."

"Seems to me like killing Skip is our best shot at that."

"If you kill him, it will never come down. Think about it, Jennifer. Edmund wanted sacrifice, and he got that. He wanted Glory dead, and he got that. He wanted Skip protected, and he's got that."

"Sounds like a dead guy's getting all he wants. When's my turn?"

"It's about what you give, Jennifer. Forgiveness. Edmund Slider cared about that, too. We have to forgive."

Turning to look at the icy statue of Skip, Elizabeth relaxed, took a deep breath . . . and walked forward.

Ten steps later, she was through.

The shimmering barrier disappeared, leaving behind a ruined town that suddenly seemed to breathe in. The river's current shifted, the trees bent inward, and the sunlight played longer on the rooftops.

The doctor kept walking, until she was in front of Jennifer and Skip.

"Mom . . . *how*?"

"I realized, as Andi was dying, that Edmund cared about three things. First, he wanted this town to experience sacrifice. It has certainly done that. Second, he wanted Skip to reach his potential." She nodded at the moon. "Check. And third, he wanted a different Winoka. He wanted a town that was built on forgiveness, instead of retaliation. It's the only logical kind of civilization . . . and Slider was all about logic."

Jennifer shook her head. "We've been trying to pass through this wall for months. You can just walk through it, and it's gone?"

"Listen to me, Jennifer. I couldn't walk through it before I lost something precious—even more precious than Glory had been to me. And I couldn't walk through it until I had forgiven that enemy. Your father's death, the seraph's sacrifice, Skip being at our mercy—these all had to happen. Without that sequence, we'd still be stuck."

"So we just forgive Skip, and it's all over?" Jennifer looked warily at where the barrier used to be, as if it would reappear at any moment. "That sounds too simple, Mom."

"Then why has no one tried it? We've thrown fists and shot bullets and even wheeled minivans into that dome. *No one* on the inside, who has lost what you and I have lost, has tried forgiving anyone else."

"I haven't forgiven anyone."

"But I have. It only takes one. That's all Edmund needed to see: a glimmer of hope. A touch of humanity."

"And he killed all those people."

"He killed no one. He isolated us, and left us to make our own choices."

"Mom. You can't seriously expect this is over. Things like this are always more complicated. Dad *died*. Skip *killed him*. You can't just walk across a bridge, and say it's okay, and, and—"

"What did you expect, Jennifer—that we'd have to toss a magic ring in a volcano, or find little bits of someone's soul spread out over town and crush them with a glowing hammer? Would those things really be harder than what I have done here right now? I'm human, honey. Part of me *still* wants to see you shove those blades into that kid's chest. But I can't let you. That's not your destiny. That's not the solution. That's not how the real world has to work."

"I know how the real world has to work. Bad people like Skip hurt others. Good people like you and me punish the bad people. That's justice. *That's* my destiny."

"Jennifer, honey. Put down the knives."

Waking from a gray dream, Jennifer looked at the weapons in her hands. Her fingers began to tremble.

"Kill him, Jennifer!" Dianna sounded desperate. "You must, before he thaws. Look at the moon."

Through the haze, the dark jade disk above began to yield, on one side, the slimmest crescent of brilliant emerald light.

"We're running out of time!"

"Yes, Dianna, we're running out of time." Elizabeth's voice remained calm. "We've been running out of time since the dome went up. Since before that, really. That's the excuse people like you have always used: if we don't kill now, when on earth might we get the chance again? Hurry, and kill, hurry and kill. Has that gotten us anything? Did that bring down the dome?"

"Your daughter brought down the dome, when she froze Skip." Dianna approached with an exasperated expression. "Please, Jennifer! Protect us all! Finish the job!"

Jennifer bit her lip. "What if she's right? I'll never get the chance to stop him again," she told her mother. "What else can we do?"

"Let me take him back to the hospital. We'll keep him frozen for a while. We'll talk. I'll bet you and I will come up with something."

Jennifer looked around at the clear sky. The dome was gone. It was a miracle. Her mother's miracle—that much was obvious, whatever Dianna said.

"I want to believe you so much, Mom."

"Then believe, honey."

Her mother's hand caressed her hair, and Jennifer felt a peace she hadn't felt in months. Maybe years.

"Okay, Mom. Let's take him back."

The peace deepened inside. She knew she had made the right choice.

Then the missiles slammed into the bridge.

CHAPTER 47
Susan

Susan knew three things about Apache helicopters.

First, she knew that the AH-64A was a tank-killer when first designed and constructed. They each had an array of Hellfire missiles, Hydra rockets, and Stinger missiles that worked together effectively against air or ground targets. They also each had a thirty-millimeter cannon slaved to the aircrew's helmets: where they looked, the weapon would fire. They were truly amazing military hardware.

Second, she knew an Apache battalion came with nearly twenty Apaches and about half as many Kiowas, which were scouts that often laser-painted the Apaches' targets. The Apaches could then remain hidden behind terrain and still attack the painted target with Hellfire missiles. Her father had explained this to her one Thanksgiving dinner years ago, using a turkey drumstick as an Apache, a spoonful of cranberry sauce as the Kiowa, and a mound of mashed potatoes for terrain. The unfortunate target was Susan's own pile of dressing, which had too many pieces of chopped celery. Watching the cranberry-painted, vegetable-infested concoction "destroyed" by the hidden Apache drumstick under her mother's barely tolerant gaze had made a deep and favorable impression on Susan. *Celery,* her father had explained with mock seriousness, *simply does not recover from that sort of firepower.*

Third, she knew her dad was an excellent pilot and that he would almost certainly be in the first wave of Apaches to secure the town of Winoka, once the barrier came down.

Ruddaduddaduddaruddaduddadudda

She heard the sound while sitting at Gautierre's hospital bedside. He was sleeping peacefully, though the bruises and burns on his face would take time to heal. *Certainly,* she was calculating, *watching his mother die at the hands of his girlfriend will have an even longer recovery period. Is that what Skip had to deal with, after Jennifer killed his father? Is Gautierre Longtail the next Skip Wilson?*

Ruddaduddaduddaruddaduddadudda

She recognized the sound immediately and looked out the window. The first thing she noticed was the clear sky full of stars.

No blue tinge. It took a moment to process. *No blue tinge. No Big Blue! The dome is down!*

"Gautierre!" She shook him awake. He started, and she spared him an apologetic look as she pointed. "Look! It's gone! The dome is gone. Jennifer did it!"

Ruddaduddaduddaruddaduddadudda

He sat up and smiled at the untainted sky. "Maybe we should get in a car and bug out of this town."

She considered the idea. *What if they've only interrupted the sorcery—not stopped it? We're going to feel like first-class asses if we get trapped twice. Why not get to an outside, fully supplied hospital?*

Two things stopped her. First, she wasn't so sure any hospital out there would be better than the one where Dr. Georges-Scales was in charge, supplies or no. Second, those choppers would be the first wave of the military force that would come in, secure the town, and evacuate anyone in need of medical assistance.

We don't need to go anywhere. Help is coming to us.

Ruddaduddaduddaruddaduddadudda

She could see them now—three of them, anyway. The twilight made them hard to define precisely, but she was pretty sure they were Kiowas.

"They're coming this way," she told Gautierre. "Their recon's been pretty good—they must have seen people coming in and out of here for months. They'll know this is a good place to—"

Several thundering explosions rocked the entire building. The lights went out, and Susan could hear screaming from down the hallway.

How could they? They saw my blogs. I told them all about the suffering in here. I introduced them to dragons, to beaststalkers, to all of it . . . and all they want to do is destroy it?! And Dad is leading them!

The feeling of betrayal reeled her senses, but not so badly that she couldn't keep her feet. She staggered to Gautierre's bed and began disconnecting his IV.

"Change of plan, babe. Let's blow this fucking town."

CHAPTER 48
Jennifer

"Get off the bridge! Get off the bridge!"

Dianna and Evangelina slipped out of the third dimension, leaving Elizabeth and Jennifer to drag Skip's frozen body off the creaking bridge. The volley of explosions had blasted the underside of the span, sending chunks of asphalt and steel plummeting into the Mississippi. Eddie, once again on the wrong side of the bridge, was forced to run back to the eastern bank.

Pieces of the arch support over their heads were hanging loose, and Jennifer could feel the entire western half swaying back and forth. She shifted into dragon shape and lifted Skip-sicle the rest of the way so that her mother could focus on running.

They barely reached the western abutment when a horrific screech of metal against metal signaled the death of

Winoka Bridge. The entire span plunged downward with a cascade of roaring splashes. The river consumed the lower material without difficulty, but the higher bits of the arch stuck in its craw and poked out like broken teeth from a watery grin.

Somewhere to the north, another several explosions rumbled.

"That sounds like the hospital," Elizabeth muttered.

"What's going on?" Jennifer asked.

Ruddaduddaduddaruddaduddadudda

Even with her excellent dragon vision, Jennifer could not spot the helicopters at first. Their anti-infrared shielding and low flight paths shrouded their approach. When she did spot them, she cursed.

There were at least ten of them slipping through the river valley, some larger than the others. They popped up fewer than two hundred yards away, pointed their rockets at the electricity substation on the riverbank, and let loose with a new storm of rockets. Moments later, the lights began blinking out across Winoka.

"Mom. They're going to destroy the town."

"I can't believe that, honey." In the dwindling light, Elizabeth's despair was still visible. "I see it, but I can't believe it."

"We can't let them do this."

"Agreed. How do we stop them?"

You could try forgiving them.

"Evangelina, that sort of sarcasm doesn't help—"

Fine. Let's move to action. We must destroy them.

Jennifer and Elizabeth looked at each other. Was Evangelina right? Did they have no choice?

Surely, this time, you will not argue. Surely, this time, you see the only possible path.

"You don't have to leave it to her." They turned, surprised, to hear Dianna say this. Her hands glowed with golden energy. "You can pursue them and deal with them in any way you like. Maybe you can find a less violent way to stop them than what my daughter has in mind."

Mother. You're interfering. I've had time to heal, and I am hungry.

"Daughter. Stand still and listen. This is not our town. This is not our legacy. Those it belongs to need our help. Let's give them a chance."

Evangelina's legs twitched. Then she was gone.

Dianna sighed. "You will have to move quickly if you want a different outcome from what she has in mind. You won't be able to save all of them—but maybe you'll be able to save some of them."

"Save them? Have you *seen* them? According to my friend Susan, they top out at one hundred eighty miles per hour and have heat-seeking missiles, among other fabulous blow-uppy stuff. Perhaps you saw them take out the bridge we almost died on. Ms. Wilson, I don't think *saving* them is going to be a problem. I think *catching* them is going to be a problem. I think *not dying* is going to be a problem."

"What can you do to help us?" Elizabeth asked.

Dianna raised her glowing hands and motioned at Jennifer. "I can make her faster."

Jennifer licked her lips. "How much faster?"

"Fast enough. You could take your mother with you. Perhaps together, you will find a way to disable one or more of the helicopters."

Another volley of missiles smashed into the center of town. Jennifer figured it was the armory, an opinion confirmed by a rapid succession of subsequent explosions.

"Faster." With a single word and a burning touch, Dianna transferred a jolt of energy through the limbs of the Ancient Furnace. Jennifer immediately marveled at how slow the rest of the world seemed to be going. *Let's race,* she told everyone and everything she could see. *Let's race race race!*

She turned to her mother. "Ready!"

"Jennifer, honey." Her mother was clearly torn. "I can't go with you. I need to get to others, form some sort of defense. They're going to come after the hospital."

Now Jennifer was racing her own fear, which seemed disturbingly up to the task. "How will I do this alone?"

Her mother motioned across the river. "You don't have to. Take Eddie. Take out as many as you can, hurting as few as possible."

"What if I don't have a choice?"

"I trust you, Jennifer. Make the best choices you can. It's all anyone can do."

Suddenly, a helicopter over their heads spun out of control and careened into a building. The resulting fireball lit up the streetscape enough for them to make out a shadow of a dragon slipping away, looking for its next kill.

"Hurry, honey."

Jennifer sped away, shouting across the river for Eddie as she cruised over the watery wreckage.

He was waiting for her, bless him, halfway up a tree and poised to jump. She hovered for half a second, caught him on her back as he leapt—

"Hummmph!"

—and then they were off.

CHAPTER 49
Jennifer

"So. What do you know about Apaches?"

"Nothing Susan hasn't already told you, I bet." Eddie shouted against the rushing wind. He clutched her neck with one gloved hand. "She told me they've got two crew—pilot and weapons. Each weighs about fifteen thousand pounds, standard loadout. They have a thirty-millimeter cannon with about twelve hundred rounds, up to sixteen Hellfire missiles apiece, and a bunch of Stinger air-to-airs. They're pounding the ground with their Hydra rockets, and their tactics are to hang back while the Kiowas—y'know, the smaller ones—paint the targets. The Kiowas themselves are less heavily armed, but you still don't want to hover in front of one with your ass showing."

"I think sometimes you pay more attention to Susan than I do."

"Can you see them?"

"Barely. My infrared vision only picks up smudges, instead of full shapes."

"That's their AN/ALQ-144 infrared countermeasures."

"Seriously. Susan told you about all this? *When?*"

"Couple of years ago. Her father took me on a tour of the base. Dad loved the idea of me going into the military. Okay—I think I see them about a mile away, eleven o'clock."

"Yep, got 'em. Looks like nine left."

A swirling explosion lit up the ground beneath the others.

"Eight."

"What's the plan?"

"I get close to one and bust open the cockpit. You jump in and convince them to set down. We disable the chopper, rinse, repeat."

He actually laughed. "Fine. Leave the hard work to me."

"I'll try to help you convince them that landing is a good idea."

They had already caught up—Dianna's sorcery powered Jennifer over the blurring rooftops—and the tail of one Apache hung tantalizingly close. It was in the rear of a formation targeting the grain elevator, half a mile beyond.

"Eddie, we've got to—"

The choppers fired. Jennifer and Eddie watched in horror as the rockets sailed into six concrete silos, ruptured the exterior, and ignited the grain dust.

CRAK-KLAM! KLAM! CRAK, CRAK-KLAM! CRAK-CRAK-KLAM!!

For a long moment, a new sun appeared on the surface of the earth—a rumble of brilliant explosions that spat flame onto everything around it. Trees, restaurants, automobiles, gardening shops, all of it began to catch fire.

"Get ready!" She came at the hindmost Apache from

a rear angle, grasping the chassis with her hind and wing claws and keeping her tail clear of the port rocket pod. The rotor blades roared overhead, and Eddie nearly lost his grip on her. She hissed fire over the cockpit glass, shattering it. She could not read the expression of the chopper pilot in the rear seat, but from the jerk of his head, it was clear they had surprised him.

Eddie squeezed into the space behind and above the pilot, drew a knife, and held it against the pilot's throat. "Set it down, set it down, SET IT DOWN!"

Jennifer braced herself in case the pilot decided to plunge too quickly. As it turned out, their altitude was too low for anything worse than a rough bump as the pilot drove the joystick forward. The landing gear screeched against hot pavement.

"Out, out, out! You've got ten seconds before she blows this thing! Out, go, go!"

Both crew members unbuckled, slipped out of their seats . . . then pulled their sidearms and aimed them at Eddie. Jennifer turned her body and her tail had enough prongs to knock both of them out in a shower of sparks.

"Pull the pilot out, Eddie. I've got the weapons officer."

From above, a hail of bullets ripped the ground near the helicopter they had forced down. Eddie and Jennifer dropped their loads and rolled under the chassis.

"What now, Sexy Beast?"

She smiled back at him. "Stick to the plan. This one's down. I punch a hole in the gas tank"—her tail spikes whipped up and punctured the armored surface—"we drag these guys to a safe place, and we move on!"

They scrambled out from under the helicopter, dragging the officers to the edge of the parking lot. By the time the bullet fire started again, he was on her back and she was in the air, circling around the attacker.

Within seconds she was on top of this one, too. This time, she clung to one of the stub wings, told Eddie to hold on, and let her skin glow gold.

"Holy crap, Jennifer . . ."

"It's not real, Eddie. Close your eyes, ignore the sounds and smells, and hold on!"

What she knew Eddie saw—and what every pilot and weapons officer in the six helicopters left in this squadron—was an endless stream of dragonflies pouring out of each of the twinkling stars above. Every dragonfly had a tiny, bulbous head and smelled like rotting fish. The streams wove a dizzying, shrieking web around every hovering vehicle. From below, the pavement cracked and gave way bit by bit to a shining, windswept field of whispering grass, each blade two stories tall.

Hide here, the grass blades promised them all. *Hide, it's safe. Safe from the flies.*

The choppers set down immediately, seeking shelter from the mystical and odorous assault from above. As they bumped down, Jennifer let the illusion go.

"That smelled horrible, Jennifer."

"Sorry. Care to take it from here?"

Eddie pulled out the sidearms he had taken off the last crew and blasted holes in the gas tanks of the nearest three.

"Out, out, out!" He called out. "They're going to blow!"

Jennifer helped him, shifting into camouflage, leaping to one of the far choppers—these were the slighter Kiowas—and reappearing on top of the cockpit with a roar. This got the crew scrambling, which she helped along as she ripped off the hatch. By the time they pulled their own sidearms, she had melted into human form and kicked the weapons away.

"I'm trying to save your asses!" she shouted at them. "Get out of the helicopter—it's going to blow!"

They emptied four of the six choppers this way. As Jennifer spat fireballs at the abandoned vehicles, the remaining two began to lift off again.

Eddie saw it first and cried out—then she saw it, too. An ugly and familiar winged shadow, slipping over the firelit pavement, leaping up and hugging the curves of the chopper as it flitted over the armored surface.

"Get down!" she tried to warn them. "Get down, get out!"

The cannon below the cockpit pointed at her and fired.

She burst into water vapor, and the bullets passed harmlessly through.

Fine. If that's how you feel. Good luck with my sister.

Descending and reintegrating, she got Eddie mounted again and headed for the last chopper, which was fleeing northeast.

Toward the hospital.

CHAPTER 50
Susan

It didn't take Susan long to find a car they could use—they had several spare vans spread across the parking lot, which they used for ambulances. It took her only a few minutes to secure Gautierre in the passenger seat. They were pulling out of the parking space when Catherine came up alongside them.

"Susan, wait!"

She screeched to a halt and opened the window. "Catherine, good! Get on in. We're heading out of town."

"No, you're not."

"Why not?"

"They've barricaded the roads. The bridge is blown. Helicopters are coming from all directions. You try to leave town, they'll kill you."

Explosions rumbled in the distance. The hospital was already in darkness; now lights elsewhere in town began to shut off. Several more blasts went off within the hospital.

"They'll kill us if we stay here! What do we do?"

"You've got to get word out there, Susan. You've got to talk to them."

"Talk to them? I've been talking to them for months! They're clearly not listening!"

"It's different now, Susan. If you go live, tell people about your friends and family, tell them about your father and his command at the local air base, tell them he's killing people, ask him to stop . . . Susan, you have to try."

They looked at the hospital, which was on fire. "All the battery-powered equipment is in there. You want me to run into a burning building."

"I'll go with you. Gautierre will stay here. Come on—it's not going to get any easier!"

With the fireproof scales of Catherine Brandfire protecting her through the ruined portions of the hospital, Susan found the equipment she needed. Fortunately, all of it was in an undamaged storage room. It took both of them to carry it all out, and Susan found her arms and fingers singed as they navigated the blazing hallways.

Five minutes later, with the help of Gautierre, they had a live feed to Susan's website.

"Go!" Gautierre motioned to her, camera on his shoulder.

"Welcome to the last edition of *Under Big Blue*, with Susan Elmsmith. I'm Susan Elmsmith. It's Day—aw, who cares! Big Blue is down, we're free, it's done—but everything has gotten much, much worse! Everyone, you've got to call law enforcement. You've got to call media. Our town is under attack from our own government! Innocent people are dying. Only you can stop it. Please, I know you haven't listened before. I know you've wanted to ignore us because we're different. But with the dome gone, we're not really different anymore. We're like every other American town—which means any other town could go through what we're going through now. Do you want that to happen?

"Worst of all . . . it's my own father who's responsible. That's right—my dad commands the air base that has sent these Apaches and Kiowas to destroy the town. Sure, he's taking orders from a politician somewhere—so call them, too! But the main reason I'm reporting now, is to talk to my dad.

"Dad, I know you're listening. You know I have a blog. You know my website. You know tonight, I'd be trying to get a message out. So wherever your command station is— you've got a computer screen up, and you're watching your daughter.

"I'm alive, Dad. I'm still here. I made it. I can't wait to see you. But I'm at Winoka Hospital, which took at least ten rocket hits. Maybe you don't understand how many innocent people are in that hospital. You've killed a lot of people here tonight, Dad. But I still love you. I still want to see you.

"But I'm not going to see you if this doesn't stop. If that hospital keeps burning, I'm going to run inside there, over and over, trying to rescue the people you're trying to kill. Do you hear me, Dad? Your daughter is going to die inside a burning building. C'mon, Gautierre, Catherine, let's go."

She moved toward the hospital. The other two hesitated.

"Let's go!"

"Susan, you're not going to last—"

"Good-bye, then!" She dropped the microphone and walked away from them . . .

. . . and almost walked right into Dr. Georges-Scales.

"Susan." Elizabeth looked at the three of them. "What's going on here? What are you doing?"

"I'm going to save them, Doctor. I'm going to save this entire town."

"By walking into a burning hospital? I don't think so."

"Try to stop me." She deftly stepped back, picked up the microphone, and flipped her hair back for the camera again. "You all remember Dr. Elizabeth Georges-Scales, don't you, everyone? She's a hero in this town. She's saved so many lives—lives my father's trying to take away, by burning down a hospital. I don't know if that's what our military is for, but what do I know—I'm just a dumb teenager who's stupid and petulant enough to run into a crumbling hospital, just to make her father stop. Anyway, let's get her take on this. Doctor—do you support the burning to death of all of your patients, or should we go in there and try to save them?"

She jabbed the microphone under Elizabeth's jaw.

"Susan. Your father doesn't want you to die. He's doing what he thinks is best. It's wrong, but you can't make him change his mind by committing suicide."

"So who will save your patients, Doctor? You?"

Elizabeth gazed at the burning building. "The thought had occurred to me. But if you pause two moments and look around, you'll see many patients are already being saved."

With a nod to the dark parking lot beyond, Elizabeth got Gautierre to pan the camera left. In the far corner of the parking lot, almost one hundred yards away, a small group of dragons had linked wings in a fireproof circle.

Within the circle were several gurneys, each holding a patient hooked to an IV. Several nurses were working with the patients—burn victims, bullet wounds, diabetics, pregnant mothers—with only the supplies at hand. It was a last stand against death. Gautierre zoomed in on it, as Elizabeth continued to speak.

"There are no enemies left in this town, Colonel Elmsmith. No one who wants to hurt your daughter. No one who wants to hurt me. Only people who want to help each other . . . and the forces under your command. I hope your daughter has inspired you to stop. She's an amazing young woman, Colonel. She has so much to look forward to . . . she just fell in love. Let her keep falling in love, Colonel. Please. I don't know how much longer I can keep her out of that building."

Ruddaduddaduddaruddaduddadudda

The sound was distant, but getting louder.

Ruddaduddaduddaruddaduddadudda

"Maybe we should seek cover," Catherine offered.

"Fuck that," Susan said. "If they're going to gun us down, let it happen here. Gautierre—keep that camera rolling. Don't you dare leave me."

"Not going anywhere, babe."

Ruddaduddaduddaruddaduddadudda

Elizabeth took Susan's hand—it was a warm, maternal touch, and Susan realized once again how much she horribly missed her own dead mother. She squeezed back.

Ruddaduddaduddaruddaduddadudda

"If they fire," the doctor told her, "you and Gautierre get your ass in that car. Catherine, you, too. Find my daughter. She'll help you get out of town."

"You know we're not going anywhere," Catherine said.

Ruddaduddaduddaruddaduddadudda

Susan braced herself.

Six helicopters roared over the rooftop and descended to the pavement between them and the hospital.

Undaunted, Susan stepped toward them.

"SUSAN ELMSMITH." The loudspeaker mounted on the center Apache blared. "DR. GEORGES-SCALES. TOWNSPEOPLE. STAND DOWN. FIRE AND RESCUE ARE ON THE WAY."

CHAPTER 51
Jennifer

By the time Jennifer and Eddie had finished chasing the helicopter to the hospital, a convoy of fire trucks and ambulances were rushing into the parking lot.

It was a moment of enormous relief for them all, not least Elizabeth, who was openly happy to see her daughter alive.

"Got most of them down without a scratch," Jennifer was proud to report. "But Evangelina is still on the prowl. We might want to get back to Skip and Dianna."

"Agreed."

The two of them, Susan, Gautierre, and Catherine returned to the bridge . . .

. . . where Skip was thawing in Dianna's arms.

"Dianna!" Elizabeth surged forward, but caught herself

as she realized what was happening. "Dianna, what have you done?"

"What none of the rest of you had the guts to do." The sorceress was crying, and her son's features were paling. Spiderwebs of black poison were streaking across his face, chasing the crystals of ice away. "I told you we had to stop him, but none of you would do it. You gave me no choice. I had to do it myself. I had to kill my own son." She buried her head on Skip's chest, sobbing. Far, far away, the sirens of fire engines and ambulances wailed.

Elizabeth knelt next to them and looked for a pulse in Skip's wrist, then throat. Dianna did not try to stop her—in fact, she smiled.

"Still trying to save everyone, Doctor? How heroic. He's past your help—the dose I had to use on him is beyond anything you can cure."

"We don't know that until we get him to the hospital. From there, they can chopper him in to the Twin Cities. Jennifer, help me get him on your back."

Jennifer wanted to hesitate, but she didn't dare. She stepped forward—

"You're too late." Dianna gently let her son's body fall to the ground and got to her feet. Venomous tears had burned dark tracks on her cheeks, and Jennifer could not tell where the woman's pupils ended and her irises began. "It's my fault. I should have stayed with him. I shouldn't have left him with his father."

Elizabeth examined Skip's body, but did not attempt any resuscitation. He was bleeding venom from his pores, and his pale skin was already starting to burn.

"I've lost him, just like I lost Jonathan . . . like I've lost everyone."

You still have me, Mother. You lost me, but you found me again.

"Look who's back." Jennifer steamed at the sight of the shadowy shape that reappeared. "Thanks for all your help back there, by the way. Nothing like trying to get those choppers landing safely while you were blowing them up. I really appreciate all that."

You're welcome.

"Evangelina." Dianna tried to smile. "I've failed you worst of all. I abandoned you to death, and death never really left you. It still seeps from your scales. You can't help yourself. I've tried to show you better worlds, better places . . ."

Jennifer looked at the sky. "Um, Mom."

"Hang on, honey." Elizabeth was closing Skip's pretty green eyes with a single hand and murmuring a prayer.

The monstrous form of Evangelina dwindled into a slender woman. Her expression was confused, and she tried to approach Dianna.

Mother. Please don't cry. I'm still here.

"Mom, seriously. Look up. Check it out."

The sorceress stepped back. "I can't do anything else for you, Evangelina. Please don't ask me. There's nothing I can do. I've failed both of you. Skip has already come to this awful end, and now you face the same."

"Folks, if you could just tilt your heads slightly up and check this out . . ."

"Maybe not tonight, maybe not for months or even years—but you are doomed, and damned. I did that to you. I'm so sorry."

Please stop apologizing, Mother. It upsets me.

"WILL EVERYONE PLEASE STOP TALKING AND LOOK UP AT THE MOON?"

They looked up.

The sliver had become a more prominent crescent, and it was leaving a trail of virulent green in its wake. Even the dark side was pulsing with color.

"Why isn't the moon fixed?" Susan asked. "Skip's dead. So is Andi."

"It's like I told you," Dianna told them. "He exists up there as well. Destroying him down here is not enough. We must do it again."

"How much time do we have?" Elizabeth asked.

"None. We have to do it now. In fact, I'm surprised we're still standing."

"We have to kill him on the moon *now*? How are we going to do that?" asked Gautierre.

Dianna wiped her face. "Someone is going to carry me up there. And then I am going to make a sacrifice, for once."

Mother. You're not making any sense. You cannot go to the moon. None of us can.

"I was thinking the same thing," Jennifer added.

"You're both wrong—in fact, you are exactly the two among us who have the strength to bring me there."

I don't see how that's possible. I cannot survive without air, Mother.

"Even if you fix that problem," Jennifer added, "It would take months to get there, even at our fastest. We could barely keep up with Army helicopters down here.

Do you have a rocket ship hidden somewhere under that dress?"

"Speed is not an issue. Nor is air. The only question would be, which one of you will bring me. I've already decided that one."

She stepped up to Evangelina.

I won't take you. Not if you're going up there to die.

"Oh, sweet Evangelina." Dianna stroked her daughter's face with both hands, wiping the black strands of hair aside. "I'm not going to ask you to take me. Instead, I'm going to give you one last gift, before Jennifer takes me."

What do you

Dianna seized Evangelina's face and explained, as the younger woman shrieked.

"I should have done this when I found you, after all those years you spent in the darkness. There's no mother I know who wouldn't gladly take all her daughter's pain away. I am ashamed that it took me so long to do this. All I can say is, I'm sorry. I wanted time with you. I wanted the time that had been taken from us. You gave me some of that time. Now, I return it to you . . . and so much more."

Evangelina's scream became higher, and her eyes brighter. Her hair shortened, and her skin tightened. Meanwhile, Dianna began to age.

"Am I seeing what I think I'm seeing?" Jennifer asked her mother.

"Kid, I have no idea what either of us is seeing."

Mooooooooom!

"I give you the gift of years," Dianna said. The creases in her face deepened, and she gritted her teeth. "All of the loneliness and misery you suffered, all of the horrible things you've done . . . I'll take it all. You have a second chance, Evangelina. Use it well."

The girl's face—for it was a girl now, no older than six—remained a reflection of pain. Her silver eyes sparkled with youth.

Where am I what is this who am when am I am why?

"Just a little longer, darling." Dianna's voice was heavy with age. Her shoulders were stooping, and she could barely lift the shrinking child into her arms. The loose clothes Evangelina had worn were now large enough to be blankets to the infant.

Finally, Dianna looked up from the wailing cloth bundle in her arms, to the others. The skin sagged from her cheekbones, and her eyes were dull with uneasy, shifting pastels. No one spoke.

Slowly, step by step, the sorceress shifted toward them. She edged by the earthly corpse of Skip Wilson, and passed the gape-mouthed Catherine. She paused when she reached Gautierre and Susan, and reached out with a hand to the boy's shoulder. Her nod passed him, acknowledging the giant black corpse on the other side of the river.

"I'm sorry for your losses, kid," she croaked. "Find family where you can. Love them for who they are. Stay with them, in good times and bad. If you need guidance . . . look to the family my first husband built."

She kept going now, passed Susan and Jennifer with a slow wink, came to the last in the group, and held out her infant child.

"Doctor. Please succeed, where I have failed."

Elizabeth staggered back a step. "Dianna. Ms. Wilson. I can't—this is—"

"We both know who the difference was, between what Evangelina became and what Jennifer has become. I have finally done something for her, worthy of your family. I cannot continue. It is up to you—the only one in this world whom I trust with her safety."

"Dianna. I can't possibly be the answer. You and I—we just—"

The sorceress presented the child again, more urgently this time. "Doctor. I would love to argue this all evening. My other child is about to ruin this earth. I know you ache for another child. I'm offering you this opportunity. If you don't want it, I'll leave it with Jennifer, and you can be a grandmother instead."

Elizabeth took the baby.

"Thank you." Dianna straightened her back and ran a hand through her gray hair. "Jennifer Scales. I am ready to go."

EPILOGUE
The Elder's Diary

I was the last person to see Dianna Wilson alive.

Since she asked, and I saw no other way, I carried her up. We went higher than dragons can, higher than helicopters or jet fighters, higher than satellites.

She whispered the sorceries I needed for speed and survival, though the words she spoke did horrible things to her own withering face and limbs.

My mother has asked me several times what it was like, up there. I find that all I can tell her was that it was cold and quiet. That's what everyone expects to hear, and so that's all I say.

The truth was, I have never felt more heat or heard more noise than I have when the earth and we raced through the sky together.

The white-streaked stone beneath us was powered by

an engine more ancient, slow, and sure than ours; but the short sprint to the moon was ours to win, and the heavens roared and the stars cheered. The more I think about it, the more I realize the heat and noise came from within—Dianna's magic was no longer what kept us alive.

She held her own head close to mine, and I began to hear her voice in my head. At first it was stuff I could understand—mostly things about her daughter, and the travels they had shared together in dimensions that existed only in dreams.

But her words made less and less sense, the farther we went. Things she said had happened, couldn't possibly have yet: a river town vanishing under a billowing cloud of fire, a dark twist of a creature obliterating herself in the midst of a holocaust, a faceless figure hunting ceaselessly for blood, a world without dragons or spiders or beast-stalkers. Maybe she was hallucinating, or peering into the future.

When the crescent moon was so large I thought its lower end would pierce us, I heard her thoughts return to me: please stop here.

Are you sure? *I asked her.*

I'm sure. You should go now. Thank you, Jennifer. Give Evangelina my love. Help your mother look after her. Help your mother . . .

I tried to hold on to her, but with one last wink and wry smile, she forced distance between us. Without my heat, her skin began to glisten with blue frost.

You've got about ten seconds, child. Move it.

I moved it, still unable to tell for sure if my newfound speed and fire came from within, from her grace, or both. By the time a cloud of emerald fire consumed the night sky, I was already piercing the atmosphere.

According to my mother, it initially looked as though

Dianna had failed, and that the moon and everything had been lost. It wasn't until her last sorcery faded enough to let the slim, white crescent shine through that she relaxed and realized all was well.

But I knew all along that Dad's first wife would do fine. That woman had no clue how to lose. Turns out, though, she did know how to die in style.

The shimmering curtain that lay over Minnesota for the next fifty nights let only two lights through: the sun, which washed out most of the aurora's colors; and the cleansed moon, which kept its crescent shape the entire time.

It turns out this was the beginning of something even bigger for all of us—but for those fifty days, it was amazing enough to see the universe bow to that martyred sorceress.

As for me, I landed safely in Pinegrove. Of course. I'm always safe. It's the people around me who seem to die.

Mom was waiting for me, holding the bundle in her arms tightly against the chill. Fog formations slipped over the river behind them, and one of them was shaped like a large bird. I thought of Sonakshi, and Xavier, and the hundreds of dragons who had followed me to the end.

I poked at the bundle and lifted the cloth from her face. Evangelina's eyes reflected all the shifting colors from the mourning heavens, until I let the blanket drop a bit. Then they were gray, just like Dad's.

Turn the page for a special preview
of the next novel in
MaryJanice Davidson and Anthony Alongi's

Jennifer Scales series

Coming soon from Ace Books!

The Last Interview of
Dr. Loxos

The following is a transcript of a recording recovered from the Saint Georges Secure Medical Facility in Cloudchester, Minnesota. According to staff at the facility, the conversation took place in a secured room in what would have been the facility's psychiatric emergency care center.

The Cloudchester Police have blacked out some information for reasons of decorum, and to maintain discretion during their continuing investigation into the death of Dr. Collin Loxos and the disappearance of at least one other patient at the facility.

[Recording begins.]

LOXOS: September 18, 5:12 P.M. Dr. Collin Loxos, conducting our second interview with a female patient, age approximately twenty, height five feet eleven inches, weight one hundred fifty-five pounds, hair black, eyes gray, refers to herself as ████████, no given surname. ██████████ has been with us at Saint Georges for just under twenty-four hours; she was a voluntary self-admit. She has barely spoken to anyone since her arrival. Her first interview an hour after entry was, in the words of my colleague Dr. Eisenstadt, "an hour-long staring match with the table." Since then patient has become increasingly agitated. Under Dr. Eisenstadt's direction, staff have attempted sedation with a progressive schedule of benzodiazepines. None have had any discernable effect. Patient has submitted to restraints, which I have recommended due to the increasing danger she presents to staff and herself. ████████ has made multiple vague references to deaths, and to the town of Winoka. This has caught our attention, for obvious reasons. I have notified local authorities, but would like to see if I can learn more prior to their arrival. ████████, I am Dr. Loxos. You can call me Collin.

[Long silence.]

LOXOS: ████████? Are we going to have another staring match with the table?

████████: ████ you, Collin.

LOXOS: ████████, I wonder if you can tell me why you came here.

████████: *I* wonder if you can tell me what you think these restraints and all the drugs are for.

LOXOS: We're taking measures for your safety, and the community's.

████████: I've heard that line before.

LOXOS: Where? In Winoka?

████████: I didn't come here to talk about Winoka.

LOXOS: But you're from there, right?

████████: You don't know ████ about Winoka.

LOXOS: I know there was a natural disaster there—

███████████: The Regiment is *not* a natural disaster.

LOXOS: What is the Regiment?

███████████: You know what the Regiment is. They probably run this place. If they don't, they know the people who do. That's why I'm here. Well, it's the first reason I'm here. You're taping this interview, which means they'll get a transcript. Right?

LOXOS: Let's suppose for now that this "Regiment" exists. What message would you like to send?

███████████: I would like to tell them they are wasting their time.

LOXOS: How so?

███████████: The people they're hunting don't have the information they want.

LOXOS: This Regiment is hunting people?

███████████: Doing a good job of it, too. I'm sure you've seen the headlines.

LOXOS: I have. They are gruesome, some of these headlines.

███████████: Nothing worse than what I've seen for years. It's easy to treat people like that when you consider them "not human."

LOXOS: What do you mean, "not human"?

███████████: Don't insult my intelligence, Collin. Everyone listening to this tape or reading this transcript is going to know who's dying and why.

LOXOS: Because this "Regiment" of yours is killing them, is that right?

███████████: It's not my Regiment, Collin. It's yours. You're a member.

LOXOS: Who else is a member?

███████████: You know it's not like I have a directory! I just know you—

LOXOS: ██████████ . . . have you considered that *you* may be a member of this Regiment? Or more precisely, that the Regiment is nothing more than a psychic construct you use to distance yourself from your awful actions? That all of the hunting you are talking about . . . that it's *you* doing it?

██████████: That's not true. That's not who I am.

LOXOS: You're so sure of that?

██████████: I'm sure. You're not going to confuse me with psychiatric games, Collin.

LOXOS: You think these are games. Yet you checked yourself in here. Nobody came in with you to Saint Georges. How long have you been alone, ██████████?

██████████: I'm not sure. A few years.

LOXOS: What about before that? Did you live in—

██████████: Let's stop talking about Winoka. You're trying to pump me for information. You're stalling until the authorities show. It's not going to work. I'm here because I want to be here, Dr. Loxos. Like I said, I wanted to get a message to your friends in the Regiment.

LOXOS: Yes, you said that was the "first" reason you were here. Was there another reason?

██████████: Yes. I wonder if you know a ██████████.

LOXOS: Of course I do. She's a patient here. Has been for years.

██████████: Why is that?

LOXOS: I don't see why that's relevant—

██████████: Let's get to the point. You preach the fiction that ██████████ suffers from severe, chronic psychosis.

LOXOS: She's been experiencing secondary delusions for over a decade. Possibly since childhood.

██████████: Her "delusions" have been documented and disseminated worldwide, using unedited video—

LOXOS: Please, ██████████. We both know the Internet

is a storage house for manufactured fantasy. Those special effects films she crafted to impress the world were nothing more than a clever stunt to get attention after the death of her mother and subsequent emotional abandonment by her father—

████████: Who believed her, after the rise of the Poison Moon.

LOXOS: You are referring, I presume, to the unusual but completely explicable phenomenon of the "green moon," which happened most notably approximately twenty years ago. Astronomers have noted that certain phases of the moon, when viewed through an aurora borealis, can give the impression—

████████: You and I can interrupt each other all day long, Collin, but we know ████████ has never suffered a psychotic episode. Neither did her father.

LOXOS: Well, he's no longer alive to tell us what he has seen, is he?

████████: Yes, that's very convenient for the Regiment.

LOXOS: Convenience has nothing to do with it. He died in a military training exercise at the air base he commanded. He was highly decorated and received a hero's funeral. I suspect he would be very sad, as are we all, to see the depths to which his daughter sank shortly after his demise.

████████: The Regiment is all over the military. All over law enforcement. All over every level and agency of government, in schools and hospitals . . .

LOXOS: You're suggesting the Regiment killed ████████'s highly trained and decorated father during a military exercise. That doing so somehow supported their false case that she should be committed. That she never suffered any delusions about dragons, and enormous spiders, and interdimensional travel, and pixie dust. That these things actually exist. That there is a conspiracy to hide this truth.

██████████: Not just hide it, Collin. Destroy it. Murder it.

LOXOS: Murder it, like you've murdered innocent people?

██████████: I've never murdered anyone. Not in this lifetime. Not yet.

LOXOS: You believe that will scare me? I don't know *who* you think you are, but let me tell you *where* you are. First, you're strapped down in a bed with steel and leather restraints. That bed is in a locked room here with me, inside the most secure wing of the most secure psychiatric facility known to North America, and likely the world. We use highly trained private security forces, at an unprecedented guard-to-guest ratio, to ensure the safety of everyone inside and in the surrounding community. You walked in here, ██████████, but you are not walking out. You're a woman with deep emotional problems who likes to hurt people to avoid the awful truth.

██████████: What truth is that, Collin?

LOXOS: You're a monster. And you belong in here, in a place far deeper and danker than any cell your friend ██████████ will ever experience. You cannot be cured of your need to kill. With luck, whatever unfortunate bastard serves as your public defender will lose his or her bid to plead insanity on your behalf, and they'll inject poison into your veins within a year or two. Meanwhile, you'll be our guest here. Get comfortable.

██████████: Are the authorities here yet?

LOXOS: Probably. What does that matter?

██████████: Because escape will be so much more impressive if I'm blowing past not just your vaunted private security guards but a couple of actual police officers as well.

LOXOS: It's more than a couple. Honestly, ██████████, it's over. What do you—*what do you think you're doing?!*

[Snapping sounds.]

███████████: I think I'm rescuing my friend from a lobotomy factory. And if I don't find her one hundred percent intact, I think I'm contemplating my first murder.

[Crackling noises.]

LOXOS: Oh, ████. Nurse!

[Struggling noises.]

LOXOS: ████. Officers! *Officers!*

[Shrieking, followed by gurgling, followed by crashing.]

███████████: Let's go find her, shall we?

[Recording ends.]

Get to know Vampire Queen Betsy Taylor
in the *New York Times* bestselling series by

MaryJanice Davidson

Undead and Unfinished

Undead and Unwelcome

Undead and Unworthy

Undead and Uneasy

Undead and Unpopular

Undead and Unreturnable

Undead and Unappreciated

Undead and Unemployed

Undead and Unwed

"Delightful, wicked fun!"

—#1 *New York Times* bestselling author
Christine Feehan

"Think *Sex and the City*—only the
city is Minneapolis and it's filled with
demons and vampires."

—*Publishers Weekly*

penguin.com

M43AS1209

Vampire Queen Betsy Taylor returns in the ninth
novel in the *New York Times* bestselling series from

MaryJanice Davidson

Undead and Unfinished

Vampire Queen Betsy Taylor is having a tough time
getting through the Book of the Dead—until the
Devil strikes a bargain. She offers Betsy a chance to
finish the cursed (literally!) thing and finally discover
all its mysteries. There's just one catch . . .

Betsy and her half sister, Laura, have to go to Hell
long enough for Laura to embrace her dark heritage
(after a rebellious youth of charity work) and finally
make nice with her mother, aka Lucifer. That means
interacting with their family's past. In doing so,
they're impacting the future in ways they never an-
ticipated. Of course, that's what Mother wanted all
along. Damn her.

M614T1209